BIOPUNK BLUES

A <u>LIQUID COOL</u> CYBERPUNK DETECTIVE NOVEL

Book Seven

AUSTIN DRAGON

Published by Well-Tailored Books, California

BioPunk Blues
(Liquid Cool, Book 7)

978-1-946590-74-9 (paperback)
978-1-946590-70-1 (ebook)

http://www.austindragon.com

Book cover design by Leslie K.

Printed in the United States of America

CONTENTS

PART ONE | BioFunk: That Endless Rainy Night Under a Milky Way Sky 1

Chapter 1 | I, Cruz 2

Chapter 2 | Punch Judy 7

Chapter 3 | Cops! 12

PART TWO | BioGenesis: The Case................................ 25

Chapter 4 | Burglar...26

Chapter 5 | China Doll 30

Chapter 6 | The Hellspawn (The Wife's Parents) 36

Chapter 7 | Two Stupid Detectives 41

Chapter 8 | PJ 44

Chapter 9 | Goat Girl 48

Chapter 10 | Twinkle...54

Chapter 11 | The Wife and The Parents (Known for Their Supreme Coolness)...63

PART THREE | I Don't Want No BioFreaks in My Future 67

Chapter 12 | Clox..68

Chapter 13 | Octane 75

Chapter 14 | Bad Bia..81

Chapter 15 | Bia's Bio-Borgs 86

Chapter 16 | Good Bia.. 90

Chapter 17 | About the Beast.................................... 97

Chapter 18 | Bia's CI... 103

Chapter 19 | Beast.. 112

PART FOUR | BioPirates Tried to Snatch My Arm 123

Chapter 20 | Officers Break and Caps...................... 124

Chapter 21 | Chief Hub.. 130

Chapter 22 | PJ... 135

Chapter 23 | Bugs... 139

Chapter 24 | Beast.. 142

Chapter 25 | Node.. 152

Chapter 26 | Bia 157

Chapter 27 | Twinkle 161

Chapter 28 | Chief Hub 165

Chapter 29 | Fraggy 168

PART FIVE | BioGenic: Wilford G's Peanut Galley.................. 181

Chapter 30 | Wize Gal 182

Chapter 31 | Wilford Jr.. 189

Chapter 32 | Quix.. 194

Chapter 33 | Prima Donna 198

PART SIX | BioTechs: Which WHO Are You Referring to? 201

Chapter 34 | Phishy 202

Chapter 35 | Three WHOs.. 218

Chapter 36 | WHO Dat.. 222

Chapter 37 | PJ... 226

Chapter 38 | Bia and Company................................ 229

Chapter 39 | One Crazy WHO................................. 234

Chapter 40 | Mr. WHO...238

PART SEVEN | The Andromeda Rain Came From BioDome 245

Chapter 41 | Raven...246

Chapter 42 | Mr. WHO...252

Chapter 43 | Fraggy 260

Chapter 44 | Zeno 264

Chapter 45 | Quix..267

Chapter 46 | Bia...272

Chapter 47 | Run-Time 276

Chapter 48 | Prima Donna..280

Chapter 49 | Run-Time and The Mick......................................283

Chapter 50 | BioTech Thugs 286

Chapter 51 | Afraid of WHO..290

PART EIGHT | BioTerror: What Does a Global Pandemic Have
to Do with a Local Street Detective?...295

Chapter 52 | WHO's Men 296

Chapter 53 | Bio-Suits...301

Chapter 54 | Prima Donna...304

Chapter 55 | Fraggy 308

Chapter 56 | Quix..312

Chapter 57 | Don't Make WHO Angry 316

PART NINE | The Part Where Those Scary Guys in Bio-Suits
Break Through Your Front Door 325

Chapter 58 | Phishy...326

Chapter 59 | Fraggy's Team...333

Chapter 60 | Fraggy 339

Chapter 61 | Corporate Soldiers 347

Chapter 62 | PJ 354

Chapter 63 | The Grapevine 360

Chapter 64 | Patient Zero 363

Chpater 65 | Decon Doctors 370

Chapter 66 | Eye Candy Crew 373

Chapter 67 | Dot 376

Chapter 68 | Chief Hub 379

Chapter 69 | PJ 383

Chapter 70 | Parents 387

Chapter 71 | Hellspawn and Cruz Jr. 390

Chapter 72 | Quix 393

Chapter 73 | A Freak Show in My Office 397

Introduction

In my last big case—***A.I. Confidential***, I had the honor of meeting my mentor, the legendary private eye, Wilford G. He had worked and solved cases in our grand supercity of Metropolis for more than 70 years. I got to partner and work alongside my hero—but then I lost him again. He was 95 years…young. He told me that he didn't expect to see me in Heaven until I had reached at least the same age. I promised him it would be so. Everyone respected him: the police, the politicians, even criminals. He was "The Man."

Now they were saying I was "The Man." But you don't replace legends. You simply continue your journey.

His death hit me hard and I was still having a hard time coping. But I wasn't a florist, or any of a million other safe jobs. I had chosen as my career one that was listed as more dangerous than law enforcement. They had advanced body armor and back-up. For the street detective, you had to rely on your own wits and instincts more than a fast draw. The "life" was dangerous and violent. I'd met hulking, scary-looking, criminal gangsters, killer robots and supercyborgs. I'd met the smooth and plotting criminals wearing silk nylons and neon lipstick. In other words, you had to forever be on your toes or death would hit hard—in the form of a bullet or laser to the head.

I had already worked a wide variety of cases from City Hall to megacorporations to shadowy criminal cartels. I'd been pulled into the world of virtual-world, gamer addicted cyberpunks to samurai soldiers to bodyguarding deranged kids of the obscenely rich. One case even involved "extraterrestrials."

Until this case I never knew what a biopunk was. After this I didn't ever want to know one again. Briefly, I had encountered this world once before in my ***Blade Gunner*** Case, where cyberpunk and biopunk merged—pulling the data out of an ancient cranial hard-drive of some poor guy. That was enough for me, but the biopunk world had other ideas.

As with so many of my cases, there was always more behind the scenes. There was the first round of criminals, easily visible. But in the shadows, there were the real criminals pulling the strings. One cabal of criminals led to another as I found out in my case of ***Biopunk Blues***. And I had to snap out of my funk faster than the speed of light. In Metropolis, depressed detectives become dead detectives. I wasn't about to break my promise to The Man.

PART ONE

*BioFunk: That Endless Rainy Night
Under a Milky Way Sky*

CHAPTER 1

I, Cruz

BioFunk.

Noun. The morose, psycho-social bad mood of Cruz, often annually, always silly, resulting in an uncontrolled desire of Cruz to hide from the world.

Wasn't this how it all started? Yes, before my Police Watch Conspiracy Case. Before I started the Liquid Cool Detective Agency. Before I hired PJ. Before I was "famous." I was doing what I was doing now—hiding from the world. Usually, I did this around my birthday, but that was childish. This was different; quite serious. It finally hit me head-on like a hovertruck: Wilford G. was dead—for real, and he was never coming back. He was dead-dead. No pretending. I think my extreme morose mood started when one of Wilford G.'s old-timer friends looked at me at the funeral and said: "Now you're Metro's main street detective. You're the Man now." He then tipped his hat—a fedora similar to mine but black, and walked away. Everyone seemed to have moved on from Wilford G.'s death except me.

How does one fill those shoes? Wilford G. wore his trademark black and white loafers, like I had my trademark tan fedora and slicker. How does one replace a legend? I was a former hovercar restorer. I fell into the street detective business like a drunk tripped over his own feet to fall onto the wet pavement. There was no plan. It just happened. I felt so...inadequate since then. I was the heir to Wilford G.? That didn't seem right somehow. It would be like someone saying they had *the* replacement for my classic hovervehicle and then showed up on a red hoverskateboard. Seriously? A skateboard to replace a classic red Ford Pony? I'd smack that person for such an insult. The successor to the great Wilford G. was me? It felt insulting. I was insulted.

So here I was—in a foul mood. It was like a personal black cloud hovering above my head. There was nothing to do but let it pass. But how long would that take? I was useless to everyone, including myself, until it did. I couldn't be anywhere near the street working a case until then. Otherwise, a five-year old robber would get the drop on me. And in this state I couldn't vouch for my own driving skills. Hovertraffic was dangerous enough. It was far more dangerous if you were in the grips of sour emotions and unfocused. Maybe that would be okay in the old days when there were vehicles rolling around on the ground on plastic tires. We lived in a grown-up world now and we "drove" hovercars. Crashing meant "returning to surface" from twenty feet up or more, maybe, if you were especially lucky, as a ball of fire and metal. Wilford G. said it to me before he died. He'd see me on the other side but not for a long time. Well, at least I could say I had one thing to look forward to when I was dead-dead too. Wilford G. and I working cases in the afterlife.

Metropolis was the supercity that truly never slept with its fifty million people but for me, these past few days, it was the loneliest place on the planet. As I sat in the driver's seat of my vehicle, I realized I was incapable of even the slightest smile. Not even a tender memory of a posthumous mentor was enough to penetrate my foul mood. Inside my vehicle, my personal black cloud and outside my vehicle was the dark rainy sky.

In Metropolis, not only did it never sleep; it never stopped moving. With the rain pouring, I sat in my vehicle, actually lying flat in the warm driver's seat as snug as a bug in a rug staring out the front window. I had literally parked head out on a huge angled ledge, quarter way up of a secluded mega-tower on a nameless street in an insignificant part of town. I lay there staring up at the heavens as the rain fell and rolled down the glass. As I watched the blue-black sky, my eyes did begin to feel heavy. Maybe if I took another nap I could shake my post-Wilford G.'s death depression. No one could find me and all devices were off, so no one would bother me. I was about fifty stories up, so there would be no stray sidewalk johnny or sally, no troll molls to encounter. Also, I didn't have to worry about any other hovercars, garbage hovertrucks, or hovertaxis spotting me. It was always when you wanted to be alone when the whole world wanted to find you. They'd fail. I had a new hiding spot—

better than all my previous ones. I had all but talked myself into taking a midday nap. The *pitter-pat* of the rain against my vehicle was but an audio sleep narcotic.

I wasn't too far from my previous birthday hiding spot. Every so often through the rain, I could barely hear the hissing rumble of the same old monorail line, about fifty feet or so away. But when you really want to sleep, the ears can tune out anything. I was almost there. But, I should've known it was all too good to be true.

My eyes darted around trying to figure out what flashed in front of me outside as I was drifting asleep. Immediately above me, the rain was coming down lighter than before. The clouds beyond were dark but I saw nothing there.

There! I saw the little juvenile delinquent zip by with his jetpack. Scraggly, spiky hair—it seemed he couldn't make up his mind. Dressed all in black, except some very bright white shoes—yes, for the police to better spot you, I said to myself, and I saw the reflection of some kind of shades on his face. He hovered around the wall a dozen feet above me, but he hadn't seen me. All I wanted was to be left alone and here I was at the mercy of some jetpacked tagger. I watched as he reached into the bag in his hand and out came the can of neon paint. Little graffiti punk. All I could think of was paint from his act of vandalism dripping down on my classic Miami Vice red painted vehicle.

I was tempted to honk my horn, but then I feared he would drop the bag onto my vehicle—crack my windshield, in addition to ruining my paint job. With the flick of a switch I started the Pony up and engaged drive mode but not moving an inch.

When I turn on my high beams, the delinquent didn't drop his bag but he smashed into the wall of the building, startled so bad, as he made his escape. I kept my eye on him as he flew higher. Then he stopped.

"What are you about to do?" I called out to myself. "Don't even think of throwing something." He did.

I didn't wait to see what "goodies" he dumped from his bag at my parked vehicle. I jetted out of there, made a left turn, and in moments merged into the regular hovercar traffic. I was tempted to call the police on him, but it would have been a waste of time. He was long gone.

"I can't even take a nap in peace!"

That meant I'd have to work. What I should have done was go straight home, but that would have been the sensible thing to do. When you're in a bad funk, you never do the sensible thing. I didn't know it then but this was going to be one evil day.

CHAPTER 2

Punch Judy

Metropolis had thousands of sub-cities or districts—each with its own name, culture, and vibe. I had been in Silver City—the center of Metropolis robot production. It was a city of robots—all sizes, shapes, and some said, personalities. Very few people worked, lived, or had any reason to be there. It also happened to be where I was shot and almost killed—my Blade Gunner Case. A psych might say that hanging around the place where you were almost killed was your inner self saying you were still screwed up. I didn't have a high regard for the psychiatric community because if it were up to them, I wouldn't be borderline OCD and a recovering germophobe. I'd be a full-blown OCD, germophobic crazy and a permanent resident in one of those Bubble colonies on the Moon. Thank God, my parents didn't believe their nonsense.

The hovertraffic was awful but moving. You'd think in a supercity where it always rained that people would be expert drivers, but they weren't. But all was in control in my classic Ford Pony. A beautiful machine. A work of art. High-performance, super-charged, advanced nitro-acceleration hydrogen engine. A sleek, bright red muscle-vehicle coupe that made the average person gawk and the genuine hovercar enthusiast and collector do a double-take.

I "liberated" the shell in a junkyard when I was a kid at the end of middle school. Over my years in high school, I built it and restored it, spare part by spare part. Few believed me, at first, that I found and built such an expensive muscle hovercar from scratch, but it was true. I established a decent living as a classic hovercar restorer. In that world, people didn't part with large amounts of cash unless you not only knew your stuff but knew more than them. My Pony was famous before I ever was, featured countless times (most without my permission) in so many hovercar magazines that I lost count.

How quickly things can change in the blink of an eye. One moment a hovercar restorer and sometime amateur (also known as illegal) hovercar racer; the next, a licensed private detective. I was so comfortable in the new life that it was like I had always been a detective. It was so natural and second nature to me but being a detective was no joke. Wilford G.'S funeral wouldn't be the last one I'd attend. My wife, the eternal optimist, scolded me and told me that everyone will have to go to a funeral at some point in their life. It was part of the cycle of life. True enough. At least I didn't have to attend my own.

I didn't even want to see how many messages I had waiting for me on my mobile. But I turned it on anyway. Immediately, my dashboard began to ring.

The call was the office. That meant P.J.

My ex-felon employee's street name was Punch Judy, but we all called her PJ, except for a few of her friends who called her Punch. Her face flashed on my dashboard video-phone screen.

"Where have you been?" she yelled.

She had short crimson hair, a simulated mole, a dot, above her lips—today's lipstick color of choice was purple, and she spoke with a distinct French accent.

"Busy," I snapped.

"A-B-C. Always be closing cases. Are you closing cases?"

"I'm busy."

"You better not be sleeping in your hovercar."

"The Pony is not a hovercar and what if I was sleeping? I am the boss."

"Ever heard of the French Revolution?"

"Which one? You Frenchies had so many of them."

"All of them overthrew the boss for not doing their job for the people."

"People? What are you talking about PJ?"

"Since you haven't been to the office in days, and your messages are overflowing, I am going to be assigning you cases. Quick cases. Quick to solve. Quick to get paid. People need to get paid."

We did things "old school" at Liquid Cool. Calls came in, PJ typed up the messages with her bionic fingers, then she sorted and stacked them on my desk. The "hot" pile, the "hold" pile, the "hell no" pile, and a few other miscellaneous ones. That's how we did things, and it worked perfectly for us. You'd often hear about some high-end detective out there getting shot because they were too busy reading messages on their mobile phone rather than paying attention to their surroundings. I grabbed a handful of messages and worked my cases in the field.

"What people? Are you the people who need to get paid?"

"I have mouths to feed, you know. And as VP of Client Services, I have a reputation to maintain as well," PJ said.

Normally, I would have been able to continue with the silly banter for quite a while, but I was not in the mood. She could see that.

"When are you going to get over it?" PJ asked me in a different voice. She was serious too now.

"I'll get over it, eventually. Soon."

"At least you got to meet your hero. How many people can say that?"

"I guess. I can't help thinking I was responsible somehow."

"You weren't and you know that."

"Yeah. What do you have for me?"

"Okay, I have a few good ones from the Hot pile."

"I'm in no mood for serious work today. Simple and then I'll go home and see what Cruz Jr. is up to."

"Simple?"

"What's in the Miscellaneous Pile?"

"There's no money there."

"Weren't you going to create a Hard Luck Pile?"

"You mean Pro Bono Pile. 'Pro Bono' is 'No Bueno.' Ask your parents what that means."

"I can't speak Spanish but I do know what 'no bueno' means. I don't know what half the population under twenty is saying, but I can still understand you even despite the accent."

"Accent? I have no accent. You do."

"PJ, what do you have?"

"Okay, okay. I got one here. Let me read them again."

"Anytime today, PJ."

"You sure you want these no-money cases?"

"Yes."

"Okay, here's one."

"Give me a few that are close together. I'll knock them all out."

"I still say this is a waste of Liquid Cool's time."

"PJ, we're doing good. Doing good is good."

"Doing good is bad, if there's no money. Liquid Cool isn't a charity."

"PJ!"

"Okay, okay. Here they are."

CHAPTER 3

Cops!

I got the idea from some of the bigger detective firms who did regular consulting work free of charge for elementary schools, neighborhood watch groups, religious groups, elderly homes, and Free City. Free media publicity always accompanied these acts of "doing good for the community," which always brought in new paying clients. I was not only a detective but a Metropolis businessman. Mostly, people just wanted to talk and ask questions related to security and crime, which I was happy to do, or meet an actual working detective. It never took too much of my time.

One stop. That's all I had to accomplish. But PJ instead was sending me on a cash-run. That was her idea of doing a pro bono case. Arrive, ring a doorbell, and pick up money for services rendered. In the beginning, I had resisted PJ's unilateral action to collect a retainer from all clients before I began a case. Now that I had been in the private eye business a few years, it was amazing how often clients would be super slow in paying for work done. It didn't matter how "poor" or how rich the client was, they would find some way to delay paying me. So far I was lucky enough not to have anyone outright not pay me. That would be a serious mistake on their part as my first client, the Guy Who Scratched My Vehicle, could tell them. But these cash-runs were an annoyance, but it was either this or not be paid this century.

I had parked the Pony in a secure parking lot, then had to ride an elevator capsule from the one hundred twentieth floor to ground level into the rain which started up again. I was not one to mind the rain, even in my bad mood, but I did mind the crowds of people all around me in their gray or black slickers and big ugly umbrellas in my face. I was wrapped up snuggly in my tan jacket, with my gloved hands in my pockets, wearing my snazzy aqua shoes so I'd never fall on my butt. It was habit to reach up and give my tan fedora a pull.

A violent gust of wind blew my hat off my head!

I ran as fast as I could to catch it while it was in the air. I jumped. I missed. My hat landed in a big puddle on the pedestrian walkway. An optimist would have said, "Oh, what a beautiful puddle with the beautiful colors." I was not that person! Any kind of rainbow display in any ground water was evidence of the chemical residue nastiness that existed on the streets of Metropolis or any big city.

"It's ruined!" I yelled as I snatched my hat up from the ground. Since it touched the ground, I was not putting it back on my head. It would never, ever go back on my head. No hat, no umbrella. I saw more than a few people laughing or smiling at me. Yeah, funny.

The important thing was that my hat had never been blown off my head before in my life and I had been in some serious storms before. I actually had my fedora fitted with an invisible band that I could use and wrapped under my chin. The band was broken. This was an omen. I should have stopped then and there and immediately gone home. But I looked up and I was standing in front of the apartment complex where my deadbeat client lived. I was there, so I decided I might as well get my money and go.

I was so tempted to toss my fedora in the big trash bin in the lobby of the apartment complex. It was not luxurious but it wasn't a dump like in Free City—orderly and trash-free. No doorkeep in the lobby or signs of any automation. No one to be seen as I walked to the elevators.

My inner voice told me to go home, but I was already in the elevator and on my way up to the two hundredth floor.

Did you ever have one of those days where you wish you could just press the cosmic "pause" button and just start the whole day over? I just stood there. I came out of the elevator, walked down the hallway, through the client's open door, and there waiting was some guy with what looked to be a spray-on tan. But it wasn't the spray-on tan that had me frozen like a statue. It was the short-barreled laser rifle in his hand aimed at the open door—well, me now.

What was strange was that he was as shocked to see me as I was to see him. He wasn't my deadbeat client, but that didn't tell me who he was or why he was pointing a weapon at me.

"Should I just walk back out and close the door behind me?" I asked. "You must have forgotten to do that."

"Who are you?" he asked.

"I came up to see my client."

"Your unlucky day."

"Unlucky? Pal, I just came here to see my client. If he's not here, then there's no reason for me to be. Should I go and close the door?"

"You can try, but I don't think you'll complete the task."

"What does that mean?"

"You're not going to talk your way out of this one, Cruz, the famous detective."

"Since you've already decided to shoot me for no reason where's my client?"

"Dead."

"Why did you do that?"

The man made a face. He didn't care in the least that he killed someone.

"Wait, why are you standing there? Who were you waiting for to walk through this door?" I asked.

"The wife."

"Oh."

He smiled. "Yes, oh."

I shook my head with a pissed off face. "I ruined my hat. Now I'm going to ruin my jacket."

"Ruined your hat?"

"Yeah, the wind blew it off my head into the nasty, muddy water. Now my jacket is going to get ruined too."

He laughed. "You mean when I shoot you."

I only fired once. The laser pulse ripped through my jacket pocket and blasted a hole into the upper top of his head. I'd already moved to the side just in case, but he didn't even have time to squeeze the trigger of his laser rifle before collapsing to the ground.

As I straightened myself up to look around the apartment, I suddenly dove for the ground as a woman's scream shattered the silence. I'd almost fired my omega-gun again but stopped when I saw it was my client's wife standing at the doorway. She had dropped her purse and a bag of groceries to the ground and stood there screaming at the sight of the dead man. The woman was like a human alarm and I could hear commotion outside the apartment in the hallway. Doors opening, footsteps, voices. "Call the police!" I heard someone call out.

Another woman appeared behind the wife to grab her. People started to file in.

"Is that man dead?" one of the male neighbors asked.

"He sure looks dead," the first woman neighbor said with her arm around the wife, who had changed from her maniacal screaming to maniacal heavy breathing.

"Is he the one who did it?" one of them yelled.

All of them turned to me sitting on the floor. They looked at me. I looked at them.

"We called the police," one of them said.

"Well, good," I said. "It saves me from having to do it."

"Did you kill this man?" the woman asked.

"What do you think?" I answered sarcastically.

"Why did you do that?"

"He was pointing a laser rifle at me," I answered. "He said he was waiting until she"—I pointed at the wife—"came through the doorway to shoot her. Do you know who that man is?" I asked.

She looked at the man for a moment, then back at me. "No."

"No?" I asked. "The police are on the way, so you might want to practice your lying so it at least appears more believable." I stood to my feet as more people came into the apartment. "What is this? This is not a house party everyone. All of you get out! This is a crime scene!"

People looked at each other but slowly started to exit the apartment.

"Not you," I said to the wife. "Don't pretend you don't know who I am. Don't you owe me some money?" She nervously glanced at the gun in my hand.

"Who is this man?" one of the neighbors asked.

"He's a private detective my husband hired."

"Is this how you conduct business?" a male neighbor scolded.

"Yes, this is how I conduct business. I collect the money I'm owed for work done."

"I'm sorry," the wife said. "My husband handles anything having to do with money in the family."

I was pissed. I knew she was going to say that. I lifted my gun arm, startling the group and I walked further into the apartment as they all watched me from the doorway. It didn't take me long but I found the husband. He was in the bedroom, on his chest on the floor, dead.

The hallway was a complete madhouse. Thick, neon yellow police tape—POLICE LINE. DO NOT CROSS—was draped across either end of the hallway with a contingent of police officers standing guard. Apartment neighbors stood outside the line trying to see what they could see, flashing pictures with their mobiles or gossiping. It would only get worse once the media arrived.

Metropolis police officers were like paramilitary soldiers. They had to be with the criminals we had in the supercity. Body-armored uniforms in the colors of silver and black, with the word "PEACE" in big, bold white letters on their chest and back. Visors concealed the top half of their faces. You couldn't see their faces clearly, but they could see everything about you clearly with their hi-tech optics.

Outside my client's apartment were a couple of officers standing guard at the door; police detectives and coroners were inside. They had covered the bodies of the shooter and my former client (who owed me money). Inside, I sat on one couch with an officer watching me. On the couch across from me was the wife, who hadn't looked at me once while we waited.

I was steaming. I wasn't going to get paid. I could tell. She had already decided and was going to use this incident as an excuse. I had lost my hat, blown a hole through my favorite jacket and I wasn't going to get any money for the first time in my new detective career. I was pissed.

"Come on, Cruz," an officer said, gesturing to me.

I stood from the couch. They were going to take me Downtown to Metro PD. I'd be cleared for the shooting but still I'd be interrogated for hours. My weapon would be taken, tested, and I wouldn't see it for at least a couple of days. Now, I realized why they gave me a gun license and concealed weapon permit. Control. Gone were the days of hiding or switching weapons. I had to register every weapon I had or I'd lose both license and permit. And no detective would last a day in the supercity without a weapon.

My dead client's wife still didn't look at me as I passed in front of her, led by one of the officers. I actually saved her life, but it didn't matter to her. If she acknowledged me, she'd have to pay me. She didn't want to pay me.

When I got into the hall, the officer stopped. "Hold here," the officer said. Clicks and flashes. That's what I heard and saw. All the lookie-loos saw me and snapped my photo. Cruz of the Liquid Cool Detective Agency at another crime scene.

"Hey Cruz! Can you tell us what happened?"

Good grief! The media had arrived too. The media jackals trained their cameras at me.

"Can't we go and get this over with?" I said to the officer.

"We're all going down together," he answered.

At that moment another officer led out my dead client's wife, but she had handcuffs on.

"Why is she being arrested?" I asked. "She's the victim."

"Thanks Cruz, but we didn't ask you," the other officer said to me.

The wife's face was red, but she kept her gaze off me.

"What's going on here?" I asked her.

She ignored me.

"What the heck is going on? Why are you arresting her?"

The police ignored me too.

"Let's go ladies and gentlemen," one of the officers said and led us to the elevators.

The police had cordoned off most of the hallway, including the elevator.

"Did you kill your husband, Mrs. Chambers?" reporters yelled.

I was tempted to answer but knew that once you engaged the press they'd never let you go. The elevator capsule arrived.

"Don't take us down together," I said.

"In you go, Cruz," my police chaperone said to me.

"Inside," the other officer said to my client's wife.

As soon as the elevator closed I looked at her.

"What did you do?" I asked.

She kept her gaze away and didn't answer. I looked at the smirking officers. "Can't you help a street detective out?"

"No, Cruz. You'll have to read about it in the news like everyone else. Just because we're cops like you, Cruz, doesn't mean we're going to give you special favors."

I looked at her again, squinting. "Did you know the shooter?"

She ignored me. Did she? The shooter said he was waiting for her? Was he? What was going on? The police wouldn't arrest her unless there was something seriously incriminating in the apartment. I noticed the two officers chuckling. No doubt amused by watching me try to deduce the crime.

"Okay, no one will tell me anything. Fine. I'll read about it in the news." I looked at the officers. "That being the case, can you at least get me home in under an hour?"

"Call your wife, Cruz. You're going to be at Metro PD awhile—a long while."

"But why? I didn't do anything wrong. I saved a citizen. Besides, I have babysitting duties tonight."

The officers laughed.

If Metropolis were a country, then Downtown Metro would be the capital. The center of that capital would be City Hall at the end of one avenue and at the other end was Metropolis Police Central, a cubical fortress of a building. It was rumored to be the deepest building in the world, burrowing endless levels into the ground—a holdover of the old days when nuclear annihilation and civil unrest of biblical proportions were the daily fear of the government. That was long before the mega-cities and supercities of today, and the rain. Police Central was headquarters of the supercity's five hundred thousand-plus police force—the largest on Earth.

There I sat in the general waiting room inside the station, which some interior decorator attempted to make as bright and cheery as possible, but it wasn't the opposite of the grimy exterior of the building; it complimented it. A constant flow of police with their captured criminals passed by. I remained in my bad mood. Why didn't they bring me back to the private waiting area? It wasn't like I was a stranger. All the rank-and-file and brass knew me by sight. I was best friends with the head of the police union and the chief of police and I were officially frenemies. I wanted to go home!

All around me were shifty, shady people. The outer waiting room of Metro PD was exactly where you didn't want to be. It was dirty and dangerous and I was unarmed. The DMV-style police behind the counter couldn't or wouldn't come to my aid, or anyone else's, if a fight broke out. I kept my eyes scanning all of them. More than a few had their eyes locked on me.

"Don't you wear a hat?" asked some old guy sitting across from me. He was unkempt, unshaven, and unfriendly.

I shook my head.

"Yeah, you do," he said. He opened his jacket and there it was. He was wearing a Liquid Cool T-shirt. He smiled. I didn't.

I promptly got up from my seat and walked to the counter. One of the officers noticed me and I could see the smirk forming on his face.

"Why can't I wait in the back?" I asked.

"Because you can't."

"How long will it be? Why can't you take my statement?"

"Because I can't."

"I have to get home."

"You need to calm yourself, Cruz."

"I can't stay here forever."

"You need to calm yourself now."

The other officer behind the counter gestured to me. "I'm buzzing you back. You know where to go."

I breathed a sigh of relief as I was buzzed in. I walked past the main counter to a single door and in I went. When I passed under the security arch, another officer was waiting and pointed me to a bench against the wall.

Security at Central was formidable—armed police guards, security cameras, armed sentries at the end of the hallways, near the elevators and scanning archways; but that was only for entering. Entering and exiting pedestrian traffic was divided by a solid metal barrier down the middle of the grand hallway. For those exiting, they walked out without any checks whatsoever.

This was much better. At least I could sit in peace away from the zoo of people outside. There were only a few other people waiting in the hallway, seated on benches. At the other end of the hallway were the bull pen of dual cubicles where the street police sat and worked when not on the beat. Further away were the elevated single cubicles where the detectives worked. The interrogation rooms were around the corner. Who knew how many hours I would be in one of them?

I hadn't seen my dead client's wife since we landed and got out of the police cruiser. One officer took her to Booking. I was taken to the main waiting area. I still didn't know why she was arrested but I didn't care. Husband, wife, and a killer. In the detective business, even your clients could be criminals. That's how the world was in Metropolis. I had more than a few clients try to kill me and I had already killed a few. I'd let the police sort it all out, not that they needed my permission. The main issue was that I wasn't going to get paid for my work. I'd sue her. That's what I'd do. Even if I lost money I would. It was the principle of the thing.

Soon I found myself lying on the bench. I wanted to go home and I wanted to sleep. I didn't want any humans or animals of any kind around me. I closed my eyes, as I yawned. I would dream of that endless rainy night under a Milky Way sky. That's what I was going to do until that tagger punk interrupted it and set off a chain of events that landed me in Metro PD.

I knew I had dozed off, though not for long. Something woke me up but unfortunately, and not surprisingly, it wasn't the police finally coming to get me. A couple of officers deposited a kid to sit and wait on the bench opposite me.

Scraggly, spiky hair, all dressed in black, wearing the bright-white shoes. His hands stained with neon paint. I sat up to glare at the tagger juvenile delinquent with a deep frown.

"Why are you staring at me old man?" he snapped.

I stood and pointed at him. "You caused all this! This is your fault! You ruined my day! I lost my hat, ruined my jacket, and didn't get to have my nap! Now I'm here! And I am not old! I'm in my thirties, you juvenile delinquent toddler tagger!"

Yes, this was one evil day. That kid stared back at me, his mouth hanging open, with eyes so wide with fear he looked like one of those Japanese anime cartoon characters. He was in the direct path of a crazy person in a foul mood.

"Quick, someone call the cops!" the tagger jumped to his feet now, about to run.

PART TWO

BioGenesis: The Case

CHAPTER 4

Burglar

ioGenesis.

B Noun. The production of living organisms from other living organisms.

Metropolis was always filled with busy vertical lanes of hover-traffic. Like any other city some districts were more congested than others. In this part of the supercity were not only personal hovercars and hoverbikes, hovertaxis for hire, and commercial hovertrucks, but not too far away were the open zone for moving hoverhotels. Metropolis had many of them for the supercity's eccentric and super-wealthy. Hoverhotels came in all different sizes and configurations. They were mobile, floating residences that slowly circled the supercity in an endless loop.

It was late at night but with all the headlights of hovercar traffic and floating hoversigns, lamps, and signals there was plenty of illumination—but only immediately around the hovertraffic. A hovervan pulled out of normal sky traffic as a passenger door opened. Out jumped a figure wearing a skin-tight leather-like black costume from head to toe. He extended his arms and was like a human flying squirrel with a membrane covering the space from his wrist to his ankle. He wasn't flying but silently gliding through the air.

The trajectory was aimed at the hoverhotels and he was coming up on them fast. He quickly moved his arms to ninety degrees, decreasing by half his gliding wingspan to slow his descent. The first of the hoverbuildings neared as he fell. Tenth floor, fifth, first, ground. He reached out and grabbed the lip of the ground floor grating, in between an array of antennas. The sensors could not see him. He was not using or wearing a jetpack or any other hover-device. He had no metal or alloy on his body at all. He looked up with his dark, enhanced goggles to see his destination. All he had were giant suction cups in his gloved hands, which he needed to get up to the first level wall. From there, he climbed using nothing more than his natural body strength and dexterity—all the way up to the seventy-fifth floor.

Click. That was the only sound he made as the large bay windows opened. The figure pushed through the drapes, crawled further inside and lay on his stomach on the carpet for a bit.

He extended his arms and contracted them. He did relaxation exercises for his legs too as he scanned the luxurious suite with his night vision. He turned to lie on his back and studied the room. No one was home but he slowly rose to his feet. "No one home" didn't mean without security. His eye caught at least two motion-and-sound sensors. He returned to a prone position on his back. His suit had no metal but it was not without its own special qualities. He lay still as he slowly and quietly "crawled" across the carpet. When he reached the first sensor he reached for his mouth with one hand. He pulled out a concealed dart gun—technically nothing more than a long wooden straw. He blew once and disabled the ceiling sensor with one shot. He turned his head, put another dart in his mouth, and blew again. The second sensor was disabled. There was no guesswork involved; he knew where all the sensors and alarms were in the suite. It took him less than two minutes to disable them all.

The burglar's suit had all the conveniences. He pulled one tightly-packed bag from each elbow pocket, opened them up and was ready. The bedroom was a Taj Mahal of opulence and the owners were going to regret that they so freely displayed their jewelry and valuable trinkets from around the world. All went into the burglar's duffel bags. He moved fast—only taking what would fit into the bag and would fetch the highest prices on the black market. Less than fifteen minutes and both bags well filled to the max.

He noticed the expensive paintings on the wall. Tempting but impractical. It would take too much time to remove them from their frames and roll them up without damaging them. Getting anything but pennies on the million dollars would be the best you could hope for when it came to such "hot properties." Not worth it.

He gave the bedroom another look over. He knew there was at least one vault in the dwelling. He laid his two duffel bags on the ground and touched the nose of a Napoleon bust statue with shades on the main mirrored chest of drawers. It was a risk but one he was willing to take. All he wanted to do was take a peek. The secret walk-in vault opened automatically, which also doubled as a panic room.

He stood waiting for the light to go on. It didn't. He stepped forward and waived his hands around the vault doorway—maybe motion-activated. Nothing. He walked to the main light switch and turned off all the bedroom lights. The night vision of his goggles would switch on. He walked back to the vault.

"What!"

The burglar frantically grabbed his duffel bags, but not before tripping on his own feet. He jumped up, grabbed them, and ran out of the bedroom as quickly as he could. One of the bags hit a large vase in the living room as he was running.

Oh no!

He couldn't catch it in time. There were only seconds left. He took long strides to the bay windows, opened them. He threw both bags over the balcony and dove himself. Alarms screeched. Intrusion lights flashed. Security drones would arrive in moments.

The burglar and his bags fell through the sky, then the parachutes opened as they disappeared into the night.

CHAPTER 5

China Doll

Where did wives, girlfriends, and mistresses of Metropolis' rich and powerful go to look their movie-quality best? Eye Candy! Eye Candy Image Salon was located on Funky Circle in the ultra-hipster Paisley Parish district. The establishment was always packed with high-end clients from the time it opened until its late-night closing. Eye Candy's "fashion police" of makeup artists, hairdressers, manicurists, pedicurists, skincare techs, tattoo artists, wardrobe stylists, wardrobe collators, and dressers always attracted high demand.

Working on a snow white-haired female client—haircut, wash, blow-dry and style, was Eye Candy's chief fashion officer, China Doll. Female clients called her China; male clients called her Doll. Family addressed her by her real name—Dot. She was already famous in the image and fashion circles, when she met Cruz. She was now Mrs. Cruz.

As the consummate fashionista, every piece of clothing, accessory, and piece of jewelry on her person was the trendiest and most stylish. Today, she wore a white halter top speckled with red stars, black skin-tight pants with a skinny red belt, and red heels. Her jet-black hair was pulled back with the ponytail resting on one shoulder. She always wore a colored neck scarf—today was a sheer light gold one. Every finger had a white ring, and each wrist had multiple red and white bracelets.

The interior of Eye Candy was designed like a beehive design, with every section visible to every other section, due to the transparent walls, except the break room, full body baths, and the bathrooms. Eye Candy was nothing but carefully coordinated chaos—clients sitting on chairs getting their hair and makeup done in one section, their nails and toenails in another, facials in another, tattoos in another (always temporary to change according to current fashion trends), skincare consultations in another, and style analysis and wardrobing in yet another section.

China Doll worked quickly on her client, who had a flight to catch, blow drying the woman's hair. They were in the main row of the hairdressing section with colleagues and clients all around her.

"Ms. Seven, I'll have you on your way in ten minutes," China said to the client.

"China, you're number one with me. Last minute flight to Shanghai. Barely had time to pack, but it's a big, big client," the woman said in the reclined chair.

"Big client equals big money," China Doll said.

"Could mean the difference of having a one month whirl-wind vacation or having to work twelve hour days for the next year, if I want to keep my job."

Another woman holding a silver, diamond-studded mobile phone walked to them. If China Doll was Eye Candy's Chief Fashion Officer, its founder, Prima Donna, the boss, was its Chief-above-all, the Matron Queen of Metropolis fashion. She was in a glittering electric blue outfit with black, knee-high boots.

"Ms. Seven, we have a premium hovercab waiting at the door," Prima announced.

"Thanks Prima."

China completed her final touches, including a complimentary make-up touch-up and topped it off with a splash of glitter. She grabbed a large hand mirror from the back of the beauty chair. "How's that, Ms. Seven?"

"Perfection as always, China."

For long-time clients like Ms. Seven, they paid and tipped before they even sat down. Eye Candy was nothing but perfection to all its clientele.

China Doll was not done. She chatted it up with Ms. Seven as they walked to the main entrance and outside to a waiting Let It Ride premium hovertaxi.

China strolled back in and yelled, "Mrs. Charge, come on down and get that beautiful self in my chair."

Prima had joined the floor to work alongside China Doll and other Eye Candy staff. There was Cyan, who had a million outfits, but all were the same color of cyan; Pinkie, known for her bright pink hair; Goat Girl, known for the large ring hanging from her nose septum; and Lipps, who had quite the set of augmented lips.

"How's that famous husband of yours?" Prima asked as she brushed then clipped her client's hair.

"Cruz is fine," China answered, doing the same with her client.

"I've heard things."

"What things, Prima?"

"That he's still stewing over Wilford G.'s death, which is strange since I knew the man for sixty years and your husband only knew him a few months. I hear he's still in a state over it."

"Wilford G. was Cruz's hero. It's different."

"I know, but I hear he's not doing much detecting as a detective these days since the funeral."

China sighed. "He'll get over it."

"He's been brooding for much too long. Snap your man out of it."

"He'll snap out of it on his own."

"Help him. We both know why."

"What does that mean?" Cyan and Goat Girl asked at almost the same time.

"China and I are having a private conversation here," Prima said.

Employees and clients chuckled.

"Private?" Pinkie said.

"Yes, private," Prima said. "Well, China. What's the plan?"

"He'll snap out of it on his own. He needs a bit more time. He probably shouldn't have gone to the funeral. It only made it worse."

"The funeral was a while ago now. What about his parents? Can't they help?"

"They're trying."

"I won't even bother asking about your parents."

China held in a laugh. The others laughed out loud.

"Parents-in-law?" Goat Girl said. "I don't know any man who ever wants to hear from his parents-in-law about his business."

"I know!" China said. "Cruz needs a case."

"Isn't that what he's been doing since then?" Prima asked.

"He has been less than interested in the cases that have been coming his way."

"I thought you hated him working the big, high-profile cases."

"I do, but I think that's what he needs. That will take his mind off things."

"What about PJ?"

"She's tried too, but I'll see what she can find. She knows the kind of cases that he can't resist."

"With all the criminals in this supercity, finding a good case should be easy," a female client said from the chair.

"Exactly."

"But he's already done the super assassin and flying saucer extraterrestrial cases already," Cyan said. "And the super cyborgs too."

"Yeah, you're right," China said. "It has to be unique."

"Not unique. Strange," Goat Girl interjected.

They all glanced at her. She was probably the biggest extrovert of the group but on the floor conversed only with her clients.

"Strange?" Prima asked. "Do you have a case for China to take to her husband?"

Goat Girl smiled. "Maybe."

The workers stopped and the clients looked at her too.

"Well?" Prima put her hands on her waist. "We're not mind-readers."

"Yes, we're waiting," another client in a chair added.

CHAPTER 6

The Hellspawn (The Wife's Parents)

Finally, I got out of Metro PD. I was steaming mad that they kept me there so long when I thought I was doing a good deed by saving them the trouble of having to have a shootout with a bad guy. Not to mention the fact I wasn't going to get paid money due me for the first time. One way or another I was going to get my money and I didn't care if one was dead and the other had something to do with the murder.

I calmed down a bit as I was on my way to get my son. My wife's parents were babysitting him, which I hated but what choice did I have? I drove into the booshy district of Elysian Heights—one of many wealthy, bourgeoisie, upper-class areas of Metropolis. Their mega-apartment complexes were triple and quadruple the size of a football stadium and were over two hundred stories high. Each tower was like its own country, with its own dictatorial semi-autonomous residential government, its own paramilitary security force, and its own pleasure world. My wife's parents lived in the building known as New China. They didn't like me and I didn't like them. They were the Wans, but I called them by the more appropriate name—Hellspawn.

To this day I didn't know what business the Wans had made all their money in. They owned a few major restaurant chains but it had to be more than that. I surmised that it had to be some illegal business, but Dot flatly denied any such thing, though she wouldn't tell me what.

Security knew who I was, but they still escorted me to the Wan apartment. I kept knocking on the door and ringing the bell but no response.

"Where are they?" I asked the two security guards.

The two young Chinese guards just looked at me—one emotionless; the other with a smirk.

"No speak the English," one answered sarcastically.

"Will you speak the English if I put my foot up your backside?"

The guard gave a high-pitched scream and took a kung-fu stance, facing me.

"I'm in no mood to play martial arts with you. Take me to them so I can get my son and get out of here. Now!"

The kung-fu guard stood up straight, and they both reluctantly led me down the hallway.

All this time I didn't know the building had its own interior botanical park. It was huge. We had exited twenty floors shy of the roof and the guards led me out of the elevator capsule into what was like stepping into a picture of the rustic outdoors from the past. Running and bike paths were on the outside, but most of the people I saw were simply walking, whether for exercise or while meditating; mostly alone. There were park benches and tables with people playing chess, cards or other board games. Large bamboo trees dotted the park with grass too green to be real which was a relief because real plant life attracted critters. I was in no mood for bugs or vermin.

There were a few groups clustered in different areas laughing and talking. But it was the one in front of me that caught my eye. I spotted the Wans. Mommy Dearest was holding my son, but that's not what made my mouth drop open, aghast. There were all these people around my son, poking and prodding him. I dashed to them.

"Why are you exposing my son to these nasty people?" I yelled at Mommy and Daddy Dearest—the Hellspawn.

The crowd stopped and looked at me. One of the older ladies, who was pinching my son's cheek, glared at me. "Nasty? You nasty!"

"How do I know where your hands have been? Touching my son with those hands. How do I know they weren't in your nose or in your pants?"

"My hands weren't in my pants. I'm not a dog. I'm not a man!"

"Go away with your nastiness!"

"You nasty!"

"Get away. Be off with you woman."

"People like touching babies. That's what normal people do!"

"Not my baby son." I took a karate stance.

"Are you going to kick me?" the woman asked, also taking a martial arts stance.

"I might."

"Who dis man!" one of the men asked Mr. Wan.

Mr. Wan yelled something to him in Chinese.

My eyes narrowed as I looked at him. "I don't need to know Chinese to know what you said. You know exactly who I am."

Mrs. Wan tightened her grip on my son and began to step back from me. She yelled something at me in Chinese.

"I know you speak better English than me, you fakers! Give me my son!" I moved to them quickly.

"No! I will take him," the older woman said to me, stepping in front of me.

"Go away nasty hands." I stepped around her and grabbed my son from Dot's mother.

I held my son up in the air to look at him. Was he getting bigger or fatter? I hope they weren't feeding my son inappropriate food like dog or snails. He looked at me as he started smiling. He probably barely recognized me without my tan fedora on my head.

"What kind of funny clothes do they have you in? I know your mother wouldn't dress you so shabbily, so it must have been them. And where's your hat? At least you have all your fingers and toes. No bruises or marks of violence."

Some in the crowd burst out laughing and starting talking to the Wans in Chinese. My parents-in-law just glared.

"You a bum!" Mr. Wan yelled at me.

I held Cruz. Jr. on my side. "That's no way to talk to your jail buddy."

"Jail buddy?" one of the men asked Mr. Wan.

"Yes. Didn't they tell you? Mrs. Wan too. We were all arrested one time by the police."

I saw mouths drop open wide in surprise as the frenzied chatter of Chinese increased. I saw Mr. Wan reach into his jacket and Mrs. Wan reach into her purse. When someone has you locked in a death-stare as they reach for unknown items in their pocket, you'd better run. If it were out on the streets, I'd already have drawn my omega-gun on them. But I had a toddler in my arms and I couldn't shoot my wife's parents. Or could I? I ran away with Cruz Jr. in my arms. The two young Chinese security guards followed, smiling. My psycho parents-in-law liked their guns, so I wasn't about to wait to see what they were reaching for.

CHAPTER 7

Two Stupid Detectives

Cruz Jr. had been rescued from the Hellspawn and their nasty hand friends! Now, I drove back to Buzz Town. The business district wasn't one of the best areas, but it wasn't one the worst. It was one of those in-between places, like my own residential Rabbit City. I had reached the Circle, or Circuit Circle to the uninitiated—the main thoroughfare that my building and others faced.

"Cruz Jr., I'll get you to the office and get you dressed properly and then I'll get dressed properly."

In my office, I always had a few sets of clothes in hermetically sealed bags in my desk for those times when I had my son. The boy was in desperate need of a wardrobe make-over. Hopefully, I had a little black fedora for him. I always had a change of clothes in the office too.

Cruz Jr. was buckled in nicely in the back seat. He was looking at me—I could see from my auxiliary rear view mirror on the side, so I could glance at him. But he was more interested in the toy hovercar he had in his hand.

We'd be at the Liquid Cool office soon.

Liquid was on the 100th floor of the tower, and after all my high-profile cases, was its most famous tenant. We still didn't have real building security like a real high-class commercial building, but I just made sure that the security for my floor and especially my office was state-of-the-art.

Unfortunately, that meant that some of the floor's tenants took full advantage of their "free" security and my firm's reputation. Some even went so far as advertising: "Right down the hall from the famous Liquid Cool Detective Agency." Swine! I had to ignore them all, but one new tenant particularly annoyed me: another detective firm. I hated them and they knew it.

"Mr. Cruz, the man himself." I heard as I exited the elevator holding Cruz. Jr.

It was two detectives in black slickers with suits underneath walking to the elevator. Both were wearing colored eye wear. They worked for this new detective firm on my floor. Vacancies were rare in the building as most of the offices were in decades-long leases or more. Likely, an existing tenant was sub-leasing space to their firm for some recurring monthly income.

"And we see you have the next generation in training," said the other one.

I said nothing. They were amused.

"Mr. Cruz, we can try out our new material on you. How many detectives does it take to screw in a light bulb?"

Every time I saw these detectives which wasn't rare enough, they had some dumb joke to tell me.

"That's stupid," I said. "There's no such thing as light bulbs."

"None," said the first one.

"Yes, there are. You can see them in museums," said the second one.

"Because Cruz already did it," finished the first one.

"You two are the worst joke tellers in the universe," I said. "Bad delivery. One guy steppin' all over the other's non-existent punch line."

"Cruz, you're like an old man in a young body," the first guy said. "What will you be when you're old?"

"Far away from you two."

I should have known by now not to engage with the human animal life in conversation. A curious Cruz, Jr. watched them with a smile as I side-stepped them to get into the office quickly.

"See ya around, Cruz."

Again, I didn't answer. All I heard was chuckling as I heard the elevator arrive. I glanced back to make sure they were gone. They were; the elevator closed and was descending.

"How do I get those guys off my floor?" I asked Cruz Jr.

He looked at me and then started giggling.

"Don't giggle. I expect an answer, sir. They're stealing business from your pops. And I don't want to hear about the virtue of the free market."

CHAPTER 8

PJ

Finally, my long ordeal was over. The night from hell at Metro PD in Downtown Metro, a super-shower at home in Rabbit City, rescued my son from the Hellspawn in Elysian Heights, to the sanctuary of my own office in Buzz City.

The moment I entered the office, there was a beep. We had our own scanning arch above the door to detect weapons, cyborgs, robots and androids. Obviously, I was now packing.

At her reception station was PJ in all her glory. She stood up as soon as she heard the beep. One hand was behind the wall of the reception desk so you couldn't see it. But I didn't need to see. She had a laser rifle.

"Oh, it's you," she said.

She had a purple sleeveless top to match her purple lipstick.

"Yes, it's me. Only the guy who pays your salary."

"Hey, Cruz, Jr." She acknowledged with a smile. "Are you tired of him yet? Come to auntie PJ." She held out her arms—her buff cybernetic arms. The rest of her outfit were leather pants and knee-high black boots.

I laughed. "Auntie PJ? Stop confusing my son with falsehoods."

"I am Auntie PJ."

I relented because Cruz, Jr. was already trying to wriggle out of my hands to be held by her. She took him and started speaking French.

"Good grief! Chinese from the parents-in-law, French from you…"

"Spanish from your parents," PJ interjected.

"My son will be so confused."

"Confused? Cruz, he'll be able to speak 10 languages before he's ten. That's ten more than you."

"Yeah, funny. I'm going to get him out of those horrible clothes from Dot's parents, so I don't want to be disturbed by anyone. No clients. And you have my permission to punch anyone who tries to disturb me."

"What a way to talk. If you're in the office, you're working."

"No. I was at Metro PD all night thanks to you."

"Thanks to me? Cruz, with your bad attitude lately did you really expect me to send you to a no-bueno, pro-bono case. If you're going to do things for no money, you need to at least get a benefit from it, like free press and good client reviews. No, with your bad attitude, cash runs only for you."

"Did I say I was at Metro PD all night thanks to your cash run?"

"Who did you shoot this time?"

"I didn't shoot anyone. Well…I did shoot someone, but it was a bad guy and I was saving the life of one of our clients."

"Oh, that's good. That means we'll get a good review."

"No, she won't. The police arrested her."

"Arrested her?"

"Yeah. The bad guy I shot, but he already shot the husband."

"Which one is the client?"

"The dead guy and the wife they arrested."

"Oh no."

"Yeah."

"You were supposed to pick up our money."

"That's why I was there. You sent me there. The bad guy shot the husband and was going to shoot the wife. At least that's what I thought until they arrested her too. She and the bad guy knew each other."

"*Incroyable!* Did she pay us?"

"No! She said he was supposed to do it, but he's dead."

"Why can't she pay?"

"Exactly! She's not going to pay us."

"Why didn't you shoot her?"

"I would have, if I knew she was going to do that."

"Incroyable."

"Well, just don't shoot me." The voice came out of the waiting area and startled me.

"Oh, I forget," PJ said. "You already have a client waiting—a potential client."

I looked at the young woman. She was dressed in a dark blue slicker and had really dark short hair. But there was something about her.

"Do I know you?" I asked.

She smiled. I looked and PJ was smiling too.

"Okay, what's going on you two? Who are you? Wait, you're Goat Girl. Where's your nose ring and why is your hair so short?"

"Yeah," PJ said to Cruz Jr. in her arms. "Your daddy can live up to his reputation sometimes."

Cruz Jr. started giggling and clapping his hands.

CHAPTER 9

Goat Girl

Obviously, my funk hadn't left me yet; otherwise I'd have noticed Goat Girl sitting in the waiting area. PJ had turned the reception-waiting area into a shrine of sorts, to me. Framed pictures hung on the wall of news stories of my famous cases and me with notable people like the Mayor and other politicians, business leaders, and average people like the mother and daughter from my very first case. Other than that, the waiting area had a few geometric, purple couches around a glass table on a shimmering, neon powder blue rug. The lobby table had PJ's French fashion magazines and my hovercar racing magazines. My powers of observation were severely not working.

"Your wife sent me," Goat Girl said.

"Dot? Why? What's going on?" I asked.

"Mr. Cruz will see you in his office," PJ said in her professional voice and pushed open the door of my private office. I went to reach for my son. But she said, "Cruz Jr. can stay with auntie until you finish speaking with the client."

I lowered my hands as PJ walked to her desk. Psychedelic posters hung on the wall behind where she sat, her fancy "modern" glass desk with see-through glass drawers, and, on top, her mobile computer and retro boom-box, which meant anything old will become new again, just give it a century or two. Her entire workstation was behind a metal barrier, but it didn't look like a barrier at all with the decorations.

"My son better not be calling you auntie when he gets to his double digits," I said.

"Cruz, I do have to get back to work," Goat Girl said to me.

"Oh, sorry. It's another full-time job protecting my son from all these unhealthy outside forces. Follow me."

On the wall right outside my office was our official LIQUID COOL neon sign, with the smaller neon letters of DETECTIVE AGENCY underneath.

"Where's your hat?" Goat Girl asked as she followed me.

"The wind blew it off. That's never happened in my life. But it happened today. A bad omen."

"Or a good omen," she said as she walked to the chairs in front of my desk. She sat down as I took off my tan slicker and hung it up on the coat rack near the door.

"Why a good omen? And why are you in disguise? Or do you work in disguise?"

She laughed. "I work in disguise. Most of us at Eye Candy do, except for your wife and Prima."

"Why?"

"Cruz, Eye Candy is our life, but we do have a life outside of the salon. We prefer to have some semblance of a private life."

"I can definitely relate to that. I knew it! I knew those big lips on Lips couldn't be real," I said.

Goat Girl laughed out loud. "In her case, they're real. All her parts are real, Cruz. But you wouldn't recognize her out of disguise, believe me."

"I'm good at recognizing faces, in or out of disguises."

"I see that, Cruz. You recognized me right away."

As I walked to my desk, I glanced out my droplet covered window with its overcast view of the other monolith towers on the Circle before sitting down behind my desk. My eyes went to the item as I sat. A block of wood on the corner of my desk. It had a baby isopod encased in a clear, solid resin in the middle. Wilford G. had given it to me when we worked our A.I. Confidential Case. Funny, I thought, he gave it to me to snap me out of my funk then. The block of wood had an engraving: "YOUR DAY IS MUCH BETTER THAN HIS—OR WOULD YOU LIKE TO SWITCH PLACES?"

It brought a slight smile to my face. A nice little gift from my posthumous mentor and a nice memory of our time working together.

"What can I do for you?" I asked.

"Firstly, Cruz, I'm here because of your wife."

"Okay."

"I mean, she said you need a real case."

"I work real cases all the time. What's she up to?"

"She said you needed a unique case."

"Unique cases are usually unique for a reason. No one wants them or they're too dangerous."

"It's not too dangerous and you might want it."

"Let's hear it then. Did you tell PJ the case?"

"And she collected a retainer."

"That's PJ."

Goat Girl grinned. "It's okay. She gave me a special discount and I pay my way. Anyway, I'll be reimbursed."

"As long as the client is happy. Let's hear it."

"I know someone who's kinda a criminal. But, it in no ways means I'm one. I'm not a criminal and I don't associate with them. Unless they're a client and come into Eye Candy for a haircut, facial, styling or one of our beauty services. Or...Christmas dinner. But that's only once a year."

"Is this person whose 'kinda' a criminal a family member?"

"Yes, but don't tell your wife. I have nothing to do with them. I went to college to better myself. They went to prison, the lot of them."

"You're like the white sheep of the family."

She thought for a moment and smiled. "Yeah. I like that. White sheep. That's me. No, a white wolf. Because if I were a sheep then that would make them black wolves and wolves eat sheep. No one's eating me. I can beat up the lot of them, even the cyborg ones."

"Are you going to tell me what this is about...today?"

"Your wife said you're in one of your bad moods, like around your birthdays, so she wanted to get you a cool case. I got one."

"From this 'kinda' criminal family member?"

"My uncle."

"What does your uncle do?"

"Don't tell your wife and no talkin' to the cops."

"My conversation with clients or potential clients is strictly confidential. The only exception is if they attack me or try to kill me, of course."

"Yeah, like that NeuroDancer chick."

"Yes. Is your uncle going to do something like that?"

Goat Girl laughed. "Him? He wouldn't hurt a fly—literally. It's better if he tells you personally, straight from the horse's mouth."

"Wolf."

"No, I think he'd be a sheep since he's non-violent."

"Then bring him in. Let's see what he's got."

"Good. It's a weird case."

"Weird? I thought you said unique."

"That too. I think you can help him. And it's so weird it's the kinda case you can sink your OCD teeth into."

"I don't have OCD anymore."

"You're cured?"

"Yeah. I only have OCD tendencies these days. I'm too busy with Cruz, Jr. for any of that anymore."

"Good for you. I'll get him in. I'll set it up with PJ then. And Dot says to call your parents over for dinner."

"Dinner? Why?"

"I don't know. I'm just the messenger."

"What are you all up to?"

Goat Girl laughed. "That's why you're a good detective. You're suspicious of everyone."

"Exactly."

She stood from her chair. "I'll see PJ then say good-bye to the little man, Cruz Jr. You call your parents, then call your wife. I'd get my story a bit more compact about why you were at Metro PD all night. What I heard you telling PJ isn't going to cut it with her. Just take my word for it."

"It isn't a story. It's the truth."

"I guess you'll be sleeping here in the office tonight."

"Okay, okay. The story will be compacted, and I'll play up the 'saving the client' angle, but keep the 'client gets arrested too' part to myself."

Goat Girl smiled. "That's why you're the famous detective—adaptability and natural intelligence."

"My Ma didn't raise no fool."

CHAPTER 10

Twinkle

I tried to get more detail from Dot when she returned home from Eye Candy. I was relaxing watching TV and Cruz Jr. was in his bedtime clothes playing with his toys on the carpet. Unfortunately, Dot told me that I'd have to wait until tomorrow. I preferred to talk about this secret, "unique" and "weird" potential case, but instead the conversation at dinner was all about her parents accusing me of all kinds of nefarious things, like starting rumors about them with their friends.

"But we were all in jail together," I defended. "You bailed us out."

"Cruz, the issue isn't what's true," she told me.

"What's the issue then?"

"My parents do have business competitors and your comments found their way onto various Chinese-language news sources."

"What?" I began to chuckle. "How? I just said it to them and their friends. Sounds to me that your parents have some fake friends around. Besides, I was speaking English."

"Cruz, everyone speaks English."

"Next time I'll speak another language. Maybe baby language so only Junior can understand me. What am I supposed to do? Why are we talking about them?"

"Yes, you're right. Let's talk about you spending all night at the Metro police station. What did you do this time?"

I could feel my stomach tightening. "I changed my mind. I want to talk about your parents."

Goat Girl had her uncle show up a nine a.m. sharp the next morning. When he strolled into the office with PJ's French ska music playing, I was standing at her desk, talking.

"Hello, lady and gentleman," he greeted.

The man wore a casual pin-striped brown suit under a black slicker. He was very lean, almost cat-like in the way he moved. There was an infectious friendliness to him with his smile. He wore a tweed flat cap, not stylish like my best friend, Run-Time, but his fit him nicely.

"The uncle," I said.

"That would be me, sir."

"I need to get you signed in," PJ said.

"If I could," he said. "I'd like to talk to Mr. Cruz to make sure there's even something to investigate. Also, in my line of work, I'd rather not be in any database anywhere. That's why I had my niece pay my retainer."

"What's your line of work?" I asked.

"Cat burglar."

PJ and I looked at each other.

"Fair enough," I said to him. "What's your name?"

"Twinkle." He extended a hand to shake mine. "Everyone calls me Twinkle. I'm light on my toes."

This time, rather than sit at my main desk. I led Mr. Twinkle to the corner lounge area of my private office where I had my own arrangement of plush chairs around a glass table; the whole set-up on another neon dark blue rug. I sat across from him on adjacent chairs.

"Is Twinkle your street name or real name?" I asked.

"My real name."

"I won't ask if it's first, middle, or last since I know you'll lie. So why did your parents name you Twinkle?"

"My mom said when I was born, I had a twinkle in my eye, so she named me Twinkle."

"Twinkle?"

"Yeah. Better than naming me after computer software, games, or some sci-fi meme or character."

"True. How can I help? A unique and weird case your niece said."

"Yeah. You have to know Mr. Cruz that I wanted to go to the CDC but they only have the general number and email. You can't connect with a real non-robot person. And again, for obvious reasons, I can't leave a message or email."

"The CDC? Centers of Disease Control?"

He gave me a toothy grin. "We told you it was a unique and weird case."

"If you thought of the CDC…Mr. Twinkle, is this a dangerous case? I mean, should we call the CDC?"

"I'll tell the story and you decide."

I sat back and got comfortable. "Tell me the story, which I'm assuming has to do with your chosen vocation."

"It does. I was on the job last week."

"Robbing a place?"

"Only from people who can afford the loss. Their insurance always pays."

"You're an ethical cat burglar."

"I am."

Being in the detective business was about living and dealing with the world of moral ambiguity. If you only saw the world in black and white, you couldn't survive. I had previous training in this world of gray when I was a kid working in the hovercar restoration and racing scene. There you met lots of people who looked like they'd laser-shank you in the alley but you became good friends with them. Then there were those who looked respectable but were the ones who would try to shank you in the alleyway.

However, that being said, I wasn't cool with stealing stuff that didn't belong to you. Whether the victim was rich or not, insured or not, a jerk or not was irrelevant. One could justify doing bad things all day long. Do it long enough and you were no longer doing bad; you were bad.

But I believed Goat Girl when she said her cat burglar uncle was the furthest from violence, so I'd give his profession a pass this time. I evaluated each potential client on a case by case basis. He gave me the run-down of the night he broke into the hoverhotel suite of his target. He knew everything about them—studying the mark for months, learning their routine, knowing all their friends and associates, scoping out the suite, detailing all their prized possessions, and even lining up black market buyers before he stole a thing. He did only target those who were super-wealthy and knew for a fact that the items were insured. That meant Mr. Twinkle was working with more than a few insurance agents on the inside who probably sold him the info for a cut of the action.

"There was no chance anyone was home?"

"No chance. I even watched them get on the plane at Metro Space International. The family was taking a trip to one of the space station colonies."

"And you know exactly which one. Did you have someone Up-Top to call when they docked?"

He smiled again. "You're good at this. Yes, I made sure of it."

"You knew all the security measures for the suite too."

"That always takes the most time. Sometimes wealthy people get paranoid so they get additional security without telling anyone, so you have to be careful. I always scan for robots, no matter how tiny they might be. I know every model there is."

"Easy break in?"

"A breeze. No different than any other job. Got all my items but...I should have just left." Twinkle started shaking his head.

"You know what trips up high-end cat burglars like me? Greed. You're supposed to grab your items and go. Nothing more. But I had to at least take a look."

"At what?"

"They had a secret vault. I had to see what was in it. It could have been an added bonus."

"What was in the secret vault?"

"Not money or jewels or anything like that."

"What?"

"Bodies."

I leaned forward. "Dead?"

"Yeah."

"How many? I mean, give me all the details."

"The vault wasn't a vault at all. It looked like a lab, a private lab. All kinds of strange flasks and glass containers, microscopes, scientist stuff. But on the floor were two bodies."

"People?"

Twinkle hesitated and that made me nervous.

"They looked like people but—"

"Twinkle, did your niece tell you about me and my past."

"You were a Bubble Boy weren't you?"

"I had severe germophobia to the point doctors wanted to send me to a Bubble Colony on one of the space colonies, where they house mental patients. My Pops wasn't having any of it and got me away from those doctors. I beat it but I am very, very, very, very nervous about this story. You tell me there are two dead people in a hotel suite, but won't say they were people. And there's the fact you first wanted to contact the CDC. That means germs! Killer germs."

Twinkle managed a smile. "No, no, Mr. Cruz. I'm sorry to alarm you. The two people were people but they looked to have been modified."

"Modified? Cyborgs?"

"Bio-modification. I think they were those biopunk people."

I could feel my skin crawl. In the past, the cyberpunks with intrabody hard drives and brain plugs had their venal period. I knew very little about the biopunk scene—genetic engineering for the low-class, low-rent set and I didn't want to know anymore. They were crazy. Sewing on an extra ear just because they could, extra thumbs, all kinds of venality. Cyberpunks put hardware on the body where it shouldn't have been. Biopunks put extra organic parts where they shouldn't be. I wanted nothing to do with them, but there was no such thing as upper-class biopunks. If the wealthy wanted real genetic engineering and organic manipulation, they'd go Up-Top. Space people— from the space station and lunar colonies to Mars—were the masters. They wouldn't waste their time with some amateur, wannabe Frankenstein kid in his parents' basement. Twinkle piqued my interest.

"You said the suite belonged to a wealthy family," I said.

"Yes."

"Why would a wealthy family have biopunks...did they look low-class?"

"Very low class. Street people even. They actually looked like they were gang members—tattoos and piercings galore. But they were in bio-containment suits, the ones with the transparent helmets so you can see their faces clearly."

I could see him recalling the moment, thinking.

"Twinkle," I said in a very nervous tone. "Modified how?"

"One had very long pointy ears. The other had a cat nose and whiskers."

"Do you know how they died?"

"I think they killed each other. Laser blasts to the chest of each guy. The weapons were at their sides. I should have looked around more, but I got spooked and some secret vaults have a nasty habit of closing on you when you enter and you can't get out unless you have the code. I wasn't about to take that chance."

"Twinkle, what you've said is a reason to get the police involved, not the CDC?"

"There was a big silver briefcase on the table near them that said: "PROPERTY OF THE CDC. DO NOT REMOVE FROM THE PREMISES." It had one of those serious biometric key locks. Since I was in someone's hotel suite and not the CDC, you could see why that would be a concern."

"I would say a big concern."

"Unique and weird. What do you think?"

"I think it's unique and weird. But who would be my client? What about the family?"

"Funny you should ask. The scene startled me and I guess I screamed out, triggering the alarms. I barely got out of there but—"

"You set off the alarms?"

"Yeah. The place was crawling with suits, my guess private security, the next day. The family returned two days later and cleared out the entire suite. And Mr. Cruz, when I say empty, I mean empty. They took the carpet, drapes, the paint off the walls, and some of the walls too."

"But who'd be my client on this?"

"I'll be the client for you to look at this for at least a couple of days. Make sure the CDC isn't missing some kind of bio-toxin or something. It's the least I can do as a citizen. Metropolis has been good to me over the years."

I laughed. "I take it you were able to sell all your stolen loot that night."

"Absolutely." He gave me another toothy smile.

CHAPTER 11

The Wife and The Parents (Known for Their Supreme Coolness)

Twinkle had been gone for hours when I heard more than one person come through the door. I was working at my desk. I had Twinkle draw me the tattoos from the two dead biopunks and I was researching databases on line. Cruz Jr. was playing crash up with his two hovercars in my lounge area.

"The famous detective is working!"

I looked up with a smile. "Pops!" I stood up and walked to my father. "Ma!"

My mother walked in too, holding her little purse in front of her, like she always did. This one was a dark blue. My parents seemed to dress alike when I saw them. Both had matching black slicker coats and black boots over their pants, instead of under. My Ma smiled at me as I hugged her and gave her a kiss on the cheek. She never wore much make-up, but had a perfect complexion; her black hair was always pulled back in a braided ponytail. They were practically the same height—shorter than me by an inch or so. My Pops with his graying mustache and beard, wore a fedora that looked suspiciously like mine, but was black. He had started to do so after I officially became a detective. He had always told me growing up that he hated hats. In his hand was a sheathed sword. Yes, my father carried a sheathed sword everywhere he went. I had also thought my Ma was making things up when she said he was a Kendo master, only to find out he actually was in my Police Watch Conspiracy Case. I also gave him a big hug.

"We're here to see Junior," Pops said and he and my Ma walked to the son. Cruz Jr. was a giggling mass of flesh as he ran to them and jumped up to be picked up by my Ma.

Then my wife came into the office. Well, of course, I greeted her with a proper kiss.

"Why am I so lucky today?" I asked. "Wife. Parents. Son. No Hellspawn." Dot slapped my shoulder.

"Be nice to them," she said as she walked over to Cruz, Jr. who was now being held in one arm by my Pops.

"Why be nice?" I asked.

Dot walked back to me. "Because we will be in need of more, not less, family babysitting."

"More? Why?"

I could see my Ma and Pops looking at me shaking their heads, disapprovingly.

"Because the Cruz family will soon have a new member—a female member."

I laughed. "A daughter. Hear that Ma. Pops where's the cigars."

They both were smiling.

"Cruzalina is coming!" I heard PJ call out from her desk outside.

"PJ, we are not naming our daughter Cruzalina!"

"I always wanted to have a girl named Ripley," Dot said with her arm around me.

I gave my wife an askance look. "We are not naming our daughter Ripley," I said.

"You don't like Trinity. You don't like Ripley. We need a name. Or should we take PJ's suggestion?"

"We are not naming our daughter Cruzalina. You want her to disown us when she turns eighteen?"

"Why female pop culture names from so long ago?" PJ asked Dot.

"I've always liked that century. People back then actually knew all the same movies. Not like now. There are so many movies made no one knows all the same movies anymore unless it's one of the megacorp studios," Dot said.

"Until your husband came along," PJ said.

"That's not my fault," I said. "They shouldn't have been involved in crimes and trying to do me violence. Blame NeuroDancer. It was her fault."

"Maybe that's a name," Dot said.

"A psycho client?" I said.

"With all this babysitting your mother and I will be doing, we should start our own daycare," my Pops said.

"Cruzalina is coming!" PJ yelled out again.

"Good grief," I said.

"I found you a case," Dot said with a smile.

"You did."

"Taking it?"

"Already have."

"I knew I could find you an interesting case. So no more bad moods."

"The funk is gone."

"Good."

"Are we all going out to dinner to celebrate or what?" my Pops asked.

"Sure. We can even take PJ."

PJ appeared at the doorway, smiling. She wrapped her arms around herself. "I'm going to be an auntie again!"

I shook my head as Dot and my parents laughed.

My post-Wilford G. bad mood was officially gone. New case, new kid on the way, renewed spark. I was back! My posthumous mentor would expect no less.

PART THREE

I Don't Want No BioFreaks in My Future

CHAPTER 12

Clox

Biopunk.

Noun. Street subculture, sometimes criminal or gang-related, obsessed with bio-hacking, biological and genetic manipulation, and synthetic biology.

Philosophy and ideology focused on the implications of biotech rather than infotech, especially the misuse by groups, governments, and megacorporations.

Fuzz Beach was a party district in Metropolis frequented by the wannabe criminal crowd. Lots of flash, bare chests, lots of cleavage, shiny clothes and shoes. The Average Joe and Jane wouldn't go there, but there were plenty who would. I had been there only once before when I was a kid on the hovercar racing scene. I didn't like it then; I didn't like it now, but it's where I had to go.

Twinkle gave me plenty to work from for the investigation. Sometimes you had a case that was vague. You knew it would lead to something important, but you didn't know what. The plan was to run down the leads, see what I had, then turn it over to Metro PD. I had to give Twinkle some respect because he did expose himself by reporting what he'd seen. Not many Metro citizens would have done the same if they had seen something suspicious.

My goal was to find this particular biopunk gang. I knew their tattoo so all I needed was to find out where they hung out at. My first call was to my associate Phishy who gave me the lead to the person I had to find in Fuzz Beach. However, he did warn me to be careful with the guy as he didn't have a very stellar reputation. I didn't trust anyone so that was fine. If I needed to find some secretive biopunkers, it was to be expected that I'd have to chat with some unsavory characters. That was the detective biz.

Fuzz Beach was not a neighborhood I felt comfortable driving my Pony to. Unfortunately, it was exactly the kind of place that I'd get far more attention because the average person on its neon streets knew their hovervehicles and could spot a classic five miles away. I had people snapping pictures of my Pony when I finally parked at a secure public parking bay with its own security guards. I had a crowd forming up around me before I had even stepped out of my vehicle.

"Nice car," said one man in a yellow suit under his black slicker.

"Apologize," I snapped as I stared at him. "My Ford Pony is a vehicle not some hovercar. Give my classic its due."

After a few chuckles from within the crowd, the man said, "Nice vehicle."

I shook the man's hand.

It took me nearly forty-five minutes to get out of that lot. The crowd included even the security guards and they all wanted to know it. If I had told them that I had built it as a kid in high school, I would have been there all night.

The streets in Fuzz Beach had a lot more steam vents than other parts of Metropolis. It did give the neighborhood a "film noir" feel, I guess. All I know is that vents in the ground meant to watch out for backwash from nasty drainage. As I walked, I kept my eye out.

I entered the club Musicality and felt the vibrations of the techno beats from outside its main entrance. Inside was dim and the dance floor was packed. What I wanted was the upper dining area. Upstairs was where meetings happened. Food and drinks were incidental.

"Do you know a Clox?" I asked a waiter as he hopped down the stairs.

"You'll notice him when you see him. Upstairs." The kid was gone.

Since I didn't know what Clox looked like that was a very unhelpful response. I continued upstairs and it was like one of those optical illusions. The upstairs looked far bigger than the ground level. The dining booths went on forever, row after row.

How exactly was I going to find this guy? There were far too many people to scan.

"Who you looking for?" a thug-in-a-suit asked sitting on a stool right next to the stairs.

"Clox."

"D-44," the man answered.

"Thanks."

"Don't mention it."

I smiled. All the booths were numbered. How efficient, I thought.

When I made my way down and over to D44, there was a single man with a single glass in front of him, watching me.

"May I sit down?" I asked.

The man gestured but didn't answer.

"Clox, I presume." I now saw what the kid meant. The man's jacket was a glowing digital clock with the current time and the time for all the major cities on the planet.

"How did you guess?" he said as he took a drink. "What are you having?"

"I'm okay."

"I don't talk to people unless they're drinking."

"I have to work late so does this place have any silk coffee?"

"That's a drink." The man raised a hand and a waitress appeared from nowhere. Seriously, I didn't see where she came from. I watched her walk away. "What brings you to my place of business, Mr. Cruz?"

"I hate when everyone knows who I am."

"You're big time. It's to be expected."

"I don't know about big time."

"Back in the day, it was G-Man."

"You knew him?"

"Everyone knew Wilford G. He was a walking legend. I'm being told you're the man now."

"Give me a few decades and we can talk about that."

My silk coffee arrived. The waitress set it down in front of me and he tapped the table to signal he wanted another drink.

"How did she know what I wanted? Never mind. Before we begin, here's to G-Man," I said.

Clox smiled. "To G-Man." We both drank. "Maybe he'll come back from the dead again."

"Not likely."

"Too bad."

The waitress appeared with another glass of alcohol for him and disappeared.

"Best service around," Clox said as he finished his first glass then took a swallow from his second. "They keep the booze flowing fast here the way I like. That's why this is my place of business. What can I do for you, Mr. Cruz?"

"Looking for a biopunk gang and I was told that you might know where I could find them."

"Who's the gang?"

I had already touched the screen on my mobile to show him the photo I had taken of the picture Twinkle drew of the holo-tattoos of the dead men he'd seen in the vault.

"Yeah, I know them." Clox took another drink. "Why should I tell you?"

"Obviously, I'd pay for the info."

"Obviously. But that doesn't answer my question. Who are you working for?"

"Confidential."

"In my line that doesn't get you to first base. Are you working for the cops, a rival gang, who?"

"Why does any of that matter? Cops don't need me to find a gang, so it's not them. Again, confidential. I was told you were an information man. You'd be the first information man I ever met who cared about the particulars of who wanted the info."

"In my line, things like that matter. Give the wrong info to the wrong person and you might not live another day."

"It's no one who has any connection to anyone you know. So, no, not a rival gang."

"How do I know that?"

"Because I said so."

"I don't know where that gang is today, but I know a person who does."

"You're going send me to another intermediary."

"Yeah."

"Does that mean I don't have to pay you?"

"You pay me to see him and you pay him for the info to the gang you're looking for. That's the way it'll be, or you can just go back to that fancy red vehicle of yours. That wouldn't be for sale by any chance?"

"I'm going to ignore your last question."

Clox laughed under his breath as he took another drink.

"What's it going to be, Mr. Cruz?"

"You do know my reputation, don't you?"

"You mean if you pay me and he doesn't give you the straight info you need? Yeah, I heard about you. I'm sure you've been told about me too."

"That's why I said what I said."

"Don't worry, Mr. Cruz, the friend of every cop in Metro, all half a million of them. I'm not looking for any enemies tonight, especially after hearing that you ran down the guy who killed G-Man at three hundred miles an hour without flinching an inch. Death by your cop friends or death by hit-and-run. I'll skip both, thank you."

"How much?" I asked.

CHAPTER 13

Octane

When Clox told me he was sending me just down the street to another bar-club to see a guy named Octane, I wasn't happy. I had paid him a wad of cash to be simply sent one building down. He knew I wasn't happy but laughed anyway. He said my silk coffee was on him.

I got out of there before I did something foolish. I was able to glance over at the garage as I walked down the street. The security guards had created a circular cordon around my vehicle to keep people away. Those security guards I didn't mind giving wads of cash to. They were doing a stellar job. Clox was a bum.

Whenever you went to an establishment that didn't have signage to its name, it meant trouble. I told the cyborg bouncers at the main entrance I was there to see Octane. Instead one of them pointed me to the end of a long line of clubbers in scantily clad outfits under their slickers waiting to get in. There was no sense arguing. I marched to the end of a long line.

"You're clubbing in that?" some kid said to me with two giggling girls around him.

I wanted to say something like "when was the last time someone shot you?" but that's how street punks talked. I smirked and simply ignored his existence, exuding the kind of bravado a gangster would. Truly dangerous people didn't have to prove it. Everyone knew it and didn't cross them. I scratched my side, which I'm sure he took to mean I might be packing a weapon. He got the message. He laughed nervously but turned around and minded his own business from then on. One of the girls shot me a dirty look.

I had to wait thirty minutes to make my way back to the entrance.

"ID?" one of the bouncers asked.

"You didn't ask any of those kids for ID. Obviously I'm older than them."

"ID?" the bouncer repeated.

I flashed my ID card in front of his eyes. I had been ready for him. "Can you tell me where to find Octane now?"

"Now as in now? Or now as in later?"

"Why are you giving me a hard time when I told you that someone sent me here to ask for him?"

"Who sent you?"

"Clox."

"Why didn't you say that from the beginning?"

"You didn't ask me."

"Ask any of the staff inside and they'll tell you where he is."

They finally let me in and as I entered I was immediately hit by a wave of heat vapor. I covered my mouth and nose with my hand and held my breath. I stood there wondering if I should continue inside. I could see this was a hookah and dancing joint, but I knew that no one cared about the dancing, it was the seriously illegal hookah that people wanted here. I walked back out into the fresh air.

The two cyborg bouncers were allowing a few more couples in as I brushed past them.

"What's wrong? You don't like our hookah."

"I can't take the chance," I said. "I'm allergic to most of the brands (lie). It won't do your business any good if I collapse and you have to call the cops and hospital."

"No, it wouldn't," one of them said.

"Can't you have Octane come out to see me? Explain the situation. And that Clox sent me. It'll be five minutes tops. I'll pay you."

The bouncers were annoyed but as soon as I laid a few bills in their hands one of them took out a mobile phone and made a call as he stepped away so no one could hear him.

The bouncer returned. "Go around back. He'll meet you there. You can get there two ways: the short way, through the club. Or the long way, all the way the hell around the entire building. Will take you about an hour on foot."

"I'll take the short way." I pulled a handkerchief from my jacket and covered my nose and mouth.

"What's wrong with him?" one of the kids in line asked aloud.

Back into the dark, damp club hit once again with a blast of heated vapor to the face. I moved quickly through the crowds watching the drugged-out dancers on the floor. I noticed that the dancers had portable hover-hookahs as did everyone else. A million uses for hover technology.

Out the back I came, relieved at escaping the claustrophobic, vapor-contaminated inner sleaze pit. I was in a back alley. I didn't like back alleys at all. Bad things tended to happen in them. The ground was littered with trash, including cigarette butts.

At that very moment, the door I exited swung open hard and a large man came out. He had shoulders like an ox, huge hands and forearms, wearing a dark shirt a size too tight.

"Here I am! Octane!"

I didn't know what to make of his wild yelling.

"Clox sent me."

"Here you aren't!" he yelled and pulled a laser pistol from his back waist.

"Clox sent me!"

"Octane!"

He started firing before he had even aimed at me. I, however, wasn't so stupid. I fired my omega-gun once and there was no more Octane as he fell to the ground with a metal thud—literally. Another cyborg. I ran as fast as my legs could carry me. I heard the door open. Commotion. Men yelling. As I turned the corner, both gunfire and laser fire whizzed by me.

"Get him!" I heard someone yell.

I stopped, ran back, and started firing.

I doubt I hit any of them. But I did hear them rush back to the door and bolt back inside the establishment. With that, I ran away again.

I marched back to the Musicality with seething rage. But, I didn't have to go far. There was Clox waiting for me at the ground floor bar.

"You don't play nice with people," he said.

"Why would your friend try to shoot me when I told him I was sent by you?" I yelled.

"I didn't set you up if that's what you're saying. Double-crossing information peddlers also don't last long on the street. Maybe he thought you were a cop. Maybe he thought you were a process server. His wife does have a restraining order against him. Who knows? Octane was always crazy. Now he's crazy and dead. At least you saved some money."

"I still do not have what I came here for."

We both stopped as we heard police sirens erupt outside.

"I better not get tangled up in this."

"Don't worry, Mr. Cruz. I made a few phone calls."

"How did you know to do that? This all just happened."

Clox smirked. "Cameras. This whole block has cameras." He pointed.

I noticed that his holo-jacket had more than the digital time on it. On his sleeve were vid-cam feeds of the whole street outside, the parking lot across the club—there was my Pony, the alleyways, including where Octane's body lay and was now being swarmed over by police.

"Cute," I said.

"I own this place, the hooka bar, the parking lot across the street and every other business on the block."

"I see."

"Do you want the info?"

"Why didn't you do this before?"

"There's protocol to follow. Something you wouldn't understand. The biopunk gang you're looking for is—was his connection. Not my place to disclose."

"Yes, I want the information still and I want it now so I can be on my way."

CHAPTER 14

Bad Bia

The rain was back with a vengeance. Hovertraffic crawled along, but I didn't let it slow my mission. My destination was another party district but far seedier. I hadn't been to Utopian End before but heard of it. All the districts in this part of Metro were known for punkers, hackers, stoners, and gamers.

I was already apprehensive about having to be around the biopunk scene but that was heightened to the nth degree when Clox gave me the name of the club I had to go to find my biopunk gang in question: The Freak Show. I wasn't happy but again I had a mission to complete. What was my case exactly?

This time I had to park the Pony quite aways from the club. I couldn't find anything suitable close because all the parking garages were packed. Maybe it was "ladies' night" or some other special event because the streets were equally more congested than expected. The crowds did give me a feel of the neighborhood I was in. Mostly a young crowd in their best dancing attire, not wealthy, not criminal, more likely a college crowd or recently graduated crowd. That put me more at ease as I neared the club.

I had expected to be in another line of clubbers but four bouncers waved people in quickly, not even carding anyone. When they grabbed and held one young male who was almost running into the club, he didn't say a word. With a smile, he turned and strolled away into the crowd. I stopped myself and then noticed that the men either had metal bionic hands or metal gloves. They could care less about under-age boozers; they did care if someone was carrying weapons. I too turned and disappeared back into the crowd. I'd have to walk all the way back to my vehicle to deposit my own weapons in my in-car gun safe. I had done it before and was sure I'd have to do so many more times in my career.

Walking the streets without my weapons was worse than being naked. I was walking into an unknown place to find some gang members without the "tools of my trade." If the club was their turf, they wouldn't be without their weapons. I was a paranoid guy by nature so any whisper of trouble, I'd be out the exit faster than Superman.

I returned to the club and before I got to the door the bouncers waved at me.

"Sorry we inconvenienced you," one said. "Having to dump your illicit guns someplace else. What is the world coming to?"

I gave him a smile. "Do you want to see my ID, sir?" I asked in a sarcastic voice.

They waved me in.

Thankfully, I wasn't smacked in the face with any nasty drug smog, but I stopped in my tracks and tried not to burst out laughing. There were a million sub-cultures in Metropolis, like every other supercity and megacity in the world. Cyberpunk hackers, grunge hoverboarders, hovercar racing groupies, and biopunker nihilists. Biopunk fashion was lots of ancient-style gas masks, plastic tubes connected from one spot to another on their clothes, and a lot of "bio-hazard" symbol logos. They loved that symbol and all its variations.

Dot and I wanted to feel the music when we went to a dance club. No such thing here. I was in a "silent" disco dance place, and it was the funniest thing. There was silent salsa, silent swing, silent tango, you name it, but I always thought the retro disco places to be the most fun. A gigantic floor with people wearing V.R. ultra-light helmets dancing. There was the tap of feet on the ground and people talking to their partners, but there was no music whatsoever.

"Sir." A waitress was standing next to me holding a VR helmet sealed in a plastic bag.

"Thanks," I responded.

I wasn't taking off my hat but VR helmets were adjustable. I ripped open the bag, fitted it, including the ear buds. I had entered the virtual reality disco town! It was quite compelling because the virtual world wasn't a dark, dank dance club but the lights were bright, changing to different neon colors, the liquid floor was a vibrant pink, and the music was loud. I almost felt like dancing myself because I actually liked the song. But I was working!

Clox told me the name of the biopunk gang's leader—a woman named Bia. The dance floor took up most of my view but on the left was the bar area. People drank, watched, and rested from going a few dance rounds. I could see that one woman was watching me, even though she was wearing dark wraparound shades. She had a spiky Mohawk hairdo and wore an all-black leather outfit. She also had a white glowing T-shirt with the word BIA.

It didn't take long for me to notice other people near her watching me too. I knew instantly what they were up to. They assumed I was plugged in fully into the VR world but, especially after my ordeal with a crazy maniac named Ichi Jumper from my Electric Sheep Massacre Case, I never fully plugged into any virtual reality device or chamber. I had one eye socket on and the other off. I watched as Bia and her comrades appeared in the VR to be watching me, while in the real world she had been sneaking up on me and was now about five feet away.

I knew it! She reached into her jacket and out came a small laser gun. So much for the Freak Show's no-guns allowed policy.

I ripped the VR helmet from my head and threw it. I hit her squarely in the face shattering her own VR helmet. I bolted out the door, running head-on into the four bouncers. I tried to get up but one grabbed me. Big mistake because he wasn't unarmed. I knew they all were packing when I walked past them, into the club. I grabbed his gun before he realized what was happening and the four of them couldn't run away fast enough, as did clubbers walking to the entrance.

Bia burst out of the club. I shot her but she blocked the shot with her own gun. (Hmm. No one had ever done that before). What happened next wasn't as psychologically damaging to me as my Jabba the Butt encounter in my Blade Gunner Case when I broke my own life rule and entered a public restroom to be so horrified that I ran miles on foot to get to a CDC gel pool. This incident would be the second most horrifying thing I experienced in terms of its weird nastiness.

Tiny hands rose from below my line of sight and grabbed my gun. When my eyes looked down, I couldn't quite understand what I was seeing. I beheld some kind of human spider—midget from the waist up and double-jointed, half-legs below the waist. I'm sorry. I can't explain it. This was why I stay away from biopunkers. All I heard was a blood-curdling scream when I kicked whatever monstrosity it was with all my might.

I was about to run when I saw three more people running to me. I turned and bolted away at hyper-light speed. It was a race. Could I get to my vehicle before they could catch me?

CHAPTER 15

Bia's Bio-Borgs

"We're not going to let you kill us!"

That's what I heard one of them say as they chased me through the streets. The only reason I was able to stay ahead of the trio chasing me was that I was familiar with them. I also used both the crowds and my heightened adrenaline at the sight of the human spider to finally get to the parking garage.

I had parked away from all other vehicles. I jumped in my Pony. As I waited, I had my pop-gun re-attached to my left forearm under my sleeve and my omega gun rested on my lap. I knew my "friends" were coming—as long as I never, ever saw the human spider again I could handle anything else. I was trying to purge all visual images of the monstrosity from my brain. Thank goodness I didn't get a clear view of it.

The trio came around the corner and stopped. I wasn't sure if they knew my vehicle or could see me with my tinted front window screen but I had my omega gun in hand and was ready.

When I saw the guns in their hands and they walked forward, I didn't wait. I pushed my driver's door open and popped out. There was no way I was going to let these biopunks, with whatever sick body modifications they had, shoot my vehicle. They could shoot at me but not my vehicle.

My omega gun wasn't an Earth weapon. It was an Up-Top weapon and spacemen knew how to make weapons. I let loose a torrent of weapon's fire and the trio found themselves on the receiving end of one explosive charge after another. Deafening sonic blasts, blinding photonic blasts, then every audio alarm system in the parking garage erupted all at once.

The three men were on the ground dazed. The tallest man, blond mustache, beard and braided hair tried to reach for his gun. I could see the holo-tattoo on his forehead. The same one Twinkle had drawn of this specific biopunk gang.

"You touch that and where you lie is where the coroner will be finding your body today!" I stood above all three of them.

"We're not going to let you kill us!"

"What are you talking about? I'm not trying to kill you. I was trying to talk to your pal, Bia, but we're past all that."

"The Beast sent you."

"The Beast? Who's that?"

"We know he sent you. We told Octane to take care of you."

"Oh, so you were the ones who got him killed."

"You killed him."

"Yes, I did. He tried to gun me down in an alleyway. I don't like to get shot. And I don't know anyone named Beast. A nice little world you little gangsters live in causing your own chaos wherever you go. I came here for information about your fellow gangsters who killed each other in that hoverhotel secret lab—"

"How do you know about that? The only way you could know that is if you killed them."

"Your friends killed each other."

"Our men didn't kill each other. You killed them and came here to finish the rest of us."

"It wasn't me who killed them because I wasn't there. Someone else was. That person saw them."

"You're lying."

"That same person tripped the alarm trying to get out of there."

They looked at each other from their positions on the ground. I could see their brains working.

The other two men besides the blond one looked average to me in their dark clothes, but I knew that was deceptive. They had the same holo-tattoos on their bodies—one had it on each hand; the other on his cheek.

"Your friends killed each other. But that's not my concern. What is my concern, is the CDC briefcase. That's what I want to know about. What were you crazy maniacs planning to do? Are you criminals or terrorists? I need to know so I can get you into the hands of the proper people," I said.

"You don't know anything, do you?"

"What's there to know?"

"Our guys didn't kill each other. They were killed and staged. Your friend interrupted the scene."

"Oh, so you believe it wasn't me after all. How do you know that?"

"Because the Beast recorded what he did. He recorded it live when your friend came into the lab vault in his ninja outfit."

They saw my concerned look.

"He's not the guy," another one of the biopunks said to the others. "He's shorter than the one in the outfit."

"You're with the guy in the black outfit?"

"Yes," I answered.

We stared at each other.

"What's going on here?" I asked. "And what was in that stolen CDC briefcase. I swear if I don't start getting answers, I'm calling everybody—police, Feds, CDC. They'll plastic wrap you three, handcuff you, ankle-cuff you, quarantine you, dump you in a deep underground cell. That's what happens to bio-terrorists. They'll also make sure to pick up Bia, that disgusting human spider, and whoever else you have in your cell."

"Cell? We aren't terrorists. We were trying to stop them."

"Stop who?"

"Talk to Bia. She'll tell you."

"She better tell me."

CHAPTER 16

Good Bia

Being a detective is as much about instincts as anything else. You have to know how to read people. If you can, you'll stay alive and go far. If not, you'll probably end up dead. Of course, you need more than that, especially good weapons and excellent shooting skills, but instincts are the foundation.

I decided to trust them. They knew I was telling the truth and I knew they were. We each knew that the other party had desired information. I confiscated their weapons and had them walk in front of me.

"When we get there, I want one of you to move ahead and make sure I don't see that human spider again."

"What do you have to be afraid of? You kicked him in the head. He's probably on the way to the hospital."

"You three should also know that I have no problems with shooting unarmed people in the back." They glanced slightly back to sneer. "Also, I don't miss."

"You missed Bia."

"I didn't miss. She blocked my shot. Next time instead of firing once, I'll fire ten times. Let's see if she can block that."

"Maybe someone else will grab your gun and beat you to death with it."

"Yeah, but that someone won't be you because you'll be dead on the ground with a laser blast to the back."

Normally, you don't under any circumstances return to a scene where you just had a shootout with a gang of dubious characters only moments before. However, strangely, I felt it was safe, or safe enough. This time I had my guns.

When we returned to the Freak Show. There were no bouncers or clubbers lining up to get in. There was Bia leaning against the wall on the side of the main entrance smoking a cigar. She clutched it when we were close enough; her eyes locked on her people.

"Sorry, Bia," one of them said.

"I'm sorry too," she said. "The Bio-Borgs can't take down one normal."

"You should talk to him."

She dropped her cigar to the ground and stepped on it, crushing it with a few foot swivels. "Why should I talk to him? I thought the Beast sent him."

"He doesn't know who the Beast is."

"I'd say we're even," she said to me. "You got the drop on me, them, sent a comrade to the hospital."

"He killed Octane."

"Oh," Bia said.

"Maybe he shouldn't have tried to kill me."

"Maybe he shouldn't. Okay, we're even. We're going to check you out thoroughly."

"You do whatever you want but I want to know about that CDC briefcase."

She stared at me.

"That's why we said you should talk to him," one of the biopunkers said to her. "I think he's a cop or something."

"Yeah, something. I'm a private detective."

"He's with the guy who was there in the suit."

"The thief?" Bia asked.

"Yeah," the biopunker answered. "But they don't know anything."

"Where's the case and what was in it?" I asked.

"You don't know anything," she said.

"Tell me what I want to know and I'm gone. I don't care anything about you or your gang."

"You'll have to be gone now, until we check you out, Mr…"

"Cruz."

I could see the surprise on their faces.

"That detective guy from the news," another biopunker said.

"The detective from the news," Bia repeated.

"You're trying to kill someone and you don't even know who they are," I said.

"We knew some guy wearing a stupid tan hat was looking for us."

"It's called a fedora and I'm not stupid."

"Yeah, you're not that," she said.

"Listen to me," I said. "Tomorrow afternoon a hovertaxi will land here at five in the afternoon. Follow it. The diner it stops at will be where I'll be waiting. If you aren't there, I'll go straight to Metro PD and the CDC. When you check me out, you'll see why you wouldn't want that."

"We're not scared of the cops," she said.

"Oh, did I mention I also know the Chief of Police." That got her attention. "Be there."

"Why trust us?" she asked.

"I've dealt with hardcore gangsters and you're not them. Terrorists? I doubt it. But my trust ends five pm tomorrow if you're not there to tell me what this is all about."

"Why didn't you tell the cops already?" she asked.

"Tell them what?" I asked. "The entire scene, including that case, is gone. The police act with evidence. We have nothing. We're the only ones who know anything about the scene, besides the people who made it disappear."

"Yes, that's true." Bia's tone was more conciliatory.

I pointed at them. "I don't want to see that human spider again. Who knows how long I'll have nightmares."

"If we show up," Bia said.

"You'll show up," I said.

The first time I'd been to the diner and bar club I swore I'd never return, but I did. I returned with my posthumous mentor so I had softened to the place even though it was where criminals hung out. The music was awful but no one met here for the music or the food; it was for business. The Sketchy Squirrel was exactly the safe place I needed to meet the biopunks. I wouldn't be without my weapons and no one could sneak up on me from the booth I sat in.

It was exactly fifteen after when Bia and her three friends strolled in looking around, their forehead holo-tattoos glowing. I had sent some sidewalk johnny friends of my own to fetch them in a rented hovertaxi. I waved from my booth at the back of the diner section of the establishment, but the place was so dark they wouldn't see me—well, a normal person wouldn't be able to. I was about to flash my mobile when I saw that Bia was making a beeline straight to me.

When they reached me, she slid into the booth, followed by her friends. She kept a good distance, which was appreciated since I didn't want her sitting right next to me. The guy with the braids sat next to her. The other two grabbed some chairs to sit and block anyone from walking to the table.

"The waitress won't be able to serve you," I said.

"We're not hungry," one of the biopunks said.

"You're not surprised to see us?" Bia asked.

"Should I?" I asked.

"I wouldn't know of a place like this," Bia said.

"I know lots of places."

"I've decided to trust you," Bia announced.

"Why?"

"I told you. We had to check you out and we did. I was told you never let something go and you do have a lot of friends in cop-land and Up-Top too. You were the guy who took down the Alien From Mars."

"Yeah."

"The first true bio-borg," Bia said with a hint of reverence. "If I could have met him."

"If you did, you'd be dead and you know that. I was there."

"I guess I do. I heard you work for criminals too."

"I evaluate every client equally. I learned quickly that if I want to be a detective in this supercity and only want angels for clients, it means I won't be in business long, or at all."

"Isn't that the truth. I've tried to kill you twice now and that doesn't seem to be working. New approach: how much do you charge?"

"Just like that?"

"It wasn't personal. Someone starts sniffing around your business who you believe has been sent to permanently retire you from life, what would you do?"

"Permanently retire, huh? If I were a criminal, maybe the same thing, but I'm not a criminal. I don't do things like that."

"Word on the street is you've sent plenty of criminals to the morgue. Well? How much do you charge? I should have thought of it before. If we hire you to do our work, the cops can't touch us."

"What work? I'm not helping you do any crimes. What about the CDC briefcase? And who's the Beast?"

"We aren't a gang. Lots of biopunks are but not us. We protect humanity. We don't prey on it."

"Protect it from what?"

"The nemesis."

"What? You mean this Beast?"

"Our nemesis. I'm sure you've had to deal with a few of those already. Only we can't seem to destroy ours."

"Destroy meaning what?"

"Destroy meaning shooting him dead."

"Why would I help you do that?"

"I'll convince you. We all will convince you. You may even help us for free."

"I doubt that. I'm waiting for answers—"

"Bio-terrorism," she said.

"Isn't that one of the possibilities I said before?"

"Before you say anything about the cops or the Feds, we've tried. They don't believe our nemesis even exists. Or they refuse to tell us that they know he does."

"You do know I'm a private detective and not some bio-terrorist hunter."

"He's a bad guy. You hunt bad guys."

"Maybe. If I have a client."

"You have one client already on this. I'll be your second one. I'll ask again: how much do you charge?"

CHAPTER 17

About the Beast

As I sat there, Bia watched me, waiting for any positive sign. The other three biopunks did the same. They desperately wanted me to sign onto their cause. A gang with a cause. In fact, Bia was right. They weren't a gang. They were some kind of quasi-religious freedom fighters. I had to decide if I wanted to proceed further.

"If I get access to your criminal jacket what will it say?" I asked Bia.

"My criminal record will say what you'd expect from an ex-gang member. Drug-running, illegal gun possession, illegal weapons possession, theft, burglary, grand larceny, criminal mayhem, attempted murder. That's it."

"That's it?"

"That's all. I never said I was a perfect being, far from it. We all evolve."

"What are you now?"

"Defenders."

"Of what?"

"Humanity."

"I get very nervous when people talk in lofty terms. I'm a private detective and everything you've told me so far seems to place this situation far from my simple street detective world."

"You have to help us," one of the biopunkers said.

"Why? You tell me that this Beast is a bio-terrorist—"

"No, that's too simplistic a term," Bia said. "He's a genetic manipulator, a dark evolutionist. That's why we've sworn to stop him."

"Why would a gang change their vocation of crime to being a defender of humanity?" I asked.

"A person doesn't have a very long life expectancy as a gang member. You die and that's it. It's like you were nothing. We have a purpose now. Something real that matters. Before I was never scared of dying because we had nothing to live for. Now, I'm terrified of it, because I have a purpose. You must be able to understand that."

"I do. But that's for the average person. What really happened with you? Something happened. What happened? You said that you didn't know what was in the CDC briefcase, but you knew it was key to his terrorist plot. You sent two of your people to steal it from him. How did you know he had it? How did you know where he was? How did he know you sent two of your guys to be waiting for them to kill them? Why don't you know where he is now? Why not call the CDC on him, or the Feds and be done with it? I can keep the questions going for a long time."

"The biopunk world is a small one. We all know each other. There are doctors and receivers."

"You mean freak show makers and those who want to be freaks like that human spider of yours."

"Six-Legs is harmless. He doesn't care if you don't understand—"

"Why did he make himself into a human spider?"

"It's not important," Bia said. "What's important is the Beast. We know he exists and so does everyone in the biopunk community but not the authorities. They should be as scared of him as we are, but they don't even know that he's real. The Beast used to be only talk, but then things changed."

"Changed how?"

"The Beast found a funder. Someone to turn his words into reality."

"Who?"

"Who else but one of the megacorps," Bia replied.

"You know this or are you guessing?"

"One of the biotech firms. They're the only ones who'd be interested and would have the money to finance him. Before it was all theoretical with him, but then he magically had knowledge of the inner workings of different biotech megacorps and the labs at the CDC. He knew what to go after. He never knew that before."

"What's the name of your gang, or your group?"

"The Bio-Borgs."

"How do you know so much about this Beast?"

"He ran the Bio-Borgs before me. He was our leader before me."

"Why didn't you just say that?"

"It's a hard thing to say for us."

"You do know that this is far beyond me and you as well."

"It's not. We can still contain this."

"Contain what? He's out there and you don't know where he is. You don't even know what he's doing exactly."

"But we can find out. Your client knows."

"My client?"

"The burglar. We should all meet."

"That will never happen."

"Then we'll give you all the info we know about the Beast and the hoverhotel suite. You get all the info about the owner of the hoverhotel suite and compare the details."

"You think the owner of the hoverhotel suite is this Beast's funder?"

"We're positive. We found out about it because we finally were able to follow him there. It took us months. He used every tactic to lose any kind of tails but we were better. Six-Legs was able to sneak in and later find out about the lab."

"That lab is larger than what your burglar friend saw," one of the biopunks said.

"Okay, what are your names?"

"Why?" they asked me.

"I know Bia, but I can't keep calling you the biopunk guys. You do know I'm going to check all of you out before I do anything."

"I'm Bolt," the one with the braided blond hair, mustache and beard.

"I'm Handy."

"I'm Zip."

I closed my eyes trying not to freak out.

"I take it you don't want to know how we got our street names," Bolt said.

I opened my eyes. "Please don't tell me. I'm still recovering from Six-Legs."

"Will you help us?" Bia asked.

"I will compare notes with my other client, but I don't think we can do much."

"Did your client try to track down the suite owner?" Bia asked.

"We both did. On day one. Vanished."

"Not surprising," Zip said.

"Which means," I said, "whatever details my client had was a cover."

"An alias," Bia said with a sigh.

"A false identity so if he were ever discovered nothing could lead back to the real person or people. A dead end."

"We could put the word out that we're looking for him. Spread some cash around," Handy said. "We may get lucky."

"We need to be realistic here. If this Beast is as good as you say and he has all this funding you say he has, he could disappear and we'll never find him, especially if we don't know who the funder is. What if it's an Up-Top megacorp? If that's the case, it'll be impossible to track him."

"What about the CDC briefcase you were focused on?" Bia asked.

"The CDC isn't a Metropolis government agency. It's a global one with division offices Up-Top as well. A missing confidential silver briefcase. Firstly, they'd never admit to it and secondly, which they? Here, Asia, Europe, Africa, the space stations, the Lunar colonies?"

"You make it sound hopeless," Bolt said.

"Because it is," I said. "Unless we get lucky. Otherwise, there's nothing to investigate. You can't even tell me what this Beast's plot is, so we can't even warn the authorities."

The biopunkers were clearly distressed, but that meant they were genuine. But as my posthumous mentor said in his 60-page book titled, *How to be a Great Detective with 100 Rules*, "sometimes there isn't anything to investigate. Either the case will come back for you to solve, or it won't. In the meantime, work your other cases."

CHAPTER 18

Bia's CI

My wife hated my high-profile, save-the-world cases, but honestly people hired detectives thinking they could solve any problem under the sun, whether it fell under "standard" private investigation duties or not. Twinkle's case made sense, but Bia and her Bio-Borgs wanted me to do what? Save humanity? What on earth is a "dark evolutionist" anyway? I told Bia and her group that I'd see if any leads turned up, but really, I was moving on. My real case was finding out about the CDC case and nothing more.

Over a week had passed since my dinner meeting with the biopunk gang or whatever they were calling themselves. Frankly, I never expected to hear from them again. With nothing to follow-up on with the "unique and weird" case, I had real cases to investigate, solve, and get paid for.

Usually, I divided up my office time between field and desk work. If I was in the field in the morning, I'd stay out at least half the day. If I came into the office, I'd stay in to get all calls, research and the dreaded bookkeeping done before going anywhere. Nothing fancy which was why it worked perfectly.

Unfortunately, I was being pestered by PJ who knew Dot and I had settled in on the name for our daughter-on-the-way.

"What makes you think Dot and I would name our daughter that? She's not a cyborg," I answered from my office. I had been working on a records search on a particular business to find out what other businesses they owned or were owned by. The preliminary stages of a "follow the money" investigation.

"If her auntie is a cyborg, and her mom is a cyborg, then she'll want to be one too." PJ stood in the doorway of my private office, smiling.

"No, she'll want to be like her father. Pure and au so natural."

"That's boring." PJ disappeared to her domain.

The phone rang at her desk. Some days the phone rang incessantly, but today was fairly quiet. It seemed that's how it always was—peaks and valleys.

PJ's voice came over the speaker on my own desk vid-phone. "Line one!"

It always made me want to laugh. "We only have one line! And why use the speaker when I can hear you fine."

PJ was at my doorway again. "That would not be professional. This is a professional place of business."

I grinned, shaking my head. "Are you going to tell me who it is on Line one?"

"A woman name Bia. She said she was a client." PJ stared at me.

"What?"

"Client? Did you collect the standard Liquid Cool retainer?"

"I'll take care of that now," I said as I touched my vid-phone.

There on the vid-screen was Bia. "We're on," she said.

"On?" I asked.

She smiled. "You didn't think this was done, did you? We found him."

I leaned forward. "How?"

"The street sees and hears all. You only need to know where to look."

"Bia, you painted a very scary picture of this person. Did you find him or did he let you find him?"

"I hear you. I was suspicious too, but we checked out the lead. We think he's legit."

"Why are you calling me then? He's your CI. Run down the lead."

"Isn't that what you do?"

"I run down my own leads, not the leads of other people I barely know. See what he gives you, then we can take it from there. I still feel this Beast is off-world."

"You've been looking for him too."

"I have, and got his full criminal jacket from Metro PD."

"Anything you want to share?"

"Bia, you already know I'm a bit queasy when it comes to this extreme body modification of your biopunk world."

"We're an acquired taste but as you've already observed we prefer a more normal outward appearance, to better blend into the crowd."

"Except for human spider man."

"Except him."

"I also reviewed yours."

"I told you everything I was arrested and convicted of."

"You did."

"You also saw that I haven't had so much as a speeding ticket from the cops in at least five years."

"That's true too. But Bia, I know what you told me. But—"

"But what?"

"I still can't figure this whole thing out."

"You're a private eye."

"At first I thought this might be a bio-terrorist thing, but this is all off."

"I never thought I'd meet a person more suspicious of things than me. Why the hesitation? We have a lead to the Beast. We have to see where it goes. If we find him, we can stop him, whatever he's plotting."

"What is he plotting?"

"I told you already."

"Forced evolution. Bio-terrorism by another name. Yes, his rantings were in his criminal files too."

"What's wrong then?"

"Let's just say I'll keep it to myself for now."

"Something must have upset you."

"My mind is stuck on that CDC briefcase."

"That's why we can't let this go."

"You don't understand. You can't steal a case from the CDC. They will track you. And even if you got it, they're tagged."

"Tags can be removed."

"The entire case is a tracking sensor."

"You are the right person to help us. You know all about this."

"Bia, it's much more serious than that. It means they have to know."

"Know?" Bia had a surprised look on her face.

"I've made plenty of jokes about the CDC myself, but they are very good at what they do. Their record is better than any other division in the government because they're so good. If not for them, especially in Metropolis, humanity would have been wiped out by some virus or nasty bug centuries ago. They'd have to know.

"You, me, the burglar, the owner or owners of that hoverhotel suite are not the only ones who know what took place that night. Most people don't know this but if needed, the CDC can commandeer Metro police officers to arrest and detain people. If I'm right, why aren't you, me, and everyone else involved, not sitting in a CDC detention center?"

It was early morning but looked like the night from the overcast. I landed the Pony on a wide pedestrian street in an empty space of a busy parking lot. A man in a hooded slicker and a neon handled umbrella walked to me.

"How long will you be?" the attendant asked.

"Do you have a day rate?"

He nodded. I paid him with a card, he gave me a stub, then I walked to my party.

I was to meet Bia's three friends and there they were as I came out of the lot. Bolt, the guy with the braided hair, had real bolts in his neck and wrists. Why someone would do that or what was the point was beyond me? Zip had zippered pockets on his very skin, which creeped me out to no end. Handy had hand-like feet, which I tried not to think about.

"I really feel uncomfortable walking with you three," I said when I reached them.

"Our feelings are hurt, Cruz. Don't you know we're all riding the same friendship train," Zip said.

"I only have one question, because I wasn't too impressed with you three in our last encounter. If we get into a shootout or street fight, can I count on you?"

"Don't worry about us," Bolt said.

"I have to worry. I don't like this at all. We get lucky and you find someone to lead us to the Beast. I don't believe in luck. I do believe in set-ups."

"We have to risk it," Handy countered. "Luck does happen, but we're ready if it goes south."

"The place where we're meeting this guy, have you been there before?"

"Many times," Bolt answered.

"Does he know that?"

"Know?"

"Does this street informant know you know the place we're meeting? If he knows that, then we could be walking into a trap."

"Cruz, you worry too much," Bolt said.

"You three are the worst gang members ever. Let's get this over with."

"We're not gang members," Bolt said.

"That's obvious. I'm more 'gangster' than you. That's not a good thing."

The street we took to our meeting place was more like a river. With the poor drainage, the water was up to our ankles. Flash floods were not uncommon in Metropolis. But I wasn't worried with my proper footwear—soft boots that reached to my thighs under my pants and my pants were waterproof.

I read the neon signs as we walked. Clinics galore: medicine, drugs, body modifications, bionic adjustments. I noticed quite a few cyborgs amongst the crowd, but then anyone could be a cyborg. You never knew, which is why I always preferred to shoot rather than fight—or run.

My three biopunk friends slowed down.

"What are we doing?" I said.

"He's waiting at the entrance," Bolt replied.

I looked down a long alleyway and could see the silhouettes of people hanging around.

"We're going to purposely walk down a dark alleyway?"

"Yes, Cruz, we are." Bolt led his guys past me.

I pulled my special glasses from a pocket and put them on. At least I could see the men waiting down the alleyway more clearly. They didn't seem to be paying us any attention. I looked behind me and saw nothing of concern from within the crowd. I followed.

"Node!" Bolt called out with a smile.

One of the men waiting at the alleyway entrance stepped to him and the two greeted each other with a combo of fist pumps and forearm shakes.

"The Bolt man. Hey Zippy. Handy man. Who's your fourth wheel?"

"Along for the ride," Bolt answered. "Bia sent him. He's okay."

"He doesn't look okay."

Node stepped closer to look me over. He was tall, gaunt, and had spiky hair like Handy and Zip. However, all his fingers were metal.

"My secretary has bionic fingers too," I said to help ease the tension. His men were watching me closely too.

"I don't trust normals. Humanity is about enhancing oneself."

"That's what push-ups and pull-ups are for," I said.

"One day, whether through hardware or genetics, we'll be able to enhance the human brain. From there, the inner universe of the mind."

"Oh, boy," I said. "Didn't your mother tell you not to listen to that megacorp biotech propaganda. The only thing you'll get from all that is dain bramaged."

Node started chuckling. Soon all the bio-borgs and cyborgs were laughing.

"I like that one. Dain Bramaged." Node smiled again. "He's okay." He turned his attention back to Bolt. "I got what you need."

Bolt pulled a square device from his jacket. Node snuck one of his metal index fingers into the center and there was a loud click. He pulled his finger out and tossed it to Bolt.

"You'll have payment by midnight as always," Bolt said.

Node nodded. "We cyborgs and bioborgs have to stick together in this mad, crazy world."

"We do indeed," Bolt said.

"Later," Node said as he gave a casual salute and went back into the building with his cyborg men.

"We told you there was no need to worry," Bolt said as he brushed past me.

I followed Zip and Handy behind him. A few times I glanced back just to make sure but no one was there. I looked up.

"What's wrong now?" Handy asked.

"Nothing," I said.

"It has to be something if you're looking around like a scared deer."

"I like to be aware of my surroundings."

Actually, they were right. It was more. I felt we were being watched. I was almost certain of it. Though I was looking around with my enhanced eyewear, I didn't expect to see anyone. These days, with modern tech, someone could be watching us from Mars through a nano-camera.

"Let's get back—" Bolt began.

"We all know where we have to go," I interrupted. "No need to say it out loud."

CHAPTER 19

Beast

I was along for the ride, but it was their show. Normally, when I did field work I was solo, the way I liked it, unless I had bodyguards. Bia had convinced me to tag along and I had my own reasons too. I wanted to talk to this Beast for myself. If I left it to Bia and her biopunks, I'd probably be at home and see some news report that there was a big shootout and they were all dead and the Beast was in the wind. Then I'd have no way to find him. I didn't know the biopunk world and didn't care to. I had to hold onto Bia and her people.

I followed closely in my Pony. The sky lane traffic wasn't too bad. They had a big clunker of a hovercar and drove slow like a senior citizen and jerky like a teenager—easy to follow. But their lack of driving skill wasn't my concern; it was where they were going. I saw the district's skyline in the distance and my chest tightened. The official name was Mad Heights and the last time I was there I experienced more mayhem than ten cases in one. I took that as my quota for the decade. That was normal in Mad City.

Fortunately, I was being spared another encounter. My new biopunk "friends" turned and descended from the hovertraffic. We weren't going to Mad City, just some place close, which was still not good.

We landed our vehicles on a huge, empty street. There was nothing around—no people, no neon signs, only two street lights, nothing in the air. It was one of those spaces between districts. Some had names; most didn't. On city maps they simply had numbers.

I sat in my vehicle and waited. My three friends exited their clunker carrying laser rifles. So even they didn't like the place the cyborg had sent us to find the Beast. I got out of my vehicle, closed the door, and walked back to the trunk, which I had already popped open. If they had rifles, I'd grab one too. My Pony had a trunk safe and I opened the biometric door and reached for the weapon.

The three biopunks waited for me. My laser rifle was, of course, bigger than theirs. I could already hear them making jokes when I reached them.

"Cruz, you have all the tools of the trade," Zip said to me.

"You may talk like a cop, but at least you have the hardware of the streets," Bolt added.

"I don't want to get shot and left dead or bain dramaged," I said and got some chuckles.

"I'm glad we're working together, Cruz," Bolt said. "You're not as bad as I thought you'd be."

"Let's hold off on the praise for each other until after we finish this. I see you all have your big guns. How much resistance are you expecting?"

"None," Bolt answered. "But in this part of town, you better be ready."

"Where did Node say he's at?"

"There's a black market clinic with its own private lab over there," Bolt said as he pointed with his rifle. "He's supposed to be there."

"Ever heard of this place?" I asked.

"No, but if we had, we'd know the lead wasn't legit. Beast wouldn't be anywhere we'd know about or anyone in the community."

"You have the full layout?" I asked.

Bolt smiled. "This isn't our first freak show, Cruz."

"Just checking."

"Shall we go gentleman," Bolt said as he led the way.

An interesting image flashed into my mind as we walked across the wet asphalt to the black market clinic. It was of four cowboys—tall, mean, able to shoot the wings off an insect—marching into the OK Corral. But this wasn't the Old West fabled story. We could have had full detailed photos of every inch of the clinic; it didn't matter. We didn't know where we were marching into nor who was inside. It was exactly the type of situation I avoided. The four of us stopped and listened. Bolt slowly reached for the door's handle and pulled.

The joke was on us. We weren't walking into the OK Corral; we stepped into the DMV. The lobby was packed with people with all kinds of wounds: cuts, stabs, gunshots, fractures. Blood dripping on the gray floor. Bloodied bandages. Everyone waiting in their chairs were criminals of some sort, and we thought we were hard with our laser rifles. In this place, we might as well have been naked and unarmed. The women in this place had bigger weapons than us.

"Calling number 87," a female voice echoed over the speakers. We all looked at each other again. We had frozen like statues at the main entrance but no one paid us any attention.

A huge bald man with gunshots to the chest and arm stood, then hobbled forward dragging his rifle on the ground. We watched him make his way to an inner door which opened. Nurses in black helped him in.

"Do we need to get a number?" Handy asked.

Even my biopunk friends didn't know if we should laugh at the absurdity of this place. We did grab a number from one of the dispensers at the counter. The counters lining the outer area of the lobby were manned by young, cute females. In a place like this I had no doubt they were daughters of local street gangsters working a simple part-time job. Young women their age of the Average Joe and Jane wouldn't be caught dead in this part of town. The four of us sat down in some chairs at the back of one section.

I leaned over to Handy. "How are you feeling since you were poisoned by those crazy maniacs? Do you think you'll make it to when we can see the doctor to have your stomach pumped?"

Handy gave me a smirk. He got into character fast and soon looked like he had contracted the Plague. The performance was solid—occasional moaning, slouched down in the chair, head back, eyes closed.

No one was talking here so we were not about to be the outliers. We were quite satisfied with waiting without conversation since we were the outsiders. Blending in was what we wanted, and great thing about it, was we didn't have to hide our rifles. We were four normal criminals waiting for emergency health care.

"Calling number 305," a female voice echoed over the speakers.

We had been waiting for nearly three hours. All that time, people stood up when their number was called and disappeared behind the inner door to the back of the clinic area. Every so often, the main entrance door opened and a new patient would arrive, grab a number, and sit.

Bolt and Zip played their role to the fullest, both of them helping a moaning Handy to the door. I followed behind them holding all the rifles.

"Hold on," I said as I moved ahead of them and waited. They looked at me. "The nurses will open the door for us."

We stood there. The door didn't open. I looked at one of the counter girls. She stared at me.

"What are you doing?" she asked with attitude. "Open the door and go through."

I dropped our rifles to the ground, except mine, startled everyone in the lobby. I gestured my three friends to move away from the door. I knocked on the door. "Can we come in!"

It was a good thing I pulled my hand back as fast as I did because I liked my hand and its fingers. A pulse blast ripped through that door and it was gone from the hinges. Bolt and Zip dove for the floor, dropping Handy.

For the entire time we waited, I carefully watched the clinic's routine. A person's number was called, they walked to the door, and nurses from within opened it and led the person back. No one opened a door. I had also observed every new patient that had showed up after us. They all looked fine to me. No cuts, stabs, shots, bruises or anything else. You don't come to a clinic to hang out, whether it's for criminals or normal citizens. I already knew all my targets.

One of the key traits of police, fire personnel, and first-responders was a conditioned instinctive mode of behavior that was definitely not normal. Normal people didn't run to where the gunshots are coming from or into a fire-engulfed building. In my case, I dove into the path of a doorway that had been pulse-blasted to bits. But that was my window of opportunity. I was also still wearing my visually-enhanced eyewear and saw what I expected—a lot of gunmen waiting. I flipped my left wrist to engage my pop-gun—definitely not the kid's toy version—and fired. Three down and while the other five were stunned, I was already firing from my omega-gun to put them in desirable horizontal and dead position.

I heard a gun blast from outside and could tell my biopunk friends were also quick to react. I joined them in the gun battle that was just beginning in the main lobby. Unlike Bolt, Zip, and Handy, I didn't have to wait for the other gunmen to fire first. I leapt out and started firing, hitting those standing, about to fire, crouching behind chairs about to fire, those lying on the ground about to fire, and that one young girl who was sending us through the door to our deaths (but I only shot her in the leg).

"Out of here now!" Bolt yelled.

Handy ran much faster than us, even alternating to run on all fours. All the gunmen in the lobby were dealt with but gunfire erupted from the dark of the clinic area. Also, one or more of the other counter girls seemed to want additional college credit by joining in the shootout. With a quick finger-flick, my omega-gun went from laser fire to explosive round firing mode and I blew the hell out of those counters as we got out of the "OK Corral" fast.

Handy had already reached their hoverclunker. Bolt and Zip jumped in.

"Great!" I yelled as I neared my Pony. Now I wished I hadn't parked so far away. If they sent in gunmen into the clinic to get us, did they also have some outside waiting for me? I got my answer.

I heard the gunfire. I turned and fired back at the entrance of the clinic. The hoverclunker came around the corner ten feet in the air giving me cover with a hail of counter-gunfire. I was in the driver's seat of my Pony and in moments was in the air.

We accelerated out of there like rockets into the sky lanes and were gone. But as my biopunk friends drove back to the Freak Show, I pulled away from them toward the exit route.

Inside the main lobby of the black clinic, people were collecting their wits and slowly standing to their feet, getting back into their chairs, and making sure they had no new wounds.

"People, we're sorry for the disturbance. None of our clinic doctors were wounded or killed so there will only be a brief delay for clean-up. Thank you," said one of the female counter girls.

One young woman, white hair under her hoodie, looked around as she sat back down. A clinic nurse in black arrived and dragged away one of the dead bodies, another nurse sprayed the area through a nozzle on her bio-backpack, a third nurse wiped up the chairs, then the floor.

Bia noticed a man in black wearing a white mask sitting in a chair facing her two rows away. She smiled and walked to him, even though he held a silver gun in his hand.

"Beast," she said happily. "Similar minds think alike."

The man pulled off his mask. He looked normal except for his albino eyes. "Bia. My protégé has managed to evolve despite her imperfections. However, you were always brilliant in your beginnings but not so in your conclusion to things."

"You mean you have a gun and I don't."

Beast pointed it directly at her.

"I wouldn't do that. You remember how attached Breech was to me."

Beast glanced over his shoulder to see the human spider biopunk aiming his laser shot-gun at the man.

"Good effort, Bia, but this is my turf, not yours. Also, Breech was never very good at marksmanship."

"True, but my new friend excels at it," Bia said.

Beast noticed the laser dot on his chest and looked across the lobby. There I was pointing another laser rifle at him. I had thrown on a black hooded slicker before I came back in—after taking care of the other gunman guarding the entrance.

"That's my new friend," Bia said. "His name is Cruz."

"The detective." He slowly let his gun drop to the ground. "Was this your plan, Mr. Cruz? Far beyond Bia's capability, I'd say."

"No need to insult Bia, but yes, it was. How do you like it?" I said.

"As I was telling my protégé, you are in my turf, not yours. This place can withstand a full assault by an army of Metro police."

At that very moment, armed men started filing in from everywhere—the main entrance, the clinic area in the back, and another secret door. I counted over thirty men and they were still filling in. Beast reached to the floor and picked up his silver gun.

I saw Breech, the human spider, drop his weapon and put his hands up, and I did the same.

"Mr. Cruz, it was a good try." He stood and Bia instinctively raised her hands in the air.

The only beast-like thing about Beast that I'd noticed was his icy albino eye, but when he stood from his chair, I saw something else. Men with big bellies were as old as the human species, but his pot-belly also included a rotund back under his clothes.

"What are you planning?" she asked him.

"Do you really expect me to tell you?" he asked.

"You're going to kill us anyway, so why not. It's not like we'll be able to tell anyone."

He smiled. "I'll play. My dear, Bia, we have simply switched places in life. You started out as a criminal with simple materialistic desires. I started out as wanting to change the world. Unfortunately, I was born on the dystopia of Earth not off-world where I could have had my chance at making human genetic enhancement accessible to all. That is where I must be, where I must."

"Money," Bia said.

"Are you surprised? You shouldn't be. Since I know you're stalling, let's end it now."

"Don't you want to know how we found you?" Bia asked.

"I will find out. That is a certainty. But I will do that after you're dead."

"Uh, Mr. Beast," I called out.

"Yes, Mr. Cruz?" Beast said.

"I'm sorry."

"Sorry for what?"

"Every criminal says they can take on the full army of the Metro police, but it's not true."

"This is the police! Drop your weapons or you will be killed!"

It was like the voice of God or a two thousand foot giant outside the building. The directive was so loud the building shook, then the entire roof exploded.

The gunmen smart enough or fast enough to drop their weapons lived. Those who weren't or didn't were cut down before they took another breath. From above, one silver-and-black police "PEACE" officer descended after another wearing silent jetpacks like wingless black angels.

I looked across at what had been the lobby of the black clinic, but was now a mess of rubble and bodies. Beast had his hands up high in the air too and was looking straight at me. The Beast was going to be put in a cage where he belonged.

PART FOUR

BioPirates Tried to Snatch My Arm

CHAPTER 20

Officers Break and Caps

Biopiracy.

Noun. The commercial exploitation or monopolization of biological or genetic material.

The police weren't hard to figure out. If you called the police to catch the bad guys, they liked you. If they showed up at a crime scene and you were there, even if you were a "friend" as I was, you were just one of the suspects or persons of interest to be swept up and hauled down to Metro PD. My last visit was awful; this one was the opposite.

One did have to be careful even as a Good Samaritan, which I found out the hard way. Any contact with the police was recorded and if not justified, more than three contacts in a thirty days period would land your butt in an all-day anti-criminality class. I believed the City purposely found the worse, mind-numbingly boring instructors on the planet to teach the class to make you want to set yourself on fire or commit harakiri. They wanted the class to leave such a putrid taste in your mouth, burn such a hole in your mind that you'd think very long and hard about calling the police to be a "good citizen" ever again. But it was for a good and legitimate reason. They didn't want the average citizens pretending they were police officers and ending up dead.

Instead of sitting in the open "zoo" of their main lobby, I was in the private one casually sitting on a bench where I could see not just the police officers but the detectives and an occasional police brass. The officers who escorted me to wait even allowed me something to drink from the vending machine. I was happy with my cup of silk coffee.

Bia and company, along with the Beast and company, weren't so lucky. Everyone was officially arrested, booked and in holding, except for me. I did tell Bia that I'd straighten it all out and that seemed to reassure her and the other biopunks. I did feel bad for them. Since Handy had hands for his feet, he was double-handcuffed and sequestered away from the normal population in holding. Bolt and Zip had less drastic body modifications but were sequestered too. I never knew what Bia's modifications, or enhancements as a biopunk would say, were until I arrived at the station. She struck me as a serious adult. Having three breasts was not something a serious adult would do. But she did say she had planned to have a breast elimination operation this year. Yes, this was my life as a detective in Metropolis.

I never did see the human spider man or the Beast. I had no doubt they were hauled off to a special unit within Metro PD.

There was a special gang unit to deal with cyborgs so there had to be one for biopunks. For those unlucky two, they were probably in a steel box container somewhere deep within until they were cleared. Unauthorized cyborgs could have their bionic parts removed without permission. I'm sure the same laws applied to biopunks. No matter how silly or serious, they could be removed too if a judge authorized it.

"Cruz!"

I recognized that voice. I turned with a big smile to see my two police buddies—Officers Break and Caps.

Officer Break and Officer Caps, who I secretly called Ebony and Ivory, escorted me to one of the empty interrogation rooms. It was one of the nicer ones so that meant I wasn't in trouble. They had been partners for nearly a decade now. Officer Break was a Black policeman on the Force for, I believe, over fifteen years. Officer Caps, the White policeman, was a year less in seniority. Most policeman couldn't wait to get off the beat to work in Homicide, Vice, Sex Crimes, White Collar, or anything else. However, they both preferred to work the street as patrol officers. I knew why. It meant do your shift, go home, and nothing more. Paperwork but no politics. Sounded good to me when you had wives and kids to raise.

I sat at the table facing the door and set my cup of coffee in front of me. They both sat in the chairs opposite me.

"Are you detectives now?" I asked.

"No, we're just babysitting you until the detective arrives. Have you solved your 100th case yet?" Officer Break asked.

"Oh, yeah. Months ago."

"You're a real detective now then," Officer Caps said.

"I am."

"What brought you into this situation?" Break asked me.

"A client started the ball rolling, one thing led to another, met the biopunk gang."

"The three-breasted lady?" Break asked.

"Yes, but I didn't know that."

"Says you. Does your wife know your running around the city with a three-breasted lady?" Break said.

I laughed. "I didn't know that until you brought her out in a T-shirt, which I know you all did on purpose. Besides she and her guys did their part in taking down these bad guys."

"Bad guys? Who are the bad guys? I only see a bunch of bio-freaks: three-breasted ladies, half-humans looking like a giant spider, retractable men, zippered and metal bolted people. Cruz, you're running around Metro with crazy crews now?" Break said.

"What's this about, Cruz?" Caps asked.

"That's what we're here to find out," I answered. "The retractable man's street name is the Beast. All the gunmen were his. We were tracking him down to find out what he was up to."

"Why? You're not a police detective." Break was annoyed.

"I couldn't leave the situation as is because I had to find out if it was basic robbery or a serious bio-terrorism threat."

"Bio-terrorism?" Break said, but both officers were very interested. They might have been officers, but with their seniority they were as good as any Metro PD detectives.

"Yeah."

"How do you get from street detective to that?" Break asked.

"Because of a stolen item, or I think was stolen. A big silver briefcase marked 'property of the CDC.'"

"Calling the police was not an option?" Caps asked.

"Call you and say what? We had no briefcase, no suspect, no scene of the crime because they cleaned up and fled, no names, nothing. There was nothing to report. That's why I was investigating. So I'd have something to report."

"Are all your cases like this, Cruz?" Break asked.

"Hardly any of my cases are like this. They're simple, straightforward, and I solve them in days. And they don't involve any gunplay."

"That's a funny thing to say coming from you," Caps said. "How many of those gangsters did you gun down today?"

"Uh, a few."

"A few, huh?" Caps said.

"Did you shoot a college freshman girl?" Break asked.

"What?"

"Stop playing, Cruz. You heard me. That girl is going to file a complaint against you."

"Wait a minute. She was shooting at us! She also was about to send us into an ambush where we would have all been shot to death. The nerve of youth these days."

"Laugh it up, Cruz," Break said.

"All you have to do is check her hands. She fired her laser gun at us."

"She said you shot her before she did that."

I smiled at Break. "You know she shot at us, and she's an employee of an illegal emergency clinic. Who's the judge going to believe? Me or the criminal youth."

"She doesn't have three breasts but she's prettier than you," Break said.

"I think I'll be okay. If it gets to court, I'll have my wife and Cruz Jr. sit right behind me as character references. And!"

"And what?" Break asked.

"And my two best police friends Officers Break and Caps will vouch for the impeccable character of their best-est friend Cruz of the Liquid Cool Detective Agency."

"Let's get out of here before we vomit all over the place," Break said.

They couldn't leave fast enough as I laughed.

CHAPTER 21

Chief Hub

I didn't have long to wait and it wasn't the detective-in-charge who came into the room. It was the Chief of the Metropolis Police himself. To say I was surprised was an understatement. Why would the head of the largest police force in the world be involved in my case, which was nothing more than suspicions at this point.

Chief Hub was six feet, lean, a muscled veteran officer of more than two decades. Dark hair, thick mustache, and his dark green eyes squinted at me as he sat. What I didn't like was that he was alone. He was the Chief. There was always at least one sycophant around him at all times, and it wasn't procedure for any officer to speak to a subject in the interrogation room without at least another officer present...or watching. I looked up at the single tiny black ceiling camera. I returned my attention to him.

"Hi Chief," I said. "This is a surprise."

"I'm sure it is, Cruz. Lots of people in jail and lots of bodies in the morgue. I thought you would be behaving yourself more now that you're a family man."

"I was the one that called the police."

"Yes, after you and your friends engaged in a grand shootout with other gang members. Speaking of friends. They're not the most disgusting bunch I've come across in my years. The cyborg gangs still got most of them beat in the most disgusting body modifications I've seen category but I wouldn't be hanging around them if you paid me."

"I needed them for this case. I'm not exactly familiar with this sub-culture and I have no desire to learn. This is a one-off. Do my investigation and that's it."

"Who's your client?"

"They are," I replied.

"They hired you?"

"Yes."

"To do what?"

"Find this character who calls himself the Beast."

"Then what?"

"Turn him over to you."

"A group of biopunk gang members hired you to find another group of biopunk gang members to turn them over to the police. Cruz, your lies have always been much smoother in the past. Are you slipping? Are you not getting enough sleep with the changing of diapers?"

"Okay. I know it sounds unbelievable, but it's true."

"Fortunately, this time I have the whole picture and you don't. Cruz, you need to understand that this is a very, very serious situation. You can talk to me or I can turn all this over to the CDC's Bio-Hazard Division. Metro PD has a Hazmat Team. We deal with substances but not micro-organisms like Bio-Haz."

"The guys in the scary yellow space suits."

"Yes, and they can quarantine guys, their wives, and little sons, and parents, and parents-in-law when they're concerned—"

"Okay! What do you want to know because I don't know anything. Again, I called you. I gave a full statement, twice, to the officers at the scene. We told you that this might be a bio-hazard situation."

"This Beast is a bio-terrorist?"

"Yes. That's what we believe."

"We? What do you believe?"

"I don't know. That's why we turned him over to you. You can find what's what."

"Cruz, guess where I was before I came here?"

"I have no idea."

"I was in the bio-haz detention facilities. Something like this involves me, the Mayor, City Council, Feds, CDC, and a whole bunch of others you don't even know about. I sat across from this Beast. Told him the situation. Basically that his life was over. Told him about all the evidence we collected on him and his gang from his illegal clinic. You know what he said to me?"

"No."

"He swore to me that he was set up. Then he stopped talking. He looked real mad to me."

"What did Bia say?"

"His former underling. She told my detectives he's a lying psycho."

"What will happen to Bia and her people?"

"They'll be held and let go when we're satisfied they had nothing to do with this Beast. Then they'll have a few operations at government expense to return them to the form they were born as and put on probation."

"Good. You have the Beast and his gang. That's what we wanted. Bia will be able to tell you if we got all his people."

"Anything else?"

I looked at Hub with a blank expression, then said, "No."

"Bia hired you and no one else?"

"Correct."

"Okay. Then that's all there is. I'll get the officers and you're free to go."

"I'm glad we got a potential psycho off the streets. Another one for the good guys."

"Something like that."

Hub stood from the chair, opened the door and left. Even though the door was closed and I was alone, I made sure not to give any indications or make any facial expressions. Hub was no dummy. He knew I was holding stuff back. He just couldn't prove it. I also knew I was being watched. For all I knew it could be a room packed with police brass, Feds, and CDC agents. All I had to do was keep my composure and wait for Ebony and Ivory to return. Officers Break and Caps returned forty minutes later and escorted me from the police station.

CHAPTER 22

PJ

Any Average Joe or Jane knew that you never yelled "fire" in a crowded stadium event with no fire. All kinds of protocols kicked in that would leave you criminally charged and jailed. When that was over the civil fines came and you were broke. You just didn't do it. One word to destroy your life.

There were a few words that had the same affect for law enforcement: bio-threat, bio-terrorism, plague. All meant the same thing. In a supercity of fifty million people the only response was overkill. Usually, I got to have a few minutes of chatting with the Chief but not this time. I was very, very lucky that I had called them, even though I suspected that they had me and the Bio-Borgs under surveillance for who knows how long.

When I left the Metro PD, I went home, had my super-shower and went to bed, making sure not to wake either the wife or Cruz Jr.—especially Cruz Jr. My parents warned me. Ages two through five you'd seriously question whether your child needed to be sedated; they had so much energy. If the society could figure out how to tap into that energy, we could power the supercity.

The next day was back at the office. This time I beat PJ in and was busy doing computer research when she arrived and stood at my doorway in a puffy slicker with a bag of some kind of pastries in one hand and her oversized purse in another.

"This is very good. I like when I get to the office and see you working. It's means my training is starting to work."

I laughed. "You do know I'm the boss."

"Boss? You're an employee of the Liquid Cool Detective Agency like me. ABC. Always Be Closing Cases."

She disappeared from my open doorway.

"That would be ABCC then."

I heard her turn on the desk radio with her French-language music.

"I have a project for you, PJ."

She appeared at the doorway. "I have fresh authentic French pastries. You can have some since you came into work on time."

I laughed. "On time?"

"I'll leave them at my desk. What project?"

"How often do you scan the office?"

"There. If you came to the office early, you would know that I scan the office first thing in the morning as I get it ready for clients."

"When was the last time you found any listening or surveillance devices?"

"Why? Who's spying on us now?"

"So you haven't found anything?"

"No. I would have told you. Nothing. All clean."

"Let's have Bugs come in anyway. I want to be sure. Every inch of the office and now that I think of it, both our vehicles. And have him check out the Concrete Mama too."

The Concrete Mama was home. Where I lived with the family, but so did PJ. We were on the 150th floor; PJ lived on the 20th.

"Have him coordinate with our doorman," I said.

"What did you do now? Who did you make mad?"

"I didn't make anyone mad. I want to have peace of mind."

"Yes, we don't want any peepers listening or watching our business. Okay, I will call him and have him come in today, but I will scan too."

"How many clients are coming in today? I don't see anything on the calendar."

"Because you will be on the phones today. I have a perfectly created system that you must follow."

"What business book is this one from?"

"Never you mind what business books I'm reading. You have new clients to call, recent clients to thank for their business and to remind them about referrals, and old clients to thank so you stay top of mind."

I burst out laughing.

"You can laugh, but I expect a big bonus for my expansion of the business."

"But I have another mouth to feed."

"I have expensive tastes. Cheap salaries won't do. Do your calls *tout de suite*."

"You get this place scanned and Bugs scheduled to come in today *tout suite*," I said.

"You're speaking French," she sang.

CHAPTER 23

Bugs

PJ's scan using her handheld device found nothing in the office, which I totally expected. Bugs showed up at noon. He reminded me of Wilford G. before I even met Wilford G. Bugs was old-school. Whenever you saw him, he wore overalls over his suit, usually purple or blue. As so often before, he came through the door with his scanning contraptions in hand and a team of two guys—one senior staffer and a younger one still learning the business. Bugs looked unassuming and humble, but he was the master when it came to listening device detection, motion detection security, intrusion defense security, video surveillance, door and wall defense security, door and lock augmentation, trap doors and panic rooms. His business had been around for decades, but he never advertised. All his business came from word-of-mouth and all his clientele were the wealthiest of Metropolis's political, business and entertainment elite. He was always in demand as spying was a never-ending and constantly-evolving threat or as Bugs would say, the cost of doing business in this world.

It was actually my best friend, Run-Time, who introduced us. While his sweepers worked, he sat in my private office to interview me.

"What makes you think there might be a threat?" he asked.

"A case that involved the Chief of Police and the CDC."

"CDC?"

"Bio-threat Division."

His eyebrow raised. "You do know in the case of any bio-threat to the city that the CDC field division outranks the chief of police and even the mayor and city council."

"Oh."

"Very serious stuff. I doubt we'll find anything here, your vehicles, or at your residence. They don't bother with planting spying devices. They don't have to. Satellites, drone-surveillance, communication device interception, and computer hacking. That's what they do."

"Spy on me and I'd never know."

"Spy on all of us and we'd never detect it. The cost of living in the modern world, Mr. Cruz. I have another team already at the Concrete Mama."

"Good."

"We'll be done within the hour."

"Oh, Bugs, I haven't told you. Baby number two's on the way."

"Cruzalina is coming!" PJ yelled out.

"How are you hearing our conversation from out there at your desk!" I yelled.

Bugs smiled. He stood and shook my hand. "Congratulations to you and the misses."

"Thanks, Bugs. And ignore PJ. Our daughter *will not* be named Cruzalina."

"I kinda guessed that."

"I'm going to be an auntie again!" PJ's voice rang out.

"Bugs, see what I have to deal with each day," I said.

"I think you're tough enough to survive," he said, chuckling.

CHAPTER 24

Beast

The sweep by Bugs and his team did turn up nothing. Office, vehicles, and residential were all clean, which was the result we all expected. But Bugs' visit wasn't completely a waste as it was always my chance to find out the latest in the commercial spying world. It gave Bugs, who loved to tell stories, a chance to share his vocation with someone outside the business. It always fascinated me. Bugs also liked to upgrade previous work he had done for no extra charge, which meant making our office security measures even better. Both PJ and I were happy to know that our scanning arch over the main door, besides detecting weapons and cyborgs (PJ and my wife excluded), could also detect people with non-natural features—biopunks!

"Modern technology," I said with amazement after Bugs told us. That really made me feel good knowing that no Beast or human spider could walk into our office without the silent alarms going off to warn us.

Bugs and team had gone hours ago and I had settled on PJ's pastries instead of a proper lunch. I had grabbed another from PJ's desk and had walked back into my office when the main door opened. I could hear PJ greeting the walk-ins.

"Good afternoon and welcome to the Liquid Cool Detective Agency," PJ said. "Oh please, hang up your jackets, and you can set your umbrellas in the lounge area."

"Thank you," I heard them say.

As I sat at my desk to continue working, I tapped the screen of my desk monitor. There was a vid-feed of the office lobby. We had five visitors: four men and one woman. They took off their slickers, to reveal their business suits. They hung up their slickers on our lobby coat racks and leaned their umbrellas against the wall.

"Rain is heavy," the largest of the men said.

"Do you have an appointment?" PJ asked.

"No, we didn't, but we did need to speak with Mr. Cruz right away. We do have an urgent deadline to meet." The large man reached into his jacket. "Here's our card. We're attorneys representing a Mr. Doubletree."

I was now standing at the doorway of my private office. "I'm Mr. Cruz."

The attorneys looked at me and they smiled.

"Mr. Cruz, nice to meet you. Sorry for the intrusion but this is a time-sensitive matter."

"You said your client is named Doubletree?"

"Yes, sir."

"Do you have a client named Doubletree?" PJ asked me.

"No," I replied. "Would your client also go by the street name of the Beast?" I asked the lawyers.

"That is correct, Mr. Cruz."

"How could someone in government custody on suspicion of bio-terrorism have been allowed to retain defense attorneys?"

"If we could have a moment, Mr. Cruz. Our client wishes to speak with you."

"What?" I said surprised. "Why would he want to speak with me? He tried to kill me."

The large man swallowed. "Give us ten minutes of your time, sir."

"PJ, you know what to do."

PJ walked to them with a flat rectangular device in her hand. "Please lady and gentlemen, stand still while I scan you all again and your possessions."

"After she does that, have a seat in the waiting area while I make a few calls to verify your story," I told them.

We had added a few chairs in front of my desk to accommodate all five lawyers, then closed my office door. The five lawyers sat there nervously.

"I take it you reached someone at the Police One," the large man asked.

Police One was the official name for Metro PD's headquarters. "Yes," I answered.

"You seem to know a bit about the law in these matters."

"The police can't hold a crazy maniac gang leader unless they are formally arrested, and even then, they have full access to defense counsel. Suspected terrorists can be held forever until the government is good and ready and they never get access to attorneys. Why did the government allow your firm to come in? Explain that to me."

"Mr. Cruz, we truly don't know. Our guess is that they believe that there are others involved and they believe the defense of our client and bringing you in will lead them to those other parties."

"Your client is guilty."

"Is he, Mr. Cruz?"

"I say he is."

"He's guilty of trying to kill you."

"Yeah, that's called attempted murder."

"But is he guilty of all the other thing's the government alleges."

"You mean the bio-terrorism."

"Yes. Conspiracy to commit an act of bio-terrorism. Our client is innocent."

"He was set-up, was he?"

"Mr. Cruz, our client wishes to speak with you."

I was already shaking my head. "No way am I helping your client in any possible way."

"Mr. Cruz, let's put our cards on the table. Our client is never getting out of jail. He knows that. However, what he does want is to bring the people who set him up to occupy the jail cell next to him."

"Mr. Cruz," the woman of the team spoke. "If I can go out on a limb here, I think you believe our client was set up too, even without knowing all the details. Our client was financed by someone else. You know this. That person or persons has not been identified and is still at large."

"Who your client claims set him up?"

"Yes," she said. "But we believe you suspect that as well."

"Why do you believe that?"

"We read the transcripts," the large man said.

"Transcripts?" I asked.

"Your interview with the Chief of Police."

"The police gave you access to that interview?"

"They did."

That really surprised me. The police could have kept those transcripts from them forever. Not that there was anything to hide, but simply not cooperate with defense attorneys. Why was the chief of police helping these defense attorneys?

"What do you want?"

"We'd like you to meet with our client. Hear him out. Nothing more."

"Why am I doing this? There's no case. I have no client."

The large man cleared his throat. "My firm often hires consultants for a fee. We would classify your meeting our client as a consultation which would entitle you to a fee."

"It better be a generous one," I said.

"It will be."

"Pay my office manager. PJ!"

First, I followed the attorneys back to their offices in Downtown Metro in my Pony. We waited on the street level of their building and a government double-decker hovervan arrived and we piled in. The windows were darkened so we couldn't see exactly where we were going and the vehicle was always shaking in erratic ways so we didn't even know if you were moving forward let alone turning left or right.

We arrived wherever we were an hour later to be greeted by well-armed helmeted guards in back of an underground parking area. We filed out and followed one of the guards. The lawyers waited in a conference room; I was led by a man in a black suit down the hallway.

"Before you can speak to the detainee, we will have you sign a non-disclosure agreement," the man said. "In here." He led me to a smaller room where a fat document rested on a desk. He gestured me to sit.

"This is the NDA?" I asked.

"Yes. Please sign." He handed me a pen.

I took the pen but rested it on the table as I got comfortable in my chair. I opened to page one of the document. The man sat there alternating between rolling his eyes, sighing, looking up at the ceiling, and gritting his teeth. I read every word on every page of the 200-page document.

"Okay, I'll sign." I grabbed the pen and did so. I was familiar with these kind of government NDAs. There was nothing unusual or outrageous, which in itself wasn't unusual. This operation was run by adults, not politicians. Everything was above board and by the book. No games, just serious business.

The visiting room was the size of a closet. They had me sit behind the table on small chair on one side of a see-through laser wall—like the bars of a jail cell only the bars were red laser light beams rather than solid metal. I waited a bit when the Beast, Mr. Doubletree, was brought on the other side of the laser wall to his seat behind a desk. He was in a white short-sleeved jumpsuit and wearing white booties on his feet.

A guard stood behind me about six feet away, and one stood behind him on his side.

"I would say thank you for coming," he said, "but I don't think you would accept it."

"I wouldn't."

"You killed most of my men." He laughed to himself. "Before the police storm troopers got there."

"What do you want Beast? Are you a Beast anymore, by the way?"

"No, my quite extensive enhancement will be removed courtesy of the Metropolis government."

"A 'retractable' body, they said."

"An amazing and disturbing effect. I could increase my height from six to ten feet."

"Yes, you were an impressive super villain. Again, what do you want?"

"Mr. Cruz, I thought, at first, I was being punished for compromising their plans. I brought Bia's Bio-Borgs into the picture, allowed them to follow me to our secret hoverhotel lab, and compromise it."

"You killed them."

"I wanted to show them that I could handle any threats to their plans, even from past acquaintances. They saw it differently. An inability to keep outsiders out of our business. The damage was done. There were other outsiders involved, or one specifically. An intruder. I assume that intruder brought you into this and you later connected with Bia."

"I'm not interested in your sad tales."

"I've been set-up so professionally that I'll never get out of here. That was their true plan from the start. Set me up to divert attention or set me up in case they had to divert attention away from themselves and their plans. It means I'm expendable to them. I always was. Their plans are too important. Set me up and send the authorities in another direction. In a direction that all the authorities would zealously pursue—all of them."

"So, you're not a bio-terrorist?"

"No, Mr. Cruz, if they want the authorities to believe that, it means that it isn't."

"Then what are your benefactors really doing?"

"Criminals want money, Mr. Cruz. Find out what the crime is. I want you to find that out. I've heard you are very good at such things."

"You want me to help prove your innocence? I thought that's what your defense attorneys are for."

"Mr. Cruz, I had them bring you down here to hire you in a way."

"Everybody wants to hire me on this same case. What if I don't believe your story? There is no 'them.' It's all you."

"Mr. Cruz, you would never have come if that were true. You also know I was set-up. Bia and her followers are good soldiers but nothing more. There are so many black clinics in Metropolis doing illegal and unethical things. How did they find mine? There was nothing special about it. That was the point. I was never seen, not even by my own men. One of Bia's informants found it miraculously? The black clinic run my me? How? I trained Bia. If I didn't want her to find me, she wouldn't and neither could anyone she knows. Her informant found me because someone, my benefactors, gave that informant the information to find me. You know that."

"What do you want me to do?"

"I want to dish out my own revenge. My attorneys will never free me. I know that. I've done so many bad things in my life that I wasn't caught for. This is simply Karma. The least I can do is set you upon those who set me up to ruin their plans. Uncover what their ultimate plan is."

"How?"

"That's easy, Mr. Cruz. I'll tell you the name of my benefactor and you'll track him down."

"If they are this good in setting you up then whatever identity you think you have is a false one."

"Of course, it is a false one. In fact, I know it's more than one person. I did say benefactors, not benefactor. I believe it's a group of them."

"Not another secret society."

"Yes, that's it. I don't know the real identity, but I do have a location. Our communications were always by phone. I always used a tracer on my phone out of habit. In the criminal world, if a 'new' business partner is calling you from a number previously used by an undercover narc then you know not to continue the conversation. I could never trace my benefactor, except twice. One trace showed the call was made from overseas, no specific building. However, another trace did identify a building. For a detective like you, that's all that's needed. I'm sure once you show up, the rats will work themselves up in such a frenzy that they'll start making all kinds of mistakes. That's when you'll catch them. Whatever the crime is or will be, you'll catch them."

CHAPTER 25

Node

I'd never believed that Bia's informant had "found" the Beast and his clinic. What I originally thought was that it was the Beast himself leaving clues to his whereabouts so we'd follow and he could wipe us all out. That's what we all thought, even Bia. We could all still be right and the Beast was playing a game on us, but he had nothing to gain. However, I came across criminals who just lied to cause chaos or make you chase your own tail. But what if Beast was telling the truth. If so, then someone else was out there. Actually, we already knew someone else was out there—the Beast's financier.

There were a few people I had to speak with first before I proceeded on with the Beast's lead. Any good detective doesn't assume anything. You follow all the leads no matter how mundane to cross them all off your list. Node first, then Bia, and finally my own real client, Twinkle for a last chat. Based on what they all collectively said, each from their own vantage point, would determine if I would accept the premise that the Beast was telling the truth. In fact, I'd add a fourth person to the list to really ensure I covered all my investigative bases.

It wasn't lost on me the fact that I was a street detective not a police detective or a CDC investigator. I really was operating outside my normal civilian jurisdiction, but I was being paid—by three people. It was not unlike accepting a job to bodyguard a little girl at her birthday party who had been stalked. Not something I'd do, but the parents were wealthy and clever PJ got them to accept an outrageous fee, but the parents paid without blinking.

There was no point going anywhere near Node's hang-out. He barely trusted me with Bia's people being there vouching for me. As a street informant, he'd know she and the gang were in jail and the police also snatched up the Beast and his entire gang too. If I showed, Node would run or shoot me.

Hiring people to get messages to people was done on the street every day. I contacted my associate Phishy, who contacted his sidewalk johnny friends on the street, who got in touch with Node's street people, who got in touch with Node.

He had agreed to speak with me by vid-phone and when I dialed, he picked up. His face stared at me from my screen. "Why aren't you in jail too?"

"Why would I be in jail too?" I sat at my desk in my private office. "I didn't do anything."

"I heard you did plenty. I heard Bia and her crew did too. Did you rat them out to your cop friends? I know all about you."

"Not that I have to justify myself to you, the only reason Bia and her crew will be released is because I vouched for them to my cop friends. The police will finish their investigation, keep the Beast in a cage where he belongs, his crew is in jail where they belong, and life goes on."

"I'll change my attitude towards you when and if Bia gets out."

"Fine. She will be getting out."

"Why are we talking now?"

"Bia and I never thought the info on the Beast's whereabouts came to you because your street resources were so good, but because someone wanted to use you to get to us."

"Bia and you thought that? Really? You two dating now? You think each other's thought? Bia and you didn't have to pay for the information. Why am I listening to you insult me?"

"I am not insulting you. I just need to figure something out. I met with the Beast."

"What? You met him? In prison?"

"Yeah."

"Why would the cops let you do that?"

"His defense lawyers brought me to see him. Node, I don't have time for all this back-story. Here's my question. The info you got was planted. Either Beast planted it on the street to lure me, Bia and the crew in. Or—"

"Or what?"

"Someone planted it on the street to set-up the Beast tighter than a cyborg choke-hold on a fat wad of cash. It's one or the other. I want to hear which one you think it is. Only you know where the info came from. Only you know the streets and the people in your turf. Which scenario do you think it is? It's important."

"Why important?"

"Because if Beast is telling the truth, we have another bad guy or bad guys out there. That could threaten you, me, and everyone in Metropolis. I got a daughter on the way so that will not do."

"I got a son on the way."

"Good. So we're fathers. Which one do you think it is?"

Node sighed and he looked around, thinking. He scratched the top of his head with his metal fingered hands.

"I don't like Beast, never did, even back when he was one of us. He was never content with what he had. It was always something bigger, something over the rainbow with him. Criminals who can't be content with what they have, soon try to take from someone they shouldn't and get themselves hurt bad or dead."

Node was still debating with himself, but I was confident I'd won him over.

"I already checked out the source of the info. Do I think the person who brought me the tip is legit? Yeah, I do. Do I believe the tip was planted or could have been planted by someone outside the community? Hell, yeah."

"Beast was set up?"

"Yeah, I think so. I think Beast pissed on someone. Beast isn't stupid. I hear that the cops caught him with every incriminating piece of evidence that could be found. That's not Beast. He's too careful for that."

"Beast is a smart one, but he could still be trying to play us. I was there. We had the shootout, and we took them down, but it could have gone the other way. Dead men can't call the police."

"You called the cops?"

"I did. Another reason why they believed me when I vouched for Bia and her crew."

"Makes sense. Okay, I change my mind about you so I'll tell you this. You didn't call the cops. They were already there."

"When the police don't want to be seen, no one can see them. Not me. Not the best criminal look-out around," I said, hiding my surprise at what he just told me.

"You can't see them when they've taken over a place. You can see them before they arrive and dig in. My source lives and works right outside Mad City. He keeps his bed right by the window so he can watch. He watched the cops fly in from the comfort of his bed. He said a lot of them flew in. They were already there when you called."

I sighed this time. "Beast is telling the truth then."

"Yeah. There's another bad guy out there."

CHAPTER 26

Bia

Before I left the office, I had PJ make the arrangements to get my original client on this case back here. I was off to Downtown Metro again to the Metro Jail house.

There were different levels of incarceration and Bia didn't qualify for the "county club" accommodations but the next best. Your own clean cell, access to books and magazines, your own TV, three meals a day without the possibility of getting shanked.

When a female prison guard brought Bia in to the visiting area—two tables facing each other between a partition—I stifled a laugh. She wasn't handcuffed but the prison guard didn't let go of her shoulder until she was guided to her chair and sat. The guard walked back out, but we knew we were under heavy surveillance. The top of the ceiling was lined with mini-cameras.

The top part of Bia's head was wrapped in bandages and her chest area was wrapped up in bandages tight.

"My eyes are up here," she said.

I laughed. "How did your operation go?" I asked.

"Leave it alone, Cruz. The government has no right to do what it did."

"Your body and all that. Did they do the same to your guys too?"

"I wasn't crying about it. And yeah."

"Bia, why would you do such a thing? You're the leader."

"I was young and stupid. I admit it. Back then I was a dancer and I wanted to be a dancer on Mars. It was my gimmick. I got used to it. But I was going to have the operation on my own!" she yelled at the cameras."

"When are they letting you out?" I asked.

"A couple of weeks. It's actually not all that bad being on the inside."

"Getting to like being in prison isn't a healthy thing."

"I didn't say I wanted to stay or return. I'm saying it isn't bad, and the food is tastier than I expected."

"Oh, you've never been to prison before."

"Have you?"

"No, but this isn't prison. You do your crimes on the outside you won't be here. I can assure you of that."

"I will not be doing crimes because the Bio-Borgs are not criminals."

"Yes, freedom fighters. That's not why I came to see you. I came to ask you questions."

"What question?"

"Do you have any idea, clue, anything on who the Beast's financier is?"

"No, none. I would have said. Beast liked to compartmentalize things. If you had no need to know, you wouldn't know."

"Do you think it's possible that his financier could have turned the tables on him and set him up to take him out of the picture?"

"Is that what he's saying?"

"It is."

"You believe him?"

"Him, by himself, no. Based on what others are saying, yes."

"It's because we found him, right? He's saying someone else leaked his location to the street."

"Yes."

"Cruz, I've known Beast a lot longer than you. He's playing you."

"Maybe."

"He is."

"He's never getting out so no need to worry there. But I do want to find his financier."

"It'll never happen. I believe his benefactor is off-world. Without Beast, there's no way to know who they are. They're gone."

"Unless they want to finance someone else."

Bia shook her head. "No, they're gone, Cruz. People like that, with that kind of money. Their little criminal venture doesn't work and they're gone. They'll put the money into legitimate resources. If they come back to it, it'll be years from now. They're gone. We got Beast though, and that's all that matters."

"Then I'll move on."

"You should. I'll do the same when I get out of here."

"Well, if anything surfaces on the benefactor—"

"I'll call you right away, Cruz. But really…it's over. Beast is as far as we go on this. Also, remember this was his show from the beginning. He found the benefactor. The benefactor didn't find him. We got him, and he'll never see the light of day to hurt anyone else or tarnish the name of the community."

CHAPTER 27

Twinkle

The Beast said the benefactor found him. Bia said the Beast found the benefactor. I felt both were telling the truth, but that didn't mean that what they thought was the truth was the true reality. Only the benefactor could tell me that.

Bia was absolutely right in that we had reached a dead-end in the case. However, I was still going to check all the boxes and wrap it up nicely by talking to my final two people.

Twinkle was out of town and the soonest he could meet was over the weekend. Though we didn't have office hours, PJ came in and opened up so I could meet with my cat burglar client in person early on a Saturday.

Our slim friend strolled through the door in his casual pin-striped brown suit under a black slicker. He sat in my office with a cup of hot black coffee in his hand. I had my cup of silk coffee.

"You don't follow what's happening on the streets?" I asked.

"In my line, Mr. Cruz, I only have time to stay abreast of the things that pertain to my business. I don't have much spare time. It takes me months to prepare for a job."

"That's what I wanted to talk to you about."

"I'll save you the time, Mr. Cruz. I went back through my notes. My mark is a phantom."

"What does that mean?"

"Like he never existed."

"You do have a picture of him."

"I do."

"And?"

"Here's the thing, Mr. Cruz. Before my job, I had the full background of a wealthy guy and his family that spent half his time on Earth and half his time Up-Top. Mergers and acquisitions were his line and after fifteen years he became extremely wealthy, and he already came from a wealthy family. The day after my job, he liquidated all his Earth assets. Once I brought you onto the case, I went back through my research and I'm very thorough, I'm not really sure if this man, or what I know of him, is real. It's like I stumbled on a guy who's in the Witness Protection Program or a spy. A wealthy guy is robbed, he's spooked and gets rid of his hoverhotel apartment. That's what I'd do, but his records of owning the place vanished. His employment records vanished, his company data, holdings. Maybe he's that good. He knows that someone profiled him, but it's too thorough, too fast."

"As if he did it before."

"Or hired a firm that does this kind of thing all the time. What I'm saying is I can't find out who the hoverhotel owner is. He's gone and all traces of him are gone too."

"Family?"

"I went down that route too and there's less than nothing there."

"Anything to follow Up-Top."

"I don't have any contacts up there. If you want those kinds of contacts, you have to visit Up-Top. I don't feel comfortable doing that—ever."

"Sounds to me like you've been targeting Up-Top business execs for your career."

He smiled. "Nothing to say."

"Dead ends all around," I said.

"Sorry, Mr. Cruz, I couldn't help."

"How about the fences you used to sell what you...acquired? Any of them received any visitors asking questions about said items?"

Twinkle shook his head. "No. I would have heard about that right away. I only take insured things. With wealthy people, it's stolen, they simply get a new one courtesy of the insurance payment, and they triple their security."

"Leave me the picture of what the guy looks like and the family."

"Right here, Mr. Cruz."

I took the photo of the man standing with a brunette wife and two kids, a boy and a girl.

"Nice looking family," I said.

"It sure is."

"Ever saw him in person?"

"Never. Nor any of the family. Which means that the photo could be fake."

"Yeah. Well, Twinkle, it was nice knowing you."

I stood and we shook hands.

"Good luck, Mr. Cruz. My niece says if there's something to uncover, you'll uncover it."

"Good luck to you, and stay out of trouble."

He started laughing. "That's funny. Stay out of trouble. Okay. I'll try—not."

CHAPTER 28

Chief Hub

I had spoken to the three people I wanted to and had officially wrapped it up. We knew who owned the hoverhotel suite, though there was a possibility the person really didn't exist, and had disappeared Up-Top. We knew who killed the two bio-punks in the suite and the Beast would be sitting in a cage for his crimes and many more. But there was one outstanding item since Beast's benefactor was a dead-end: the CDC briefcase.

Back to Metro PD I went. I asked to speak to the Chief and was surprised when an officer appeared and led me from the general waiting room, past the interior waiting area, and directly to his empty office.

"The Chief will be here shortly," the officer said and left.

I sat down, looking around to pass the time. The chief strolled in and sat at his desk.

"Mr. Cruz."

"Chief."

"What brings you down to Police One—again."

"Is the Metro PD using me to solve its case?"

He sat back in his chair with a big grin. "Don't we have an inflated sense of self-worth."

"Is it the Feds? CDC? Why did you allow a suspected terrorist to retain counsel, read the transcripts of our talk, and come down to my offices to hire me as a consultant? Yes, that's what they did."

"I didn't allow anything. My higher-ups made those calls."

"There's a CDC briefcase involved. Do you or don't you know what was in it? You're working with the CDC so you can make them tell you. They won't tell me."

The Chief moved his chair back and reached down to something under his desk. He put a silver briefcase on the top of his desk with the big initials CDC and in smaller letter underneath: PROPERTY OF THE CDC. DO NOT REMOVE FROM THE PREMISES.

"Like this one?" he asked.

"Yeah."

"My officers found this one in a drug den. It's the current rage among the dope roaches these days. Another designer drug, but this one goes by the name CDC."

"A new kind of drug."

"Yes."

"When did it hit the streets."

"No way to know. You know this. We only know when people start dying from it and the bodies start piling up."

"Well, thanks Chief for setting me straight. I've done my due diligence and have wrapped up another case to my satisfaction. I'm not really sure what the case ever was, but if my clients are happy, and they've paid me, I'm happy."

"Maybe you need speak to one more person," the Chief said.

I looked at him perplexed. "Who?"

"Don't you know people at the CDC?"

"I don't know anyone at the CDC." We stared at each other. "I don't know anyone at the CDC as a citizen. I know a few people there as a former patient."

"Don't you know the head of the Metro CDC?"

"You mean Fraggy? Call him? Why would he ever accept my call? He hates me. He's probably called the police on me a dozen times when I went to use their gel pool."

"Maybe you should call him and run your theories past him."

"What are you saying?" I asked.

"Don't call him. I'll have him visit you at your detective office."

I was in shock. But my case was over. What the hell just happened here?

CHAPTER 29

Fraggy

The Centers for Disease Control had a base in every major supercity in the world. They had command posts, research labs, vaccination storage, and, my personal favorite, Decon. In my last germophobic crisis attack after the incident I dubbed the Restroom of Horror featuring Jabba the Butt (my Blade Gunner Case), I literally ran to their Metro headquarters, breached security, outran the guards, entered, stripped off most of my clothes, and dove into their pool of decontamination gel. It was designed for emergencies if lab staff accidentally exposed themselves to deadly bio-contaminates, germs, bacteria, or viruses. I used it as my personal remedy to exposure to a level of nastiness that I mentally couldn't deal with. But that was years ago, I hadn't been back. Besides you could now buy the decontamination gel for personal use, which I did. But even that I hadn't used in over a year.

I told PJ that the head of the Metro office would be visiting us and she asked the pertinent question: "Why?"

"I don't know," I replied. "The Chief is sending him here."

"The Chief of Police?"

"Yeah."

"Why?"

"I don't know. We'll ask him when he arrives."

"You said this case was over."

"I thought so too."

"It has to be over because no one is paying anymore. Talk to him and get rid of him. You have real cases to solve with paying clients. Liquid Cool is a professional detective firm. We only deal with legitimate paying clients. Deadbeats can go someplace else."

"I'll be sure to tell him that."

"Cruz, don't get soft because he's your friend and he let you swim in that gel pool."

"You don't swim in a gel pool."

"Cruz, I don't want to know what you do in that gel pool. That's a private matter."

I laughed. "You soak in a gel pool, PJ. That beautiful, magnificent gel magically decontaminates the human body erasing all the filth, visible and microscopic. You emerge as a newborn baby after a morning bath."

"Whatever you say. Again, I don't want to know what you do in that gel. That's your business. You can tell your wife."

"I don't need to go there anymore. I have my own gel."

"That's what your spending your money on?"

"I can have my own gel pool in my own place."

"For you and Mrs. Cruz. I see. Oh, that's a baby name. Gelina!"

"Oh God!" I left to go back to my private office.

In a million years I never thought I'd see the man outside his office. But there was Fraggy, a small man wearing clear glasses. He first peeked in through the door. PJ suspiciously watched him from behind his desk. He didn't know we were watching him on our video monitors. There were hidden cameras outside the main door and the hallway, among other places.

A smile came over my face.

"Fraggy!" I yelled. "You are in my headquarters this time. Come on in!"

I got up from my desk, opened the door, and pulled him in by his forearm. I pointed him to my waiting area.

"Have a seat. PJ, get this man something to drink."

"Oh, no, please," he said to PJ. "I never eat or drink anything outside my designated schedule."

"See, PJ! I'm not the only one who has a designated eating schedule."

"Is this him?" PJ asked.

"PJ, this is Mr. Fraggioti, the head of the Metropolitan CDC. But everyone calls him Fraggy."

"No one calls me Fraggy," he said.

"His friends call him Fraggy."

"My friends don't call me Fraggy."

"Well, PJ, he doesn't mind me calling him Fraggy."

"Boss, can I see you at my desk?" PJ said.

I sat the man down in the waiting area. "Hold on a second. I'll be right back."

When I reached her desk, she pointed to one of her monitors. Anyone who passed under the arc was scanned and the results were flashing red on PJ's monitor.

I walked back to Fraggy. "Fraggy, I'm so happy to see you." PJ followed me.

"Now I see why you're so happy. When you go cuckoo, you pester this man at his office," PJ said.

"I do not pester Mr. Fraggy. He's providing a much-needed service to one of the many citizens of this great supercity," I said.

"What does he do in there?" PJ asked him.

"Mr. Cruz's favorite pastime at our facility is to dive into the anti-decontamination solution in Decon."

"The gel pool, PJ! After a swim in there all the nasty germs and bacteria and anything else that's not supposed to be on your body from a microscopic level is gone."

"Mr. Cruz, how many times do I have to tell you that the human body needs a certain percentage of bacteria on and in the body to survive? Or would you prefer to live in a hermetically sealed bubble."

"Bubble boy!" PJ laughed.

"Mr. Fraggy, what can we do for you? What brings you to my 'facility'?"

"Mr. Cruz, I must say I thought very deeply about this. The notion that I would need the services of a detective..."

"You want to hire me? Wow!" I regressed into a child with a big smile. I grabbed him by the arm to get him up.

"What are you doing?" PJ asked me with a disapproving look. "You go to your desk and do your work. Sir, have a seat there while I get my pad. We'll get you signed up as an official client of the Liquid Cool Detective Agency."

I leaned over. "She means…"

One of PJ's bionic hands covered my mouth so fast. "This is my domain out here. Your domain is at your desk. Go to your domain *tout de suite* and leave this man alone."

I strolled towards my private office, smiling. "Oh Fraggy, if I help you with your case, can I get a few free visits to the gel pool?"

"Uh… no."

"Why would you be concerned about germs? You have a small child and another on the way. How nasty is that?" PJ said.

I pointed at her. "Cruz Jr. is not nasty."

"All toddlers are nasty."

"Ignoring the zone below the waist and above the knees, my child is as clean as a newly detailed hovervehicle."

PJ laughed. "Do you know his wife once caught him changing the child's diapers wearing a bio-suit?"

"Knowing Mr. Cruz as I do, that does not surprise me in the least."

PJ shooed me away. Well, at least I could do a bit of work while PJ did her "thing": assessing the client's needs, giving an overview of the agency and me, and lastly but more importantly getting a retainer payment. It was the last part that was the important part for her—money coming into the business.

Fraggy now sat in front of my desk. He seemed more at ease as he looked around with his hands clasped and resting on his lap.

"You are most fortunate to have such an employee," he told me.

"That's why I hired her."

"Yes. Being a cyborg with two bionic arms probably doesn't hurt either."

"She can throw out the riff-raff. Lots of riff-raff in this business."

"I suppose so."

"Mr. Fraggy, what's going on? You don't look very happy."

"Because I'm not."

I could see in his face the weariness. He probably hadn't had a good night's sleep; he may not have had one for a while. He was a man who held in his emotions well, except when exacerbated by me.

"Since you're here, we've never had a chance to just chat. How did you ever become a CDC official? Did you always want to work for them as a kid?"

"Heavens, no. I was a biopunk as a kid."

"What? You?"

"Yes, me, Mr. Cruz. We called it 'body bizarro' or some such thing back then. I was...ten years old. My flirting with the sub-culture actually led me to being a bio-scientist. The reckless and dangerous body modification procedures, compromising people's immunization systems, spread of disease and infection, cross-species contamination giving humans diseases that were confined to the animal world. I went from being very liberal and laissez-faire about the subject to the extreme opposite. Half my friends had to undergo amputation and full body blood transfusions to save their lives."

"Nasty."

"There I would agree with you."

"You a juvenile biopunk. I would never have guessed it."

"We all come from somewhere, Mr. Cruz."

"How can I help you then?"

"The Chief told me to be here so I'm here, but I need to give you some background first."

"Tell me whatever you need to so I understand the situation."

"You really are the only detective I could hire for this kind of matter. You know the CDC better than most. I doubt there is another detective in the entire supercity who knows more than you."

"No doubt about that. Will this story also deal with the matter of your arm?"

"Yes, your scanning arch. You can scan for organic anomalies too. To answer your question: yes. I believe there is a problem with WHO."

"Who?"

"Yes?"

"Who what?"

"WHO."

"What is who?"

"THE WHO."

"What who?"

"There is only one WHO, Mr. Cruz."

"Fraggy, are we on a kindergarten playground here? W-H-O?

"Yes, the World Health Organization."

"Oh. WHO!"

"Yes."

"Okay, I'm following now. What about WHO? What problem?"

"You need to understand I'm here rather than Federal Investigations, because of the Chief."

"You said that. Feds? This is a Fed matter?"

"There's nothing I can take to the Feds or anyone else. That's why I feel I need your services. The background first."

"Okay."

"You well know that CDC works with law enforcement as much as it does with health providers. Is this conversation...confidential?"

"Of course."

"No one could force you to disclose it?"

"Like who? And I don't mean the organization. Who? Feds? You're starting to worry me, Fraggy."

"I have a reputation. There I said it."

"Reputation for what?"

"For 'crying wolf.' I'm overly cautious. This is a dangerous world, Mr. Cruz. Nature can be every bit the bio-terrorist as a terrorist."

"You do know I'm a local street detective? Your case is sounding like way, way above my job duties."

"It may be, but finding the evidence definitely falls in your area. You see because of my past false alarms no one will believe me. In fact, I've gotten reprimands for scaring people. I run the Metro CDC but I can't issue any health alerts without approval of the mayor and city council. What do politicians know about bio-threats?"

"I don't know."

"Nothing. Sometimes it's customary to take work home. Extremely confidential. Sometimes the work we have to do is not allowed to leave the premises, but we do so anyway. Everyone does it. It's allowed. One night, I took work home. It was stored in…"

"A silver briefcase."

He looked at me. "Yes. You already know what the warning labeling says. But I'm very diligent. I live alone. I have a home office. When I'm finished. I return the contents of my work to the briefcase—papers, notes, devices. Everything goes back. It's locked. I handcuff it to my wrist and then…I go to bed. With the briefcase handcuffed to my wrist. So if ever asked, I can truthfully say it has never been out of my sight."

"Fraggy, I am getting very queasy. Please don't say it."

"One morning, I woke up and the case was not handcuffed to my wrist. In fact, the case was gone. I panicked. I was shocked. I didn't know how such a thing was possible."

I literally held the sides of my head with my hands I was so disturbed.

"Later, I returned to the headquarters and when I went under our own scanning arch the alarms went off. Security told me why and I passed out." Fraggy's eyes were tearing up. "They removed my arm to get at the briefcase, and, maybe they thought they were barbaric, so they gave me a new one. It's not my arm, but it's somebody's. It's not bionic. Its natural. Not a perfect match but it's natural."

Fraggy began to sob.

I stood from my desk, walked to the door to open it. "PJ, I think Fraggy will have that drink now."

We all sat in my private office's lounge area. Fraggy with his bourbon in his glass, PJ on another chair with her vodka, and I had my sake.

"They stole my arm," Fraggy repeated. "The doctors said in the time allowed it was the cleanest surgical procedure they had ever seen. You hear about biopirates but you never imagine being a victim. And it's always for organs, not an arm."

"Fraggy, did they steal your arm or were they stealing the case?" I asked.

He looked up at me. "That's the question I've been wrestling with since it happened. I thought it had to be the case. The information inside would be of value on the black market, but then it happened. I was so stunned that I wasn't thinking straight. If only I reacted faster. I had them check for any biometric access I made at any CDC or related organization or lab in the world, and there it was. WHO headquarters overseas."

"What did they do?" I asked him.

"I have no idea. Once you get into the facility, there are two hundred levels of offices and labs."

"I thought government facilities did full presence scans. Not just eye-scan, palm-scan, fingerprint but everything. Photo, heartbeat. To prevent something like this."

PJ looked at me, surprised. "How do you know all this?"

"Patient. You know that."

"True," Fraggy answered my original statement, "but some places still use the rudimentary biometrics, especially where there are live guards. The access was made when the guards were conveniently called away."

"How long ago?"

"Two weeks ago."

"The Chief told you about his case and this incident where a CDC briefcase was involved?"

"Yes, we were brought into the investigation."

"You believe it was the same case."

"Yes. Though it wasn't found."

"Have you been able to find the owners of that hoverhotel suite? Or the police or Feds?"

"No. The owner was a fabricated identity. The sophistication means a foreign government or one of the top megacorps. It's being investigated though."

"You said something before about there's a problem with WHO."

"I believe I was targeted."

"You specifically."

"Yes."

"Why?"

"To discredit me. Scare me. Shock me."

"Why would someone do that?"

"To stop me from investigating."

"Investigating? You're a scientist."

"Yes, Mr. Cruz. It would seem my exposure to you over the years made me think I could be my own detective too. If you could do it, why couldn't I? I learned the hard way that it is much more involved than I thought. It obviously can be dangerous which I neglected to factor in. However, I did manage to touch the tip of the iceberg."

"What were you investigating?"

"Corruption at the WHO."

"Every government agency has corruption of some kind."

"Maybe true, but I obviously got someone's attention. I once dreamed that if I could get all their higher-ups and senior staff away from their headquarters for even a day. Get in there with a small financial and scientific team to have a look at their records and labs. I could get to the bottom of it all."

"They took your arm and put a new one because you were snooping around their finances?" PJ asked. "That don't make sense."

I stood from my chair. "Fraggy, I'll take the case."

"What?" Fraggy and PJ said in unison.

"What case?" PJ said.

"But-but," Fraggy stammered.

"Fraggy, don't speak. I'm taking the case just because I'm curious and we're friends. I'll take it from here. If I need more, I'll come to see you. PJ, walk our client out."

PJ pointed at me. "Don't go anywhere." She looked at Fraggy smiling. "We will get you on your way Mr. Fraggioti. Good Italian name."

"I have Scandinavian ancestry too."

PJ did the small talk thing with Fraggy and said goodbye. When he was out the door, she locked it and was back in my office.

"I'm sorry for him, but what case?" she asked. "You're a missing arm hunter now? Why didn't you do this when you cut off my arms?"

"What arms? They were mangled, burning strings of flesh. PJ, do you want them back?"

"No! My bionic arms are cool."

"That's what I thought."

"Why are you taking this case?"

"I met with the Beast remember."

"And?"

"He traced his benefactor."

"His money man?"

"Yes. And guess where it came from?"

"No way! It can't be."

"The World Health Organization. WHO."

PART FIVE

BioGenic: Wilford G's Peanut Galley

CHAPTER 30

Wize Gal

Biogenic.

Adjective. Resulting from the activity of living organisms. Necessary for the life process, such as food and water.

My posthumous mentor Wilford G. spoke about cases that didn't die. They plodded along with no end in sight. In this case, I also didn't know what the actual beginning of the case was. I had pseudo-clients, lots of opinions, my own theories and suspicions. First a burglar, then biopunks and a supposed bio-terrorist. Now, according to Fraggy, biopiracy too for some unknown but likely illegal plot.

I'm glad Fraggy revealed what he did. If he was on the CDC's "naughty list" then the chief and others would know more than him. For the moment, I had to keep busy. Thanks to PJ, I had a day of client appointments.

PJ led the next clients into my private office. My wife had stopped by leaving me a brand new piece of room accessory—a snazzy, eight-foot tall, four-panel Chinese screen with midnight black faux-wood borders. The fabric had Chinese letter characters and pictures of animals from the Chinese calendar. I was at my desk admiring it when a man and woman entered.

"Thanks PJ," I said as I walked to them and extended a hand to greet both of them.

Just as I did Cruz Jr. came out from behind the Chinese screen, wearing his little black fedora and properly dressed, hobbling to them. His appearance startled the couple.

"What is that?" the female asked.

"Is that a midget?" the male asked.

"Yeah, I'm housing midgets in my office. It's not a midget. What's wrong with your eyes? This is my business partner."

"That is a baby," the woman said. "Why are you keeping a baby in this drafty office?"

"My office is not drafty. It's comfy." I picked up Cruz Jr. and set him on the top of my main desk. He had his toy hovercar in one hand. "Please have a seat and we can talk about your case."

"How awkward," the woman said. The couple seemed to be nervous about sitting down.

"My business partner observes strict client confidentiality like me," I said.

"Why don't you just say your son?" the woman said.

"My business partner."

"Your son."

"My business partner and I are ready to hear your situation."

"Aren't there child labor laws against what you're doing?" she asked.

"He's sitting on a desk with one of his toys in his hand. Do you have a potential case to discuss or not?"

"What are you going to do when he's bigger?" the man asked.

"A wild guess, but maybe have him sit in a chair like any non-baby person. But it's just a guess. PJ!" She appeared at the door with a shotgun. Their eyes expanded to the size of baseballs as they jumped up from their seats. "These people are wasting my time, and my business partner's time."

"Hold one second," PJ said. She disappeared then reappeared without her shotgun.

"What kind of crazy house is this?" the woman asked.

"Boss, you have to work on your client service skills," PJ said.

"Meaning you got your retainer," I said.

"Which I think we want back," the man said.

"You wouldn't be the first. Sit back down. PJ close the door. You two ignore my son and get on with telling me about your situation so I can determine if there is even a case and if I'm interested in taking it."

The couple sat back down in their chairs.

"Your business partner?" she said.

"Yes," I answered.

"Are you too cheap to get a baby sitter for your own kid? I thought this was a proper private investigation firm. I thought you were rich and famous."

"My business partner doesn't like being called a baby. How dare you. Let's get on with the details of the case so you can pay me and I can hire a baby sitter."

I had no doubt that Cruz, Jr. had no clue what the clients were saying but he sure looked like he did. His demeanor was serious, no giggling or playing. Cruz Jr. was ready for a real day's work! Though as we listened to the couple, it was clear these two had no case I was interested in. Missing pet! Please!

A surly looking man came into the office.

"Can I help you?" PJ asked, standing from her desk.

"Is the owner here?"

I happened to be at my doorway. The clients were gone so Cruz Jr. had regressed to baby mode throwing his toys out the office into to lobby for me to play fetch. I hated fetch.

"I'm Cruz."

The man walked to me and handed me a document. "You've been served." He had a device in his hand, typed something and snapped my picture.

"Served!" I yelled.

The man said nothing more and was out the door.

I had never been served before but I'd seen it done. I stood there carefully reading it.

"Well that female bum!"

"What happened?"

"That female college criminal kid is suing me and Liquid Cool for shooting her."

"No."

"Yes."

"You have insurance to protect you."

"I know how the game is played. She has a big law firm representing her. It's a shakedown. If this goes to court, we lose even if we win. PJ, I need a good attorney. One who knows how to play nasty."

"Why ask me? You already know an attorney who can play nasty."

"Who?"

"You know. Wilford G.'s friend."

"Oh. Yes! Wize Gal! But isn't she just a paralegal?"

"Call her!"

Actually, PJ called around until she found her. It was Wilford G. who introduced us. When he did, at some casino, I thought she was a waitress, but later learned she was a cutthroat paralegal attorney.

I finally got Cruz Jr. to take a nap on the couch in my private office's lounge area as I took her call on my vid-phone. She was a petite brunette and liked her sharp business suits.

"Cruz."

"Wize Gal."

"Now that you're the man, I'm going to have to come up with a nickname for you like G-Man."

"Cruz sounds like a good nickname to me."

"You're no fun. PJ says you've gotten your first lawsuit."

"I don't think it's something I should be happy about."

"Now you're a legit detective agency. If you're not sued, then you don't exist in this city. Businesses that matter get sued. The tactic from here is to win."

"How do we win?"

"We win by making sure it never gets to court."

"How do we do that?"

"I do that. I got all the details from your VP, PJ. I'll take care of it."

"How much is this going to cost me?"

"A lot but far less than what it would cost if it got to court. Cruz, did you see the name of the firm she hired?"

"No."

"Who did you piss off?"

"No one."

"Someone doesn't like you, Cruz. I mean really not like you. This firm may be in a well-to-do, upscale district but if you blend a shark, snake, slug, and rat together, this is the law firm you'd have. They specialize in tying people up in depositions forever, leaking false stories about them in the media, digging up dirt on their children and parents, and destroying them. People pay them off, pay anything, do anything to make them go away. The girl suing you didn't find them. They found her. Someone out there wants to get you."

"G-Man, told me that you're better than an attorney and if I ever got in legal trouble to call you immediately. If G-Man had that kind of confidence in you, then I can."

"G-Man was the best around. We all miss him."

"Wize, make this go away."

"Already done. Stay by your phone. When I call you to tell you to be somewhere, hop in that classic of yours and be there. No questions. No hesitations. You follow my instructions and you'll be free and clear by tomorrow. If you don't, prepare for two years or more of hell."

"I'll be ready."

"Talk to you then."

I hung up the vid-phone. So, someone out there wanted to hurt my business and me bad. Why?

CHAPTER 31

Wilford Jr.

I shouldn't have but I did. I looked up the law firm suing me and they were even worse than I'd thought. They never worked for criminal gangsters, so they'd never fall into the trap of being labeled a "law firm of the underworld" and get on the radar of law enforcement. They worked exclusively for members of the Council of Corporations—megacorps, big and small, with net profits of a billion and more, in every industry imaginable. I'd never heard of the firm before, but I, along with everyone in Metropolis, recognized their handiwork in the corporate, political, and media battlefields. Of course, I also called my best friend, Run-Time, for additional guidance. This was his world of expertise as the boss of his own megacorp. Initially, he was very concerned that I was in the cross-hairs of this law firm. However, when I told him that I'd hired Wize Gal, he laughed and said "I was in good hands." If Wize Gal, got the recommendation of my posthumous mentor, Wilford G., and the endorsement of my best friend, I would think no more about it and let her do her thing—whatever that might be.

The next day she called the office. I was on client visits, but PJ told me that Wize wanted me to go immediately to a district not too far from Neon Blues, where my parents-in-law (the Hellspawn) owned a bunch of businesses. As the hovertraffic neared, I could already see red and blue flashing lights below. The police were in force at the very building I was told to be at.

I parked the Pony about half a mile away and walked. As I neared the police scene, I saw that there were many more police officers than I originally thought. Police cruisers parked on the ground, cruisers hovering in the air. Most of the street officers knew me on sight so I pushed through the crowds of lookie-loos to talk to a few keeping them out of the crime scene.

"Hi, officers," I greeted.

They looked at me. "Cruz," one of them said.

"What's going on?"

"Bomb scare," one of the officers said.

My eye immediately caught sight of him, and I smiled. "There's G. Jr. Let me say hello."

The officers looked at me with smirks.

I raised my right hand. "I promise to behave myself. I'll walk to him, say hello, and come back here."

They chuckled. "Cruz, if it were anyone else." They waved me through and I ducked under the police cordon tape.

G. Jr. as Wilford G. Jr.—the son of my posthumous mentor, Wilford G. He also happened to be a veteran police officer and president of the Metropolis Police Union, all half a million members. This forty-something was one of the most powerful guys in Metro politics, as Metro PD was the largest police force in the world, so in some eyes equal to the chief of police. He also happened to be a friend.

"Wil," I called out.

Wil was in standard silver-and-black body-armor. I recognized him because he was wearing his black cap and held his visored half-helmet in one hand. He clearly was the scene commander until the Bomb Boys got there.

"Cruz." He shook my hand when I reached him. "What brings you here?"

"Client visit," I replied as I looked around the scene. "Serious bomb threat?"

"Likely not. We have the suspect already."

I looked over and there sitting on the steps to the entrance to the mega-tower was the college girl. I couldn't believe it. She was in a nice business dress suit under her slicker but was handcuffed and shivering. The woman at the Beast's black clinic who had planned to send me and the biopunks into an ambush to get killed, the woman I shot to teach a lesson, the woman who was suing me and my agency. She was also looking dead at me. I stepped forward and glared at her. She glared back.

"Do you know her?" Wil asked me.

"I don't think so. But you come across so many people in this world. How long will the area be closed?"

"This is not a credible threat, but we still have to wait for the Bomb Unit to clear it."

"I'll call my client and reschedule. I'll let you get to it. Say hello to your wife for me."

"Same to you. Rumor is that you're going to be a father again."

"You can't keep a secret from the silver and black for long."

"Congrats, Cruz. We'll do family dinner soon."

"Yeah, let's do that."

We shook hands again and I made a beeline back to the same spot I crossed.

"See, I did what I said I'd do."

The three officers at the cordon line smiled. "Bye, Cruz."

This college girl had now witnessed and knew that the person she wanted to get revenge on was friends with the entire Metro Police Department, and that police department could snatch her up at any time. She was the one who needed a lawyer. They'd prove she called in a false bomb scare. She'd be arrested, but it would probably be expunged from her record. She'd be in jail but not long. She'd have to pay bail, but the money wouldn't come from her. Bottom-line: a message was sent and she heard it loud and clear sitting on that cold asphalt in the rain with her mascara running down her face.

As I walked back to the Pony, I had only one thing to say: "Damn! Wize is good!"

"The firm has dropped the case," Wize said to me over the vid-phone.

Early the next morning, Wize's call was the first one of the day. I leaned back in my chair at my desk. "That was fast."

"She was their client and she told them to drop it. They had to drop it. They might try to find someone else, but since we're on to them, they won't."

"Wize, does this mean you're the official legal counsel for Liquid Cool."

"Cruz, we don't have to make anything formal. Call me when you need me, which shouldn't be too often. If you've gone this long in your new biz without getting sued, considering your public profile, I'd say you're doing something right."

"Thanks, Wize."

"Don't mention it. After all you are the Man now. Take care of yourself and I'd find out who you pissed off. They probably will try again."

CHAPTER 32

Quix

I hadn't been in Old Metropolis since Wilford G.'s death but having connected with Wize, it made me think of another person from the G-Man's circle of associates. I would never be one of those massive private investigation firms which also did security with their own pseudo-army on payroll. I was never the seedy detective firm with an office adjoined to a bail bonds outfit. If they needed security, they'd just hire someone off the street for a few bucks. PJ was more than able to do enforcer work, but that wasn't her job. I also couldn't lean on my best friend, Run-Time's corporate security led by his third VP, the Mick. I had to have my own. Call it bodyguards or full-blown security, I needed to have my own team for when I needed it. I had been talking about it for over a year. It was time to make it real.

Fubar was a very seedy dive bar of ex-military. Outside the main entrance, there were always at least several big bald guys talking in some language not English and drinking—I still didn't know if they were customers or bouncers. I approached and tried to move around them, but they blocked me.

"What you want?" one asked with a heavy accent.

"Quix."

They watched me for a long while.

"I've been here before," I said. "With G."

"G?"

"Yes."

"What you know about him?"

"A lot. I was there when he died, and I was at his funeral with his family. I don't remember seeing you.

The group of guys who were big enough to pull my arms and legs out of their sockets just for sport looked like little kids with eyes cast down as if being scolding by parents.

"But Quix was there," I added.

They let me through.

The ex-Marine cyborg was seated near the back of the establishment at a round table with other guys that I assumed were all ex-military too. They always gave clues: dog-tags hanging outside their clothes, wearing camouflaged Army hats or pants, Aviator-like glasses, though I knew no airmen ever wore them.

Quix saw me from the moment I stepped into the bar. I stuck out like a neon thumb in this place. When I reached the table, we exchanged a fist bump. He was a short, bald, muscular, cyborg with big leathery hands, an earring in one ear, part of his jaw and neck were metal, and he was wearing yellow-tinted shades.

"Cruz."

"Quix, can I join you?"

"Private conversation?"

"It's up to you."

"Pull up a chair."

I did so and joined the men at their table. Before I could agree or object, he had signaled the barkeep to bring another drink over. All the men were drinking serious alcohol and it was not even lunchtime.

"How's the cherry red Ford Pony?" he asked half-laughing as he drank his drink.

"My Miami Vice Red Pony is doing quite well."

The other men laughed and muttered to each other in some East European language.

"Remember, what we had talked about before?" I said.

"I remember."

"If I ever need muscle, I'd like you to be that man."

"G. trusted you, so that's good enough for me."

Quix raised his glass, and a waiter set a mug of some kind of beer on the table in front of me.

"We know you youngsters aren't allowed to drink real alcohol yet. You can have the beer. Beer is for children," Quix said and laughed. He raised his glass. "To G!"

We all toasted to Wilford G. and took a drink.

"Cruz, find me when you need to find me."

"Can you pay?" one of the men at the table asked.

"I can pay."

"Nothing else to talk about then," Quix said. "Call me with the job. If I'm available I'll be there. If I'm not, I will send one of my men. No more killer android zombie vampires though."

I joined them in the laughter this time.

CHAPTER 33

Prima Donna

My wife's boss at Eye Candy was Prima Donna, the Matron Queen of Metropolis beauty, fashion and style. However, if I showed up there, I wouldn't get out of there for at least a couple of hours or longer. If I had Cruz, Jr. with me, I'd never get out of there. I didn't mind it normally, I loved Eye Candy's staff. My wife worked with a great group of people and between them and their colorful clients, I always had a good time with lots of joking around.

"Judy!"

"Prima!"

That's what I heard from my personal office. I came into the main lobby to be subjected to a rapid-fire conversation of French between the two women.

"English!"

"Mr. Cruz," Prima greeted. She was dressed in a very stylish dark outfit with a plastic head scarf on.

"Cruz, what are you going to do when Cruz, Jr. can speak five languages before he's five?" PJ asked.

"I'll say in English to him: I only speak English."

"Judy, don't trouble yourself. If his wife can't convince him to learn another language, we surely won't."

"Cruz, learn it. Anyone can do it. Even a caveman can do it. Why not you?"

"Ms. Prima, office please. PJ, you study language. I study criminals so I can catch them and bring in the cash."

"Oh, forget me," PJ said. "Do that. Forget us. Bring in the cash. That's more important."

Prima couldn't be happier sitting in front of my desk holding Cruz Jr. and bouncing him on her lap. Cruz Jr. was a giggling mass of joy.

"Looking sharp little man in your black fedora," she said to him. "What you working on, Cruz?" she asked.

"Eye Candy does a lot of events around the city."

"All the time."

"And if it's Eye Candy that means high-end, high-class all the way."

"All the way."

"I'm putting together a team," I said.

Prima laughed and set Cruz Jr. to sit on her lap facing me. "Junior we need to pay attention to this." Now Cruz Jr. was watching me with his serious face.

"I want to put together a large event but I don't want anyone to know I'm behind it."

"For who, for what, for when, why?"

"The Future of Health: Challenges for Earth and Off-World This Century and Beyond."

"That's a mouth-full."

"Government agencies, non-government agencies, politicians, scientists from around the world."

"Hmm. Name fits for a crowd like that then."

"Here in Metropolis. Pick a trendy, wealthy district that everyone would want to go. For the after-hour parties too."

She smiled. "Cruz, Cruz, Cruz. But you need a headliner, someone who will get everyone else to sign up."

"WHO?"

"Someone to legitimize the whole event."

"No, I understand you. WHO. The World Health Organization."

"Ah, WHO." She leaned to look at Cruz Jr. who smiled and clapped. "Who's going to pay for this shindig?"

"I have benefactors."

"Cruz, what are you up to? Do other detectives do these kinds of things?"

I smiled. "Prima, I'm a famous detective. I have to maintain my rep."

"Yes, you're the Man.

PART SIX

*BioTechs: Which WHO Are You
Referring to?*

CHAPTER 34

Phishy

B iotech.

Noun. An industry encompassing a wide range of research and development procedures for modifying biological organisms, systems, or processes for human purposes. Includes the fields of molecular biology, biochemistry, cell biology, embryology, genetics, microbiology, bio-engineering, biomedical engineering, biomanufacturing, molecular engineering, and genetic engineering.

My friend Phishy.

If you were to ask me when I met him, I wouldn't be sure—probably on the illegal hovercar racing scene. It seemed as if I always knew him. He was crazy in a good way and gravitated towards me because I treated him with respect and as an equal when many—outside his sidewalk johnny and street hustler friends—dismissed him. Phishy was funny. His antics always brightened your day no matter how gloomy it was. Actually, he was a good counter-balance to me and my sometimes-morose demeanor. Not Phishy. He was always smiling, introducing himself to strangers, chatting it up. He was a naturally likable person. But Phishy had to be managed because he was like a hyper-active puppy. Manage the puppy and life was fine. If you didn't, you'd find it chewed up all your stuff and would stand there smiling as if nothing was wrong.

I had decided that Phishy was going to be my wingman today, which made his week, no, his whole month. My mission at the moment was to find him on the streets. I went from one of his usual spots to another. Streets in Metropolis were massive so I sat in my Pony hovering a few feet off the ground, scanning the crowd for him.

When I found him, I had to climb all the way back up into hovertraffic, loop around, and descend to where he was stuffing his face at a hoverfood-truck. The maneuver took me a good twenty minutes, but I got back to the trio of hover-foodtrucks where he was. It was actually Phishy who corrupted me with eating from the trucks. In the past, I wouldn't dare eat anything from one of them. Because of Phishy, I'd have to have a Coney Island brand hot dog about once a month.

I rolled down my driver side window with the push of a button. "Phishy! Get in here!" I yelled as I set down near the hover-foodtrucks.

"Cruz!" he whipped around and yelled with a hotdog in each hand.

Phishy wore his trademark dark colored vest and pants, with his off-white colored, long-sleeve shirt extravaganza with colored fish all over it.

"But I can't give you a proper greeting."

"Phishy, save the dancing for later," I said. "Why are you eating so late?" He suddenly bolted to my Pony. "No! No food in the Pony, Phishy! Eat your food out there."

He stopped and looked at his hot dogs. "I forgot my beverage." He ran back to the truck counter where I saw a large cup. Then he ran back to me. "Cruz, you have to have one too. It's Dog Man. You can't not have a dog too." Then he bolted away again. This was Phishy.

"Cruz!" yelled a different voice.

I looked at the hoverfood-truck and it was him. "Hey Dog Man!"

Dog Man was the king of hover-food trucks in Metropolis as far as I was concerned. He staked out the perfect corner with six lanes of pedestrian traffic on the ground. He had a fleet around town, but these three trucks on this corner was his main cash-cow because of the increase in demand 24-7. It was all about his dogs—the best hotdogs on the planet, as many of us were concerned, with any of a dozen exclusive sauces.

Since I now had to stop to eat, that meant I had to ascend again into hovertraffic to find someplace to park. Phishy!

I had my dog and beverage, courtesy of Dog Man. Phishy finished his two dogs and two beverages, but still managed to run around, saying hello to friends, slapping a high or low five as he went along. Phishy had more friends on the street than anyone.

After another forty minutes of wasted time, we had finally gotten to the Pony and were on our way.

"I'm like your partner today!" Phishy said from the passenger seat, beaming.

"You're my wingman for today, Phishy. We have a lot of work to do and it will be all day."

"I'm ready, Cruz. I'm up to the task."

Phishy was a street hustler, mostly selling info, retrieving info, a bit of courier work, whatever scam he could get to bring in some extra cash. Nothing illegal enough to get him a solid prison stint, but always at the level where if he were caught, he'd get no more than a mere misdemeanor—pay the fine and be on his way, not even a blot on the record. Cops and courts couldn't be bothered with street hustlers working non-violent, low money scams. In this vile world, you had to set your priorities properly.

Phishy was also a licensed gun dealer, which I only found out when I became a detective officially. At first, this seemed insane with his scatterbrained tendencies but he was always diligent and professional in this one area. I had him to thank for all my weapons, including my prized omega-gun from Up-Top.

"You got the boys standing by?"

"And the gals," he answered.

"Good."

"Are you going to be working the conference for the entire time?" he asked.

"All week. And you'll be on site too."

"What's the name of the conference again?"

"'The Future of Health: Challenges for Earth and Off-World This Century and Beyond' sponsored by the World Health Organization."

"Sounds stuffy, but it's Opus Fields. Free hotel for a week in Opus Fields. Cruz, thanks for bringing me on-board. We're going to have fun!"

"Fun, maybe. But it's still work."

"I understand. You can count on me."

We were headed to Opus Fields, a wealthy section of Metropolis near Silicon Dunes, Silver City and not far from Elysian Heights where my parents-in-law lived. Opus Fields was also called Movie-Town, and had been thriving until I solved my NeuroDancer Case and...well the scandal kind of sent a lot of studio heads, producers, actors, etc. to jail. I'm sure I was still burned in effigy there, but they'd never know I was there. The conference had nothing to do with the movie business. As Phishy said, it was a stuffy government policy conference closed to the general public.

When we arrived at the Utopia Conference Center in Opus Fields, Phishy couldn't stop staring at it. I had seen it before but only in passing. It looked like the moon fell to the Earth and buried itself halfway in the ground. The conference center was a ginormous, half-dome structure that had been the site of every high-profile movie and music premier and awards event, but because of the Movie-Town scandal hadn't been as busy. (I didn't mention that I—or my wife and I—killed a couple of movie stars too...but they were trying to kill me.)

At the Center, you didn't park. You pulled in and the Center's human and robotic personnel took it from there. Phishy and I exited the Pony in the flashing valet area, an attendant had me place my palm on a device and that was it. You didn't even need a ticket. We walked to a waiting hoverbuggie and we were whisked away to the main entrance lobby. Phishy was like a giggling little kid at an amusement park.

The lobby hall was empty except for human security in dark suits. This was the first day of the pre-conference when support staff would begin arriving ahead of the dignitaries.

"Please check in at the main desk sirs," a security man said as he pointed.

"Thanks," Phishy said.

We had to walk completely across the ground floor. The lobby design was a huge atrium with each balconied level rising into the air under the dome. There were only fifteen levels but it looked much taller and the ceiling was much further away. The main counter check-in area was manned by a few other security personnel. We could see the glow of their angled in-counter computer screens.

One of them motioned to us and I already had my ID in hand to give to him. Phishy was staring at him. "Cruz, isn't that your friend..."

I turned to him with my index finger over my mouth. "Phishy, where's your ID?"

"Oh." I had easily shifted Phishy's scatterbrain elsewhere as he dug into his pocket for his ID.

"Make sure it's your real one."

Phishy laughed as he handed his to the man. Quix scanned them, watched the screen, then handed them back. "Do you gentlemen know your room numbers?" he asked.

"We do," I answered.

"Those elevators will take you to the Tan Section." Have a pleasant day, gentlemen," Quix said.

I nodded. "We will," Phishy said, smiling.

We walked to the elevator area.

"We're undercover, right, Cruz?" Phishy whispered.

"Phishy, we're working a case."

"Okay. Do we have secret identities?"

"Yeah. Phishy and Cruz."

He laughed.

"Let's check out our rooms and say hello to your team."

"My team?"

"You're running our Sidewalk Johnny Brigade, Phishy."

"Oh," he said smiling.

We came out of the elevator onto the penthouse level with tan painted walls and tan carpet. Already we could hear them. On the streets they were called sidewalk johnnies—street people, Phishy's people. On the street they were always scamming and scheming for cash—hanging around, watching trouble, causing trouble, hustling, looking for a hustle. But they were harmless, not the real street criminals that preyed on people. In my short career as a street detective, they became my invaluable source of street intel. Nowadays, and thanks to Phishy's help, I had my own team of them—my Sidewalk Johnnie Brigade.

As we neared our hotel rooms, we saw them hanging out in the halls, chatting loudly, beverages and coffee in their hands. One of them noticed us, then all of them did. Phishy was already running ahead of me.

"Phishy! Mr. Cruz!"

Phishy was already greeting them.

"Boys, anything to report?" I asked.

"Mr. Cruz, quiet all morning," one of them said. "We got here as soon as they opened up at five am."

I nodded satisfied. "I'll check my room, then Phishy, we'll make the rounds."

"I'll be ready, Cruz."

I knew that I couldn't leave until Phishy greeted every last johnny first and spent at least an hour catching up with them to get all the daily street gossip. This was why I worked solo. Over two hours into the work day and I hadn't begun our real work yet, because of Phishy. Though none of it was unexpected.

I opened the door to my suite and strolled in.

"Hey, Mr. Cruz." A group of johnnies were at the living room table playing cards with plenty of food and beverages around them and the TV playing.

I walked over to the table and peeked into their cups. They laughed.

"No booze, Mr. Cruz."

"Just checking."

"We're on the job, Mr. Cruz."

"That you are."

I walked around to inspect my room. Penthouse suites were always nice. One in Opus Fields meant it was nice enough to please royalty. I wasn't royalty, but I was pleased. The suite was huge. There was also a business office so I could check messages and do a little work before I grabbed Phishy.

I had access to every floor with biometrics. We got off on the second floor and we waited at the balcony, overlooking the hoverbuggy drop-off and pick-up dock. We had arrived before the official pre-conference admittance time of four pm came— only a half hour away now. I sent Phishy to get some food while we waited.

Almost an hour later people began to arrive as Phishy and I watched, stuffing our faces with seafood taquitos. The transportation arriving weren't buggies anymore but full open cart trains. I could tell who was who because those arriving had plenty of signage with their organization's or company's name and logo. The support staff for the conference attendees came through like a flood: biotech and pharma megacorps, food growers, manufacturers and distributors, NGOs, law enforcement, intelligence services and first responders, including the CDC, political staff, air, land, and sea transportation megacorps, robotic megacorps. There seemed to be no end to the people.

There was only one group I was waiting for and it figured they'd arrive last—the staffers from the World Health Organization.

"Phishy, let's go on our tour."

"Sure, Cruz."

We were in the Silver Section of the Center. Phishy followed me out of the elevator into the hall. The walls on either side of us were glass and in the laboratories inside we saw people working on computers, holding meetings, or wheeling in more equipment and material on hovercarts.

We moved into another section without glass walls but metal doors, so what we had seen weren't the real labs. Now, we were in the real lab section. I listened as we walked for any signs of life. At the end of the hall were some double doors.

"Let's try here. I hear people inside," I said.

"Who's labs are these?"

"Government agencies. But this one should be the World Health Organization labs."

We passed through the main double doors and into a small hallway to another door. We could see people in lab coats on the other side of the door through the top glass half of the door.

"Hello," I said when we walked through.

There were about half a dozen people in lab coats moving furniture around.

"Hello?" one responded. "Can we help you?"

"Is this the labs for the World Health Organization?"

"Depends," she said.

"On?"

"Do you work for one of the megacorps?"

I smiled. "No, we're staff for the Convention Center itself. Boss, sent us down to watch over everything. It's one thing to have an event for movie stars and rock bands, but scientists and government agencies? He wants us to get a flavor of things to see if it's something we should aggressively pursue in the future. Oh, do you all need help moving the furniture?"

Before they could respond, I was directing Phishy to help move the long heavy tables.

"Thanks. What's your name?"

"I'm Cruz. This is Phishy. You can check with main security."

"We will, of course," one of them said.

"And you should. When you verify our credentials, since we're here before the start of the convention, can we get the informal mini-tour? Never been to the WHO headquarters. I actually don't know what you all do."

"If it has to do with health on the planet, we're involved," answered one of the scientists.

"You talk while I call security," the woman said as she left the room.

"But what does that mean," I asked as Phishy and I helped them move tables, then some chairs.

"We're not about health care, if that's what you mean. We deal with the health of humanity and fighting any bio-threats natural or man-made to humanity or the environment."

"I see."

"You two want any of our stash?" one of the male lab coats asked.

"Stash?" Phishy asked for me.

"Yes." The man walked to one of the plastic containers and took out a large covered glass container with what looked like yellow gummy bears. "Our stash of candy." He opened it, used some chopsticks to pick one up, toss it in the air and catch it with his mouth. "Have some," he said as he chewed.

He gave us a few each and we gladly accepted.

Phishy's face lit up. "They're good!" He ate the two he had and was already holding out his hand for more.

The door opened and the woman returned.

"Oh my God! What are you doing?" she yelled at the lab coat who gave us the candy.

"I'm sharing my stash of candy."

"That's not candy! Those are the frozen embryos from the resin of the glowing rat-worm, yellow roach hybrids!"

The male lab coat collapsed on the floor holding his neck.

I could feel every muscle from my throat to my stomach to my bowels trying to forcibly up-chuck what I'd swallowed. Phishy had doubled-over trying to vomit out the "candy."

"You have to run to the end of the hallway and get it out of you! Run and regurgitate it when you get to the atrium balcony! It's toxic! You don't have much time!" Her yelling only heightened the terror.

Phishy and I jet out of the lab, running in a frenzied panic down the hall and around the corner. Phishy was screaming holding his throat trying to force-vomit. He was making these weird sounds like a cat trying to cough up hairballs. We could see the balcony at the other end. Like a half mile away!

I stopped! I grabbed Phishy. He looked at me with wide-eyes of fear, then noticed I was no longer panicking and was as calm as a cucumber. I gestured to him and led him back around the corner.

"Cruz, we're going to die!" he said.

We reached the lab and I pushed open the door.

On the ground was a room full of scientists rolling on the floor laughing, including the woman. She saw us and stuffed a bunch of the yellow gummy bears in her mouth.

"You dirty animals!" I yelled but soon Phishy and I were laughing too.

The head of the WHO labs for the conference was a Ms. Companion. She did verify our clearance with security and what zones we could visit—all access.

"Will you be doing real lab work for the conference?" I asked.

"This will be a working conference for us. A unique opportunity to bring our work to conference attendees right here in Metropolis rather than having everyone fly to us overseas. The top people of the anti-bio-threat community in the government and private sector. The labs will be demonstrating new formulas, substances, techniques in the continuing war against bio-threats."

Ms. Companion gave us a full tour of the labs on the different levels. It was apparent that more people were arriving each hour though it was well into the evening.

"Looks like a long night for everyone," I said.

"We have a lot to prepare so none of us will be sleeping tonight. We'll be up well past midnight. I'll show you the executive offices too, then you should go down to the dining hall."

I looked at her, smiling. She knew what I was thinking.

"They don't serve glowing yellow hybrids," she said.

Phishy laughed.

When we got to the executive offices the color scheme of the floor was green. It was the penthouse level, which meant the ceiling was high and the offices were larger than those on lower floors.

"Let me show you this."

She led us to the general office of the President of the World Health Organization for us to see.

"Impressive," I said. "He's like a president."

"Or prime minister."

"Oh, I forgot you're from one of those backwards countries."

She chuckled. "Let's move to the wall here."

On an adjoining wall were pictures of several men.

"These are photos of our past presidents and our current Mr. WHO."

"Mr. WHO?" I asked.

"Yes. Inside humor for our agency. All our presidents are known as Mr. WHO."

"How interesting," I said. "Could the answer be that simple?"

"What answer?" she asked me and Phishy was looking at me too.

"I sometimes play those international crossword puzzles online and there was a question: three letters. A person who's one person and many people at the same time."

Ms. Companion nodded. "Yep, that fits."

When we exited the ground floor, we could smell the aroma of the food. We didn't need anyone to tell us where the Dining Hall was. All we had to do was follow our nose, or the people in dress attire walking to one of the hallways.

I glanced up at the main check-in area in the distance and could see Quix. I'm sure he was watching.

"Mr. Cruz."

I turned to see Fraggy!

He walked to us.

"You're here already," I said.

"Yes, I have to oversee the CDC set-up."

"Oh, this is my associate Phishy."

The men shook hands.

"We got a tour of the WHO labs and got back from a tour of the WHO executive offices."

"Did you now," Fraggy said.

"Will you be at the panel discussions or any of the keynote speaker events?" I asked.

"I'm going to try to be as inconspicuous as possible."

"Good idea."

"I'm skipping the dinner event, but you should definitely attend."

"I will."

"Goodnight then."

Fraggy walked off to the hotel suite elevators.

"Phishy, I think you should go up too, get your rest, so you're ready for tomorrow morning."

"You don't need me at the dinner event with you?"

"No. I'll be working until past midnight, I'd guess. I need you to take charge of the Sidewalk Johnnie Brigade first thing in the morning. You know what to do."

"You got it, Cruz." He shook my hand. "Night."

"Night, Phishy."

He stopped and spun around. "Don't think I forgot. I owe you two Phishy dance greetings."

"Phishy, go to sleep!"

He ran for the elevators.

CHAPTER 35

Three WHOs

The Dining Hall was on the ground level within the center of its own atrium. Lots of security guards and all the servers buzzed around in their very expensive suits and dress clothes, which I didn't expect. Government agency types were supposed to be more modest but as I saw the guests from all the private sector biotech megacorps with profits in the hundreds of billions, I realized that in a sense the World Health Organization was actually a biotech firm too, only run by governments of the world.

I mingled with my plate of assorted sushi in hand, but I didn't strike up a conversation with anyone. I was too busy eating. I was also under-dressed compared to the growing number of dinner guests gathering in little cliques to network while eating. But at least I was the only one wearing a cool hat.

"Hello there. Who might you be?"

I turned to see Mr. Alonzee. I had already memorized all the photos of the WHO presidents on the wall of their convention executive offices.

"I'm Mr. Cruz. I work for the convention center."

"Security?"

"Not really. They hired me to attend the conference, mingle, get a feel for the success of the conference."

"Seems like a vague mission."

A petite woman with blond hair joined the man and wrapped her fingers around his.

"Who's this?" I asked.

"This is my daughter—I mean wife."

I stopped eating and my eyes narrowed. He smiled. She laughed.

"My wife. I—we don't have a daughter."

"Yet," she interjected, smiling.

"Do you always make those kinds of Freudian slips?" I asked.

"You do when all you've been consumed with for endless months is adopting a baby girl."

"Oh, good luck then."

"Thank you. Very sorry. I'm Mr. Alonzee. My wife, Jennifer."

"I'm Cruz," I said to her.

"What do you do, Mr. Cruz?" she asked.

"Consulting and investigations. The convention center hired me to attend the event for all seven days. They want me to mingle, observe, and report my observations. Easiest consultant gig ever. And I get to eat good food."

"Always the best," Alonzee said. "The World Health Organization is the major sponsor of this conference."

"Really? Do you work for them?"

"My husband was a past president," Jennifer said with pride.

"Past president? Wow. Impressive. The World Health Organization is a stellar organization. Where do past presidents go when they're no longer current presidents?"

"We go into the private sector to continue the good fight."

"That's for sure. I've learned so much already and the conference hasn't even started yet."

"You're in for a treat then. We'll have the best speakers in world health and bio-threats from around the world."

"Will you be speaking?"

"No, my speaking days at the organization are behind me. Past presidents attend but don't speak. Our new president enjoys that limelight."

"Excellent. I can't wait to hear him then."

"He'll speak at the conference kick-off breakfast event."

"I'll be there."

"Mr. Cruz, we'll leave you to your sushi and mingle ourselves."

"Great meeting you both. Good luck on the adoption thing."

The Alonzees smiled and moved to another group of people. My eyes looked around and locked on a very slim Caucasian man wearing a fez not too far away. What drew my attention was I caught him staring at me. He was Mr. Geronimo, another former WHO president. Now, he was making a beeline to a server for a drink and finger food.

"Hello, young man. I saw you were speaking to Mr. Alonzee and his wife."

I turned and it was Mr. Euclid, another past WHO president, with his curly brown hair. He was one of those gregarious people who was always smiling even when he wasn't.

"Hello," I greeted.

He walked up to me with a small metal tin of something. "Jelly belly?" He offered.

I smiled. "I love candy but I gotta finish my sushi."

"Ah yes. Candy is for dessert, and dessert is after the meal. We'll have to consume plenty of appetizers for it to constitute a real meal."

"True, but we get to mingle while we do it."

"Right you are, young man. Let's mingle and see how many new friends we can make this evening."

I chuckled and that's exactly what happened. Mr. Euclid was my new wingman and we mingled through the entire crowd well past midnight. He knew everyone. I met megacorp executives, scientists, journalists, military officers, researchers, authors, and many more.

The one person I never spotted again, however, was Mr. Geronimo. He was gone—fez, bowtie and all.

CHAPTER 36

WHO Dat

It was late, but I actually had fun hanging around Mr. Euclid. I made a ton of contacts, collecting as many business cards as I could—maybe I could get a new client from the bunch in the future, but now it was time for bed.

I exited the penthouse level of the Center's tan section of hotel suites. From the elevators I could hear them even before I turned the corner. In front of my suite was a new crew of sidewalk johnnies.

"Hey, Mr. Cruz," one said. The others greeted me too.

"Hey guys. Is Phishy asleep?"

"Out like a light a few hours ago," Sidewalk Sid told me. "And your suite is all ready for you too."

"All quiet?"

"That's a different story."

"What do you mean?"

Sidewalk Sid pulled his electric pad from his jacket and began to read his notes. "The afternoon crew said about a couple of hours after you left a suit—White male in a black suit, no distinguishing marks—came around the corner, saw us and double-backed. The evening crew noticed a duo of men do the exact same thing too. Our crew heard the elevator and we noticed someone peek around the corner, when we started towards him, we heard running. Whoever it was got on the elevator before we could see them. You're pretty popular today, sir."

"Seems so."

"But don't worry about it, sir. Your crew has it covered. You get a good night's sleep."

"Thanks boys."

"Your instincts were right to have the Brigade covering the suites."

"Yeah, I hate when I'm right."

We exchanged "good nights" as I opened the door of my suite, stepped in, and closed the door. I never slept on hotel linen—I was a recovering germophobe so I'd shower, retrieve my sleeping gear from my hermetically sealed bag in the closet and get to sleep.

I had snoopers around the suite. They didn't expect I'd have round the clock personal security. I loved it when I was right.

The next morning, I came out of the elevator for breakfast. The plan was to arrive first thing and remain there until the end of service. I'd watch as I nursed my food for the two hours.

"Mister."

I turned to see Mr. Zeno standing outside the elevators on the way to the Dining Hall.

"Hello," I said.

"Mister...what is your name?"

"It's Mr. Nun-Ya-Biz-Ness. What's yours?"

He smiled. "Unfortunately, I'm going to have to insist."

"Why? Who are you? I've been cleared with security so why am I talking to you. You're not security."

"You came from the penthouse level."

"Why? Do you want to change rooms? No, you can't sleep in my comfy bed either."

"I believe you are a security threat. This is not a public conference. Only authorized attendees are allowed."

"Why are you here then?"

I attempted to walk past him but he blocked my way.

"There is high probability that you're going to get kicked in the head," I said.

"You can do whatever you like."

"You'd like that so you could call the police."

"Do whatever you like, but I will continue my conversation."

"Is there a problem, gentlemen?" The voice came from an approaching Quix.

"Yes. Good. Security, I believe this man is an unauthorized person here at the conference. I'd like him detained until his identity is verified and his purpose corroborated with the conference management." Mr. Zeno stood there with a smug, self-satisfied look.

"I've already done that, sir. Another made the same request yesterday."

Zeno was surprised. "By whom?"

"Mr. Timely."

"And?"

"Mr. Cruz is fully cleared."

Zeno was not happy. "Mr. Cruz, is it?"

"It is, Mr. Zeno."

He was visibly unhappy that I knew who he was.

"Anything else?" I asked.

"I guess not."

"I'm going to have my breakfast. Stay away from my suite. Stay away from me. When I meet Mr. Foil, I'm going to tell on you."

He started to half-laugh.

"What's so funny?" I asked him.

He ignored me and walked away. Quix and I watched him head to the hover-transport pick-up area. He hopped into a hover-buggy and was whisked away.

CHAPTER 37

PJ

Breakfast in the Dining Hall was really for the early-risers at the conference. Seating was at small square tables and the food was banquet style, which I hated. The kick-off event would be the main breakfast service with food served to attendees seated at large round tables. I was at the super-early breakfast to see who else was up and about, which turned out to be a lot of people. But everyone who showed up in the Dining Hall probably wouldn't be attending the kickoff event too.

Five minutes before the end of service, I got up and hung out in the front of the large open area of the atrium lobby. I watched people make their way to the Grand Ballroom. My timing was perfect. From the hover-transport area a giant crowd spilled off the hover-trolley. As they came around, I saw him: Mr. Foil, the current World Health Organization President. He looked right at me with familiarity but continued on, surrounded by an army of aides and media, and followed by Metropolis's Who's Who—the Mayor, city council, police brass, other law enforcement, including Feds, and Interspace authorities from the space stations and lunar colonies.

"Cruz." I heard and knew it was Phishy.

He joined me in my vigil.

"Are you getting any breakfast?" I asked him.

"Nah, I had something upstairs."

"They'll have food in the Ballroom too."

"Are we going to attend the event?"

"Yes, I am, but you have your mission."

He smiled. "I do."

"Cruz!"

We turned and there was PJ.

"What are you doing here?" I said.

"I heard you were here," PJ said.

"Are you undercover too?" Phishy asked her.

"Undercover?" She looked at him dismissively, then looked at me. "How can you be undercover with Stupid Man?"

"I'm not! I'm going to have you swimming with the fishes," Phishy yelled at her in a strained tough-guy voice.

"That's not funny, fish-Phishy. I'll punch the fishes off your shirt, then punch you so hard you'll be floating in space."

"Are you two done?" I asked. "We have work to do."

"But where are my free tickets?" PJ asked me.

"You're not supposed to be here, PJ."

"But you are all here. How come Phishy and all his sidewalk johnny friends get to stay here?"

"They are working, PJ. No play."

"I want to stay in a nice hotel suite in Opus Fields." I could see Phishy making faces at her from the corner of my eye.

"PJ, you're running the office. Speaking of which, who's in the office?"

"Oh, don't worry, I have that covered."

"I'm not even going to ask who you have in our office. Everyone here has their jobs to do. We're working here. It's not play. Phishy, go do your mission. PJ, go back to the office and run it. I have free tickets for you already."

"You do?"

"Yes, PJ."

She smiled. "That's my boss," she said to Phishy.

"I'm his partner," Phishy said.

"Partner? You're not even a sidekick."

I left the two of them there and walked to the Ballroom for the kickoff breakfast event.

CHAPTER 38

Bia and Company

The President of the World Health Organization was the keynote, but at first I wished I skipped the whole thing. The warm-up speakers were my first real exposure to the world of world health, and I was bored out of my mind. Then he began.

"I welcome you, my distinguished colleagues near and far, to the first annual Future of Health: Challenges for Earth and Off-World This Century and Beyond in this great supercity of Metropolis," Mr. Foil, the WHO President, said from the podium.

That was pretty much all I understood from there. There was a copious use of terms and acronyms unknown to me, and probably most of the population of Metropolis. A room full of egg-heads speaking their own language to themselves, frequently applauding and laughing. Mr. Foil publicly acknowledged one person or another; people applauded. I realized that this was like a Movie Town awards show but for world health and bio-tech communities. It was sickening. Also, the food was either vegan or seafood only. Never a good sign when you go to a place to eat where the vegan plate was more filling than the seafood. I realized that what we were being served was brunch not breakfast. No wonder they were all so slim; they only ate leaves and seeds and drank a bucket-full of water.

Now, it dawned on me why there were so many people in the early breakfast rush. They were the smart people. Avoid the mind-numbing kickoff event at all cost. Why couldn't I've been smart?

The upside was I was able to see all the past WHO Presidents at their own center table with their significant others—all except Mr. Timely. I watched for him, but he never showed up. Since he had security check me out, he had to be somewhere in the convention center.

After ninety minutes, the brunch event was over. How could something that could've been over and done within ten minutes take ninety minutes? I couldn't get out of there fast enough.

The convention center also had an observation level at the very top. I took the elevator and, when I arrived, looked out the windows with my binoculars, scanning the area around the building and saw them.

Any type of meeting of global governments or megacorps attracted protesters—always. So did this one, especially because it was not open to the general public, despite having plenty of media. But even if it were, these kinds of events fed the paranoid conspiracy mill. If the event were about saving kittens, the protesters would say the event was really a global conspiracy to eradicate puppies. There was no way to win, so don't even try. I laughed at the signs I saw in the hands of protesters.

"Bia!" I said to myself.

I should have known biopunks would be among the protesters. I saw biopunkers, the usual anarchists who protested everything, cyberpunks, who I imagined were just there to support the biopunks, lots of senior citizen groups, not sure why, a significant number of cyborg groups, who probably were there to support the biopunks and cyberpunks. Encircling the Convention center was nothing but crazy town. The police were out in force too, and the convention had its own security which I'm sure was on permanent high alert too. We were safe inside but you always had to keep a watchful eye.

I debated with myself for a bit then decided I would. My mission was to be a provocateur, what better way to do it.

"Let's see what happens."

I walked to the elevators.

I had to get special permission from Quix, but I exited the hover-transport area to the pedestrian alley to the outside gates. It was a long way to walk but I came out from the super half-dome structure into light rain and scrambled up an incline to the flat ground. I could see the police in the distance ahead of me, and beyond them the gates of the perimeter where the protesters were gathered on the other side.

"You sure you want to do this?" an officer asked me.

"They do throw things," another said.

"I'll be okay. I know a few of them. When the crowd sees me talking to some of them, they'll know not to attack me."

The officers smiled. "If you want to risk it, but be careful. Some of the bottles they throw aren't empty. What's in those bottles was not originally in them."

I moved to the gate quickly before I had another germophobic attack. I couldn't let my mind conjure up all the nasty things that could be "deposited" into a bottle.

"Cruz!" It was Bolt. His neck, wrists, and forearms were visibly bandaged.

Zip and Bia joined him. Breech, the former human spider, and Handy were in their own hover-wheel chairs.

"Hello," I said.

"What are you doing in there?" Bia asked.

"Playing detective."

A smile came over her face as she looked at her people. "You're still after the benefactor, aren't you? Your leads brought you here."

"I can't say anything."

"It makes complete sense!" she declared. "The global conspirators at the heart of the plot against our community and humanity. It makes all the sense in the world."

"Plot against you?" I knew immediately after I asked the question that I shouldn't have.

"Cruz, this is what we're fighting against to protect humanity. The World Health Organization is a front for the biotech megacorps. They use the threat of bio-threats and bio-terrorism as a ruse to steal the DNA of humanity for their own evil capitalistic purposes. They are the true bio-terrorists. Not nature. Steal the DNA. Use it to create bio-weapons. Unleash it against humanity under the guise of inoculations and vaccinations, when in fact the true purpose is mind-control. They've cracked the code, Cruz."

"The code?" (Shut up, Cruz!)

"The genetic code to control our brain processes. Make us stupid. Make us compliant and submissive." She smiled and looked at the others. "I knew you were our savior, Cruz. You're exactly who we've been waiting for. You're going to bring down their entire new world order. Bless you, Cruz."

When I first met Bia, after we got past her trying to kill me, I thought she was actually a sensible lady. Then I found out about the third boob and started to doubt it. I was now completely convinced she was a permanent citizen of "crazy town."

"Bless you, Cruz," the other Bio-Borgs said. Soon the words were being repeated by a whole bunch of the protesters.

At that very moment, I wondered how quickly I could get back to the convention center and away from all the mental patients I had now befriended. I had no desire to be the Messiah to crazy town? I had to get away—fast!

CHAPTER 39

One Crazy WHO

I wanted a response. That's exactly what I got.

I'd reached the pedestrian entrance to be buzzed back into the hover-transport area. I took a hover-buggy to the main lobby area and there he was, waiting with "friends." Mr. Zeno was glaring at me with five big security guards in suits, waiting.

"You again," I said as I got out of the hover-buggy. "I do seem to bother you for some reason. Who are your friends? They're not conference security."

"I observed you outside conversing with those terrorist-sympathizers through the security gates. Is that why you're here? Are you working with them? Is the plan to sabotage the event? Or maybe assassinate one of the bio-tech CEOs, maybe even the WHO President himself!"

"You are drinking far too much caffeinated beverages in your diet. You're as crazy as them. They're calling you terrorists;

you're calling them terrorists too. I think you should go out there and both of you should take your collective crazy town somewhere far, far away from Metropolis."

"You will be detained until we can get the authorities here."

"Oh, this again."

He stepped to me to block my way. "This time I will not be ignored!"

"What did I tell you I would do if you came near me again?" I asked him.

"What's that?"

It took a few moments, but one of his security men finally woke him back up. He was startled at first, disorientated, then realized he was on the ground. He sat up looking around at everyone.

"What happened?" He tried to jump to his feet but couldn't quite manage. His men pulled him up. "What happened?"

"He kicked you, sir."

"What?"

"I told you I'd kick you in the head," I said.

He charged me but was held back. Quix and the convention's real security arrived.

"You need to stay back, sir," Quix said to him.

Zeno screamed, then jumped to a Kung fu stance.

"Sir, you need to stop screaming and calm yourself," Quix said.

"I will kick you in the head again," I said, "and your paper tiger, plastic serpent, deadly pig claw, Kung Fu chicken isn't going to save you."

Zeno screamed again and charged. Quix swung his arm and smacked Zeno and all five of his men to the ground.

"Gentlemen, I'm the head of security at this center and my job is to maintain the safety of every attendee and staffer. I'm also empowered to arrest any I deem as a threat to the order and safety of this facility." He gestured to his men. "Please detain these gentlemen."

"This event is sponsored by the World Health Organization and I am its past president," Zeno said.

"In our country, sir, nobody cares who the past president is, only who the current one is."

Quix's men grabbed Zeno and the others put a hand on each security. "Take them outside until the police arrive."

"Police?" Zeno said. "There is no need for that."

"Sir, we take Center security seriously. I'll need to file a report and have you speak with officers."

"There are terrorists right outside the Center. Shouldn't you be calling the police on them."

"The police are monitoring the crowds outside and they'll be monitoring you too. Your security men will be ejected from the facility and they will not be allowed to return."

"These are security personnel under the direction of the World Health Organization."

"Sir, we are in the city of Metropolis, not your country. Do you wish to be ejected too so you may return to that country."

"No," Zeno snapped.

Quix looked at his men. "Take them all outside."

"Are you also going to take action against Mr. Cruz? He assaulted me."

"I am, sir. I will issue him a warning, but that's all. I'm not worried about him. I'm worried about you. This is the second time you've tried to take unauthorized action against him. Sir, it will be the last. I am also going to notify the WHO President of this incident."

Zeno wasn't happy. He and his men were escorted away.

A crowd had begun to form around the commotion. Mr. Euclid appeared with his container in hand and walked to us.

"My word, what came over him?" he asked as he ate one of his candies. "Jelly belly?" He offered me again. "I'm the main speaker at one of the break-out sessions. Join me."

I took one of his jelly bellies and followed him to the conferences.

CHAPTER 40

Mr. WHO

The session led by Mr. Euclid was a non-stop laugh fest. I never thought there was anything funny about nasty germs, continental plagues, and bleeding out of every orifice of the body but that's what Euclid managed to do. The discussion was supposed to be about educating the public about bio-threats but the entire room, including me, was laughing so hard we could hardly breathe. The man was a scientist with more degrees after his name than I thought possible but he missed his calling. He should have had his own prime time comedy TV show. He'd be filthy rich. At the end, he was also selling books he wrote. Even I bought one out of gratitude.

I looked at my program for the location of my next session being led by the WHO President himself. I knew everyone would be there, including the smart people who avoided his brunch event. The conference was seven days, but his half-day afternoon session was the real draw. Seating was arranged like a lecture hall. A main stage and rows in a half circle facing it, with each row at higher elevation. On the sides were the standing areas which were already packed when I arrived. The seated area was for VIP attendees only.

When I came in, Mr. Foil was at the front chatting with people in law enforcement uniforms and high-priced suits. Aides were buzzing around, as were members of the media. I had all access to the conference, but that didn't mean I had VIP reserved seating. I'd have to stand in the overflow area. The name of Mr. Foil's session: Preventing the Next Bio-Apocalypse. How uplifting.

It seemed to be standard protocol at these events wasting time thanking and recognizing colleagues. We were already thirty minutes in and he was still doing it.

"Shall we get started, ladies and gentlemen?" he said aloud.

Yes, please, right now, I said to myself.

"I have a trivia question since we are being hosted by the wonderful supercity of Metropolis. However, I dare say, most of its residents don't even know the real name of their city. It's not Metropolis. Does anyone know and how it received its name?"

He looked around the room, as did attendees in the audience.

Foil's gaze locked on me. He saw my hand raised. "We have a contestant. Yes, sir. Please identify yourself and who you represent."

"Cruz, Liquid Cool Detective Agency on behalf of the Utopia Convention Center. Not looking for bad guys, just consulting. The original name of the city, before it was a megacity or the current supercity was Ellis World. The planners wanted to create the reality that our ancestors envisioned the city of the future to be, so they turned to movies and got the people to vote on it. They named the newly merged city Metropolis."

"Very good, sir," Foil said. "An accurate history lesson from a layperson. The masses decided on your supercity's name. The beauty of democracy, but as we all know in this room there is a dark side too. The masses, laypeople, can decide some things, but they can never be allowed to decide all things. As the protesters outside the protective zone of this convention center remind us. The masses do not solve problems, individuals do. Individuals, experts, take on the burden of both responsibility and blame. The masses cannot decide some things even when the sheer strength of numbers might suggest they should. The masses are the masses. Is there a layperson among us that could do something we couldn't?"

I raised my hand again.

"Yes, Mr. Cruz."

"Build a high-end, classic hovervehicle in his parent's basement as a kid in high school."

The audience laughed.

"You got me there, Mr. Cruz. But honestly you are no more representative of the masses than you are representative of the experts in this room. You are what we refer to in biological terms as an anomaly."

"If you mean I'm unique, I'll take the compliment," I said.

The chatter in the room grew and I knew I was the cause of it. The experts didn't like a layperson in their space.

"I must ask, Mr. Cruz," Foil began, "since this is a confidential presentation with national security implications, do you have authorization to attend separate from your recent consulting contract with the convention center?"

"I do," I answered.

"May I ask from whom? Someone at a senior level in Metropolis government."

"Yes."

"Present here in the room?"

"Yes."

"Who might that be?"

A man raised his hand in the middle of the second room in full Metro PD dress uniform.

"Who are you, sir?"

"Chief Hub. Chief of the Metropolis Police Department," he answered.

Mr. Foil paused, then looked at me. "Then the matter is closed. Welcome to the session, Mr. Cruz."

"Thank you," I said.

I couldn't say I understood all what was being said during the hours of the session. Again, lots of long words, acronyms, and lots of science stuff. But one term stood out.

"This, ladies and gentlemen is the heart of bio-management," Foil said.

Bio-management? That's exactly the term that would have the super-paranoid, new world order-fearing protesters stirred up into a fit. But I wasn't from crazy town so I "bio-managed" my own paranoia.

There were moments that I definitely felt the audience was censoring what they were saying because I was in the room, especially when we got to the Q and A block at the final hour of the session.

One of the officers, I believe from the lunar colonies asked his question, "Are there any new threats we are aware of to the rain? There was an alert earlier in the year."

Foil nodded and answered. "There were two alerts we issued, but they were false alarms. There are no credible threats to the potency of Andromeda Rain, but it's monitored constantly from field agents and drones."

I almost fell down. Rain? Andromeda Rain? What the heck was Andromeda Rain?

"Ladies and gentlemen, let us wrap up the questions. There will be plenty of opportunity during the breakout sessions for further discussion. Do we have any last questions?" Foil smiled, seeing my hand. "I'd say it is more than appropriate for Mr. Cruz to ask our last question of the session."

"Thanks, Mr. Foil. Well, my wife and I are on the residential building tower council and we like to share these kinds of things with our neighbors—whether it be crime reports of interest, latest scams, new building safety measures, or emergency procedures for our district. We like to keep our building residents informed. We're a family building. What recommendations do you have for our residents, laypeople, on how to combat bio-threats?"

"That, Mr. Cruz, is a very intelligent and excellent question. In fact, WHO has community reps that come out to residents such as yours to address building councils and can answer any and all questions." He pointed to aides at the back of the room. "I'll have my staff provide you with literature too that you can distribute to your entire building."

"Thank you."

"No, thank you, Mr. Cruz."

The session was over. Most of the attendees slowly made their way out the exits, but I hung around. Foil was surrounded by people again, chatting. He looked up at me and said something to the group, then walked my way.

He shook my hand. "I'm glad you attended, Mr. Cruz. We're having a private dinner event and I'd like you to attend."

"Tonight?"

"Yes. Can you attend?"

"I can."

"Raven," he called out. A petite young woman with very short black hair with a tint of crimson appeared next to us. "The event is formal attire. I don't imagine you have a proper suit."

"I don't."

"Raven will take care of everything."

"Thanks, Mr. Foil."

"No, thank you. See to Mr. Cruz, Raven. See you later tonight, Mr Cruz."

Foil went back to the crowd of people waiting for him.

Raven shook my hand. "Mr. Cruz, let me know your room number and I'll bring a suit to you. The dinner will begin at eight. Should I stop by at six?

PART SEVEN

The Andromeda Rain Came From BioDome

CHAPTER 41

Raven

Biodome

Noun. A closed ecological system.

Raven wasn't just prompt. She rang my suite doorbell at exactly six p.m. like she was some type of android. I yelled, "It's open," and in she came holding a full suit on a hanger in a plastic see-through covering. I shuffled to her in a robe with karate slippers on my feet.

"You're not an android, are you?" I said as I took the suit.

"I've never been asked that before."

"Tell your boss that no one is more prompt than you."

"I take extreme pride in punctuality and delivering what I promise."

"Also tell your boss, thank you. I would have hated battling through those protesters outside to get home and then come all the way back though them. Instead, I stay within the circle of security of the convention center."

"You get used to them—the protesters. They are always there but never an impact on one's daily life."

"They're really angry. Have you seen them up close?"

"Yes, they are, and no."

"I'd say they need a good vacation."

"If you'd like, Mr. Cruz, I am a licensed massage specialist."

A big grin came over my face. "Are you?"

"I am."

"I admit that I'm not up on the ways of the booshy elite, but we commoners just put on our clothes. We don't get massages before we do."

"One of the perks of being a friend of Mr. Foil."

"Mr. Foil must have lots of friends."

"He does."

I laughed. "As tempting as that is—" Raven removed the band in her hair to release the ponytail and let it hang naturally. Then out came the clear plastic gloves from her pockets. Didn't seem like she was going to take "no" for an answer.

I walked into the living room and lay the suit on one of the chairs. She followed and immediately stopped.

The room was filled with sidewalk johnnies sitting in chairs facing the TV, back to her, with drinks and food. All of them were wearing VR glasses watching a movie.

"This is the part where she—" one of the johnnies began.

"Shut up!" they cut him off in unison.

"Raven, thanks so much. I'll take it from here and see you at the dinner."

"Yes, Mr. Cruz." She stuffed her gloves back in her pockets, turned and was out the door.

The second it closed, all the sidewalk johnnies stood and took off their VR glasses.

"Maybe we should have been elsewhere, Mr. Cruz," one of them said, grinning. They all started to laugh.

"You were about to get the white glove, rub down treatment," another said.

"With extras," another chimed in.

"Okay, comedians. I want you to check and scan the suit, hanger, and bag thoroughly. I don't believe for one second she came up for any massage or anything rated adults-only. But she came up here to do something, and it wasn't to add to her boss's friends list."

"What do you think she was going to do, Mr. Cruz?"

"I have no idea. There are all kinds of purposes for gloves. One purpose is so you don't leave any fingerprints."

The sidewalk johnnies looked at each other. They started checking the suit.

I made my way down to the main lobby check-in area and its hidden security command post to see Quix wearing my trusty tan fedora. I felt funny wearing the tuxedo-like suit. The fabric had a cool sensation to the touch. It was super strong but flexible and stretchable. I could probably run a marathon in it with ease; it was that durable despite the sheer weight. The boys found nothing on it, in the way of bugs or trackers, and neither did the scan.

The guards let me through to the private offices and I sat down with Quix at a side table. He rested his portable computer on the table and scrolled through his files. All around us was a massive video monitor bank with dozens of guards in front of them. There were over a hundred screens, and these were only the ones I could see.

"Why are you asking about her?" Quix asked.

"I'm not armed, so I want to make sure she's an aide rather than some assassin."

Quix smiled. "Your instincts are right."

"She's not a massage specialist."

"Massage specialist? Is there something I should know?"

"No. Nor my wife, since nothing happened. What does the file say?"

"Calling her an aide is one way to describe her. She's the head of security for the World Health Organization."

"I knew she was up to something!"

"Did you check the suit thoroughly?"

"The boys did."

"I'd scan every inch of your suite too. There are all kinds of tricks used in the spycraft game used by governments and megacorps. In fact, I'll send up a team to do it."

"Head of security means trained fighter."

"Much more than that. Trained killer, if needed."

"What's all in her file?"

"Very little, but no one becomes head of security with an empty file. This is the public file I have access to. There's another. Probably Up-Top. I heard from my guys that WHO likes to hire their security from off-world—ex-military, former mercs, soldiers-for hire."

"Are your security still the only personnel allowed to be armed?"

"Yes, that's standard. Armed security is centralized under our control and we have sensors to make sure no one smuggles anything in, including law enforcement."

"The Chief of Police is unarmed."

"He checked his weapon at the main desk like every other law enforcement personnel per the wishes of the World Health Organization and enthusiastically seconded by the Metropolis City Council."

"I feel naked without my weapon."

"Also, not all the bio-tech megacorps have arrived. In fact, all the major ones haven't arrived yet. They'll be here in force soon. All their security are cyborgs."

I smiled. "Most of our convention center security are cyborgs." He smiled too.

"This is an enclosed biosphere, Cruz. Not many places to run. Be thankful that everyone is unarmed except for our convention security. However."

"However, what?"

"Keep in mind that if she is a corporate soldier, she could kill you with a butter knife."

"Good to know. I'll stay away from her when she's at the buffet table then. Killer massage specialists."

"The stories I could tell," Quix said.

"I'll keep that in mind when I visit the Fubar again."

"I'll send my team up to your suite. I hope you know what you're doing with this big operation scam of yours." He stood from the table.

"Everything is working according to plan. All we're doing now is buying time."

"Raven could help you with that."

"Named after a big black bird that flies around corpses. I'll pass, thank you."

CHAPTER 42

Mr. WHO

The private VIP lounges were held above the convention's grand Ballroom and the lounges were every bit as grand. The men wore tuxedo-like dinner suits and the women were in slinky dresses. The second I came through the door, one waitress appeared with a tray of drinks and another with some jumbo-shrimp appetizers. I helped myself to both.

"Mr. Cruz." I turned to see Raven in a slinky black dress and she pointed to a section of the crowded lounge. I saw him—Mr. Foil—entertaining guests.

"Thank you, Ms. Raven."

Before I could get to them, Foil spotted me and beckoned, smiling.

"Mr. Cruz, I was speaking about you to my colleagues. We have a real-life private detective amongst us. He even has the nostalgic fedora to match. Bravo, Mr. Cruz. I told Raven that you'd wear it without us having to coax you."

Foil introduced me to over a dozen people surrounding him with sparkling glasses in hand. They were officials and scientists; one was from a biotech megacorp.

"What's the name of your company, miss?" I asked.

"Our biotech firm is called Biome."

"Yes. I heard of it. It means a community of plants and animals that all have common characteristics of the environment they exist in."

"Yes, Mr. Cruz," she said. "That is correct."

"I believe more than one of the past WHO presidents work for you."

"That is correct too. I hope my firm hasn't come under your scrutiny for some reason."

"No, no. Nothing like that," I said, grinning. "I'm consulting for the convention center. All security related due to all the protesters outside."

"You couldn't by chance go out there and shoot them," one of the male guests said getting laughs from the others.

"Sorry, no. Ignore them and the conference will be over and they'll have to look for someone else to pester."

"Speaking of security, Mr. Cruz," Foil began. "My aide Raven told me about your own low-tech security measures for you own suite. I must say I was impressed. She has already implemented the same for myself and all our staff, current and former. Can never be too careful?"

"You're absolutely right, Mr. Foil."

"We've also done the same for the lab and research zone too. I wouldn't want anyone sneaking in there for an impromptu, unauthorized tour," Foil said.

"Well, what I've seen of the convention security so far is that it's top-notch. They seem to run a very tight ship," I said.

"They do indeed."

"None of us have anything to worry about though. My own low-tech security measures have to do more with my personal paranoia not a reflection of the convention's security. You have to remember I work the streets of Metropolis, Mr. Foil. I sometimes have to camp out in very seedy and dangerous areas. Hotel rat traps not the palatial suites we have here. You need those low-tech security measures in place or you won't be coming home."

"You have a family?"

"I do. I have a wife, a kid, a vehicle, and a cool hat."

They laughed.

"My goodness. What a fascinating life you must lead, Mr. Cruz," Foil said. "Maybe I went into the wrong field. You're living the pulp fiction detective life."

"Fiction is fun. The reality of the streets is another thing altogether."

"Have you ever been shot, Mr. Cruz?" the woman from the biotech firm asked. I noticed that Raven was now standing nearby from the corner of my eye.

"Shot. Shot at. Shootouts. All of the above."

"Mr. Cruz, you're going to be in high demand tonight. None of us ever get a chance to meet someone like you. I'm glad you ignored my attempts to have you ejected from the conference. I'm so glad indeed. Let me introduce you to more colleagues."

As we moved from group to group, I felt like I was like the new amoeba under their microscope. They were all of the scientific world, but they were all also part of the super-wealthy set. To them, the life they led was normal. They had no contact with the normal world of the Average Joe and Jane. It was like the biopunk protesters out there. They were aware of them only from afar. They would never meet them.

I knew they were intelligent and well-meaning. They truly wanted to "save the world." But it was odd that they wanted to save the world when they knew so little of that world.

"Don't judge us too harshly, Mr. Cruz," Foil said to me as he led me to another group.

"Not judging."

"It's true that you may know more of the true way of things than most of the people in this room, but we all have our part to play in the universe."

"We do."

"Mr. Cruz, I can't help feeling like I am a character in one of your cases."

"How could you? I'm simply a consultant. I actually left my detective crime-solving costume at home."

"Of course, you have. I have always been fascinated with the crime thriller. Would I be better as the detective or the criminal?"

"I don't know. Do you think you could outsmart the detective? Or would you have the patience to catch the bad guy no matter the obstacles?"

"Interesting question. Let me introduce you to my colleagues here. I've known them for ages."

I lost count of the groups of colleagues that he introduced me to. I was definitely the star attraction. However, my Ma didn't raise no dummy. Foil wanted to keep me close and under his eye, and left hints on more than one occasion that he knew I was up to something and he'd find out what.

After all this socializing, Foil announced dinner was to be served. The joke was on me because I thought all the appetizers were the dinner when in fact the appetizers were the appetizers. Men came in with long tables and tablecloths. They turned the lounge area to a dining hall in moments. More staff came in with the utensils and the servers came in promptly after them.

Of course, I was at Foil's table. He sat at the head, I was in the seat to his left and Raven was across from me on his right. Great! She had a knife and fork in her hands.

The conversation at the table turned to a technical, scientific debate about DNA structure and genetic manipulation and compounds and chemical elements. They might as well have been speaking Mandarin or Swahili. I ate quietly, ignoring Raven who was pretending not to watch me, until there was a natural break in the chatter.

"Mr. Foil, I did want to ask a layman's question."

"By all means, Mr. Cruz."

"You don't have to answer it if you don't want to. It was a point from your half-day conference."

"Mr. Cruz, I was told you have all the proper clearances. I even was told that you were a police intern in high school. Preparation for your future busy detective life. Building hovercars in your parents' basement, interning with Metropolis's finest. I didn't even know youth could intern at police headquarters. If we're not doing that in my country, I'm going to see to it that they do."

"What's Andromeda Rain?"

The question didn't make Foil nervous, but it did seem to make the table nervous.

"How did I know that you would eventually ask me that, Mr. Cruz? Are you familiar with the concept of bio-management?"

"Yes." I smiled. "I attended your half-day conference."

"Yes, you did. Let me ask you this: if the World Health Organization identified a deadly virus and we had to inoculate the entire Metropolis population, or the entire population of any supercity, or any smaller city, you pick, how long could we reasonably expect to reach everyone?"

"Metropolis?"

"Yes."

"Never."

"Why do you say that?"

"You might get a quarter to come into the hospitals and clinics, if you were lucky. For the rest, they'd miss the message—stoned, sleeping, don't watch news, live in virtual reality, whatever the excuse. Then there are those who wouldn't accept the vaccination under any circumstances. They'd say you wanted to poison them or you created the outbreak to trick them to inject mind-control devices into their blood." The table guests laughed, but they all nodded.

"I told you, Mr. Cruz. You understand the ways of things. You are absolutely right. You are actually more optimistic than the studies. We would likely only get less than twenty percent voluntary compliance with a mandatory order to get vaccinated.

"That would spell disaster to your supercity, or any other. Nature creates its own deadly viruses from time to time. Nature is in fact the greatest bio-terrorist in the solar system. Add to that mutations as a result of flora, animals, or humans. Add to that designer diseases that could be created by bio-terrorists. You can see the true scope of the bio-threat to humans, our food, our entire ecosystem. Earth.

"With the stakes so high, Mr. Cruz, humans cannot have the choice to refuse or delay vaccinations or inoculations. Even a handful of people who refused an inoculation for whatever imaginary reasons could unleash a pandemic killing millions. Off-worlders are far ahead of Earth in genetic manipulation and engineering to create better humans, animals, plants, food, but that is a static process. Bio-threats are always changing, evolving, or mutating far faster. You can quarantine a building or district, but not a supercity. Hovercars flying everywhere to all parts of your country. Andromeda Rain was the solution. Andromeda Rain is a necessity."

"You put the vaccinations in the rain," I said.

"Yes. It has been standard protocol for far longer than you think. Imagine if there was an outbreak of the Bubonic Plague in your fine city. With fifty million people. You could see three-fourths wiped out in days, even with draconian bio-containment measures. That, of course, would not do."

"No, it wouldn't."

"I'm sure you recognize why such a thing has to be kept confidential from the public."

"I do."

"Until we can create the super human it is what we must do. But! We cannot let the dinner descend into depression. Mr. Cruz, has been so gracious to entertain with his colorful stories of the private detective world and his exploits defeating criminals, we must return the favor. Mr. Nadir, tell Mr. Cruz about the many interesting diseases and parasites that I'm sure he doesn't know exist."

"Parasites?" I asked. "As long as there are no stories about isopods. Those things give me nightmares."

CHAPTER 43

Fraggy

The time went by fast and when dinner finally wrapped up it was after two in the morning. Thank goodness the first set of breakout sessions wouldn't start until ten. The first part of the conference featured government agencies, NGOs, science and law enforcement bio-threat divisions. The final half would be the private sector megacorps. Those senior execs were arriving, but the CEOS and presidents would arrive tomorrow. My work would be increasing not the opposite, so I had to grab some sleep but...

Goodbyes took forever, but finally I was free and clear from Foil, Raven and everyone else. It seemed odd that none of the other WHO past presidents had attended. This concerned me, along with the fact that I hadn't seen the WHO past president, Mr. Timely, once in person, though I knew he was here.

The crowds would all be taking the elevators up to their suites and I didn't want to be packed into any elevator with anyone. I ran to the main check-in desk manned by two guards. Quix was off-duty but I was buzzed back. Instead of the security command center, I had them escort me to the secure phones.

I sat in one of the private booths closing the door as I sunk into the couch. I always preferred to manually dial rather than use voice. Three rings and he answered.

"How much longer, Fraggy?"

His face took up my entire vid-screen at first, then he sat back a bit. "You're over four hours late."

"I couldn't leave sooner."

"To answer your question, they've already accessed and copied everything we need."

"Then why are they still there?" I asked.

"They can do the forensics review much faster there than flying back here and starting from scratch."

"Have they found anything at all?"

"No. What's wrong? Did something happen?"

"Foil knows something is off," I answered. "It's just a matter of time."

"I never did like this part of your plan."

"It was to keep them off-balance. Distract with the right hand so they don't even know to look to see what the left hand is doing."

"If you say."

"I'm having Phishy pull them out today."

"No. Not yet."

"We shouldn't take any chances, Fraggy."

"Give us one more day."

"But they haven't found anything yet."

"Cruz, the WHO HQ database is huge, and the labs are even more vast. It's entirely possible that my team could be reviewing the data for years until they find anything."

"Have they looked at the Andromeda Rain files?"

"What? How do you know about that?"

"I was in the conferences."

"Cruz, that knowledge is extremely confidential and not for public knowledge."

"Fraggy, I've never disclosed secrets to the public before, not going to start now. Have they?"

"No, but that can be the next area they review. What about the Rain? What do you know?"

"Foil was very talkative about it. I'd like to make sure he wasn't using reverse psychology on me. Telling me everything when in fact he really wanted to tell me nothing to send me in a different direction."

"Cruz, what game are you playing with him?"

"I told you. He knows we're onto to them. They all do."

"What do you think they'd do if they found out the conference was a way to get them out of WHO headquarters?"

"React violently. Don't look at me. It was you're idea, Fraggy."

"My idea? I don't exactly remember when you said I came up with this idea."

"Don't you listen to yourself talk?"

"I ramble all the time like all scientists. I don't pay attention to any of it."

"Well you should. Who knows how many good ideas you had, but let them get away because you don't listen when you talk to yourself. One more day, but I'm having Phishy get ready today to pull them out."

CHAPTER 44

Zeno

I slept right away when I returned to my suite. Sidewalk Sid had nothing to report, which was what I'd suspect after Raven saw for herself that I had people in my suite at all times. Foil himself said he was impressed by my low-tech and would be doing the same. So I slept right away when I got into my sleeping bag on the bed, but I didn't sleep very long.

I was back for breakfast at the Dining Hall for the early-risers the next morning, or four hours later. I found myself looking at the center atrium with all its levels as I came out of the elevators. There was someone on the seventh floor, I think, leaning over but I couldn't make out who it was. I stepped back and they were gone.

The early breakfast was the same and the people I saw seemed to be the same as the previous morning. The difference was I could now put names to faces, and quite a few people greeted me as we helped ourselves to the buffet-style breakfast counter. Early breakfast was about eating and reading; eat breakfast and read the news or email on devices. No talking, which was why I liked them. I could sit alone at a small round table and not be bothered, though I was really working. This morning I expected to see some new faces as more megacorps would be arriving, but it was only us regulars.

I used the time to do my own reading of messages. There were plenty from PJ keeping me up to date on all the happenings at the office. One week was a long time to be out of the office, but I was getting paid, which was the main thing that mattered. But I also wanted a case to solve. I had a case but its solution was a question mark, especially when I was not yet certain as to what the real case was. Lots of people were watching this in Metropolis law enforcement and politics. Fraggy's team had to come through or our grand plan was going to be a big bust, and a lot of those people were not going to be happy with me.

"Hello, Mr. Cruz."

I looked up from my device to see Mr. Zeno. He wasn't sneering at me this time, nor did he have his thugs with him. Actually, he looked very contrite and was struggling to get out whatever he wanted to tell me.

"Yes?"

"I came to apologize. I've treated you horribly. Foil told me about the dinner last night. I feel like such a troll, the way I behaved towards you. You're doing your job and I behaved the way I did."

"No need to apologize at all."

"No, there is. Please accept my sincere apology. It will never happen again."

"Apology accepted."

"Thank you, Mr. Cruz. I'll leave you to your breakfast. I for one can appreciate the importance of one's quiet time. Today will be a busy one."

I nodded.

"If there's anything you need, as far as the WHO, let me know. I was always known as the historian of the organization."

"Thank you, Mr. Zeno. I do enjoy history. I'll take you up on the offer if I can think of anything."

"Good. See you at the conference."

Zeno walked off in his retro Victorian business suit. I watched him until he was out of sight.

It was a nice gesture of him to apologize. I don't think I could do that after someone had kicked me in the head, though he deserved it, but he did. Maybe it was more reverse psychology.

CHAPTER 45

Quix

When government types went anywhere, they sent their underlings first, then all the principals arrived together. Not so with megacorporations; they arrived in waves. The lowest of underlings arrived first, then came the junior management, senior management, executives, and senior executives arrived with the bosses.

The conference's hover-transportation was operating nonstop with new arrivals. Endless suits came from the arriving hovertrolleys, one after another. They reminded me of gangs because someone in the group would be carrying signage with the company's logo but no text. It was just like gangs with their symbols. Outsiders didn't recognize the symbols, but insiders knew it instinctively.

Quix was right. Their security was obvious. Big, scary-looking, and cyborg—metallic hands or entire arms. Japanese-owned megacorps loved their samurai soldiers but all companies had their version of elite corporate soldiers. I'm glad they weren't armed with guns, but at their level of proficiency in violence, did it really matter? Without my own omega-gun, the only weapon I had was the ability to run away like a rabbit.

There were no places left to sit in the main open lobby area. I stood near the main check-in area so I could see everyone, but they could see me too.

"Who are you?" asked a female security person with one of the megacorps.

"Mr. Cruz," I answered.

She and all the security looked down at the devices in their hands, typing away.

"The Metropolis private detective."

"Why are you here?" she asked.

"Conference hired me."

They all looked at their devices again and typed. She walked closer to me.

"Why are you really here?"

"Conference hired me. They're my client. Not you."

"We know of you, Mr. Cruz, we all do."

"What's the name of your company?"

"Ask your client."

"This is a conference about keeping humanity safe from bio-threats in the world. One would think that would be a good, altruistic, charitable mission. I didn't know there was money to be made in such a mission. Money enough to hire so many high-priced corporate soldiers."

"Why are you really here?"

"I answered that question already."

"You will not be successful," she said to me with a piercing stare.

"I am a successful man. Therefore, I am always successful in whatever I do."

"I would leave this conference if I were you."

"When my clients release me, then I will. As I said before, you are not my client."

"That will be arranged."

She turned away from me. The group of them all checked in at the main desk. Conference security hand-scanned their persons and their bags before clearing them. None of them acknowledged my presence again as they walked to the hotel suite elevator.

Quix was on duty but wasn't at the main desk at the moment. One of the security guards gestured to me. "Quix wants to see you."

They buzzed me back to enter the security command post.

"Cruz, what did you do?"

Quix had sat me down in one of the empty meeting rooms.

"What do you mean?"

"Cruz, it's like Defcon Three out there. Every megacorp that's arriving is asking about you. They all know you're here, want to know why, and are demanding you be expelled, along with all your sidewalk johnny friends."

"They know about them too. Quix, this wasn't unexpected. We just have to run out the clock."

"Your plan was to make them nervous. You've done that, but they're way past nervous. I expected all their security to ask to be briefed about the protesters outside. No. They're asking about you. Which is strange?"

"Why strange?"

"The size of the protest outside has increased."

"Increased? That's not unexpected either. The megacorps are arriving for their half of the conference schedule."

"Cruz, no one on the outside is supposed to know that. We may be here, but it's a confidential conference not open to the public. No one outside should know who's here and when they arrive. The crowds outside have tripled in size. Something is going on."

"We just need to run out the clock." I was outwardly calm but nervous.

"Cruz, you said it yourself. They know you're up to something. They're turning the tables on you. Something clearly was said to the megacorps last night to make them behave this way today, and something clearly was put out there to get all these new protesters to arrive this morning. Cruz, I've seen real combat in my life so outside of that I don't get nervous. Cruz, I'm nervous."

"What do you think could happen?"

"Cruz, we don't have enough security on our own to man the perimeter against those protesters massing. That means more police will have to be deployed, which has already happened. At some point, the megacorps will demand we reverse our no-weapons ban and they'll get Metro PD approval. Then both of our lives get very complicated."

"The Chief wouldn't agree to that."

"Wouldn't he? Take a look outside for yourself and you tell me."

"I know some of them so I'll ask what's going on."

"We know what's going on. The megacorps are pretending to be focused on you when they should be focused on the protestors, which means this is their doing. They're going to get their weapons, take away security control from us, get you thrown out, and have the authority to move against the protesters. When you go after powerful people, Cruz, they can play nasty too. We are about to experience them playing nasty big-time. You better wrap up. Your clock is done today."

CHAPTER 46

Bia

Today? I couldn't "wrap up" today, but Quix was probably right. I had no choice.

The gravity of the situation really hit me when I returned to the observation level at the very top of the convention center dome. Quix had tripled the standing security outside, but it wasn't enough. I had my binoculars again and when I looked out the windows, I was shocked. There had to have been at least a million people surrounding the center. Both Quix's outer security and Metro PD were so outnumbered. They were joined by a couple of Metro police gunships in the air which I was sure was the only reason the crowds hadn't pushed, scaled, or ripped apart the fencing to storm the convention center. I had to move faster than fast.

Quix and two ex-military cyborgs with heavy laser rifles escorted me from the hover-transport area to the pedestrian alley to the outside gates. The police were not going to let us near the gates at first, but I convinced them. What I was doing was crazy. As I scrambled up an incline to the flat ground, Quix and his men stayed right with me. Bottles were thrown at us. Quix actually pulled a small gun from his waist and shot them in the air before they could land.

"Bia!"

I saw her and yelled her name again. Then I saw her turn to yell at her people and they fanned out into the crowds. She too had a lot more people. It didn't look good but the biopunks were fighting the other groups. It looked like a civil war was about to break out amongst them.

"Cruz! We have to leave now!" Quix yelled at me.

I saw Breech still in his hoverchair. I raised my hand and he saw the phone in it and he waved his hands. I stepped forward and tossed it at him, over the fence. Thankfully, he caught it but several others in the crowd tried to grab it from him. I saw Bolt punch one of them.

At that point, I was lifted into the air. Quix pulled me back and I was barely keeping up with them as we ran back to and through the police perimeter, back to the pedestrian alley of the center, and back inside.

"Cruz, that was very stupid," Quix yelled at me. "They could have acid in those bottles, or one of them could have shot you."

"I need to get to the secure private booths again."

Quix led me back through the hovertransport area with his men.

"Is this what you normally do as a detective?" Bia asked me. Her face on the vid-screen of the private phone booth.

"Absolutely not," I replied, leaning forward on the couch.

Bia was talking but she was still moving to get away from the crowd. She looked up from the vid-phone frequently and at times disappeared from the screen all together.

"What's going on, Bia?"

She returned to the screen. "Cruz, it's chaos out here. No one knows who all these new groups are. They showed up this morning out of nowhere."

"It's the megacorps," I said.

"How do you know?"

"It has to be."

"Cruz, there's so many of them. I've sent for more people, all of us have, but they're arriving much faster."

"Bia, you need to be very careful out there."

"Don't worry about us. You're the one who should be worried. The cops are not going to be able to stop this crowd. They'll get to a certain size then they're going to break through all your security, cops and all."

"Were any rumors or news put out on the street to cause this?"

"No. This was going to be a normal protest day for us and these new groups showed up. We've never seen them before. They're using our slogans and same signs as us, but we don't know who they are. But they're coming in, Cruz. That much I can tell you. If you think it's the megacorps, then I'll tell my people. They've done this thing before to get the media to blame us for something, but never on this scale. Cruz, we're literally outnumbered ten to one."

"Bia. Listen to me very carefully. Get all of your people out of there now. All of them."

"Why?" she asked me nervously.

"Do it now. Get out of there now, go underground so you can't be found, destroy the phone, go now."

Bia's face disappeared. The screen went blank.

I leaned back on the couch. Quix was more right than he realized. A full out attack of the convention center by these new "protesters" was being orchestrated before our eyes.

CHAPTER 47

Run-Time

The seed of the idea had come from Fraggy, but I was the one who immediately saw how to make it a reality. I could never pull off something this big, but I had powerful friends. Prima could make the venue happen with the city eager to rebrand Opus Fields after the Movie-Town scandal. Chief Hub made the sponsorship happen, along with the endorsement and attendance of all the higher-ups from Earth to Up-Top. He knew something about all this but wouldn't tell me. I suspected he and his intelligence feared a real bio-terrorist attack. The icing on the cake was the premiere transportation. These dignitaries needed, and expected, the best in hoverlimo transportation to and from the airport, and to any place they wanted to go in Metropolis. That part of the plan fell to my best friend Run-Time and I didn't need to ask him twice.

When I came out of the private phone booth, Quix told me Run-Time was waiting for me at my hotel suite. Quix sent two armed security men with me. When we exited the security command post into the main open lobby area it was like a ghost town. The conference was supposed to be happening but there was not a soul to be seen.

We came out of the elevators on the penthouse level and could see a couple of johnnies watching at the end of the hall, but also another armed guard courtesy of Quix. We turned the corner and the hallway was filled with sidewalk johnnies and security. I saw Run-Time standing in front of my hotel suite door.

My best friend Run-Time started Let It Ride Enterprises at twenty-five. He was a middle-school drop-out at eleven years old, body shop go-fer at twelve, hovercar mechanic at thirteen, valet attendant at fourteen, hovertaxi driver at seventeen, hovertaxicab owner at nineteen. We met in high school. He only returned to get the piece of paper (diploma) but he was already on his way as an entrepreneur. He became a mega-multi-millionaire by thirty.

He owned all the top car washes, hovercar body shops, hovercar rental shops, hovercycle rental shops, hovertaxicab, and hoverlimousine services in the city. Anything that had to do with private transportation, Run-Time had his hands in it. He was founder, President, CEO, and COO of Let It Ride, and was the icing on the cake of my grand plan, which seemed to be imploding in slow motion before me.

Run-Time wore his slim fit business suits and slim ties, and his trademark flat hat. That's why we hit it off as kids; no one else wore hats. We had been best friends ever since.

We exchanged hugs when I reached him.

"Mr. Cruz," he said. "What have you gotten me into?"

We left everyone in the hall to have our impromptu meeting in my suite. Though we relaxed in chairs in the living room area, there was nothing relaxing about the situation.

"You do know that the police may evacuate all the attendees at the conference?"

"Makes sense."

"Was all this the plan?"

"This is their response to the plan."

"I hope you got what you needed because this is going to be bad."

"The protesters outside are plants."

"Plants? You know this for certain?"

"I know members of the legitimate protesters. They said these new protesters showed up in force this morning and no one knows who they are or where they came from."

"Who's behind it?"

"The megacorps."

Run-Time shook his head. "The megacorps wouldn't do this. They're part of the conference, co-sponsors, the conference is sanctioned by the Council of Corporations. The megacorps wouldn't do this."

That's why I liked Run-Time. He knew the megacorp and political worlds and could set me straight in my suspicions. I started to rethink everything.

"Cruz, this conference is going to be shut down today if I had to guess."

"Maybe."

"What are you thinking now?"

"Something is being orchestrated alright. We just don't know what yet. Do you know anything about a company called Biome?"

"I've heard of them. I believe they're one of the megacorporate sponsors of our little conference here."

"Is that the only reason you know who they are?"

"They're a leading biotech lab testing company."

"What do they do?"

"Cruz, why are you asking about them?"

"So they do something important for the city?"

"They do, and I can't talk about it. I'm not even supposed to know, but I do."

"I think I can guess too."

"You were always good at figuring things out. Isn't that what your mentor told you too?"

"Wilford G. Yes, he did say that. Can you do me a favor?" I asked.

"Name it," Run-Time said.

"Quix thinks that convention security will have to relent and allow the megacorp security to have their own weapons. If so, can you see to it that my sidewalk johnny brigade is transported out of here. They always stay away from real danger. I don't want them to find themselves in the center of it because of me."

"My security will get them out if we have to evacuate."

"Thanks."

There was a frantic knock on the door. I wished I had my omega-gun, but Run-Time had me covered. He was pulled a laser pistol from his jacket.

CHAPTER 48

Prima Donna

With Quix's two armed security guys at my side, I came out the elevator to the main open lobby, but it wasn't a ghost town anymore. Heavily armed megacorp security guards filled the space, encircling their given senior executives and staff. Every one of them staring at me as I walked to the main check-in desk.

This time Prima Donna was behind the counter, with three other security personnel. Quix buzzed me back.

He led me to one of the larger private conference rooms and there were a dozen sullen face suits waiting, both Asian and European men and women. Prima Donna walked in after us.

"We are all here," Prima said to them.

"Why is the owner of a beauty salon running a World Health Organization bio-threat conference?" a female CEO asked.

"As I already stated before, I do not run a beauty salon. Eye Candy is a global international beauty, fashion, nutrition, and wellness megacorp. We have done numerous high-level events for Metropolis and as a result of that expertise and our connections was asked to manage this event. The hope was for it to be the first of an annual event to take place in the city."

"The reason for Mr. Cruz?" a male CEO asked.

"That was my decision. I wanted someone on site that I knew and trusted, known for their keen observation. Out of the norm, granted, but I wanted a good reporting of the atmosphere of the event."

"How do we have this man fired?" the man asked.

"That would be a decision of the director of this event," Prima replied.

"Not you?" he asked.

"I am the manager, not the boss."

"Where is this boss?" a woman asked.

"Mr. Incom is at another engagement. I can get in touch with him."

"Please do. We want this issue dealt with immediately."

"With all due respect, the matter outside the Center's security perimeter is my immediate priority."

"With our security being armed, that concern is over," he said.

"Even in Metropolis, it is not customary to mow unarmed people down with gunfire and laser fire," Prima said with a glare.

"Of course," he answered.

"We only mean that if the violent protesters were to overrun the police and attempted to break through the walls of the convention center, we would respond accordingly, and within the law," the woman added.

"That is obviously what you meant."

"How long will it take for you to get Mr. Incom on the phone?" the man asked.

"I will do so now."

"We can have someone accompany you to your office."

"That will not be necessary." Prima was now mad. "I know how to make a call all by myself. I've been able to do so before you were born."

He smiled at her. "You hide your age well and no offense was meant. Security is of paramount concern to our companies and there are doubts to the legitimacy of this conference. We had paid quite large sums of money to make this conference happen and my board of directors would have my head if they learned this conference was not legitimate. You, ma'am, might find yourself in prison for fraud. This is a very serious situation."

"I completely understand." Prima responded in a soft tone.

"We shall wait here until you return from making your call."

I followed Prima from the conference room. She was seething with anger but not at the megacorp bosses—at me!

"Cruz, if there is any jail time in my future, I will not be alone."

She left me there as she walked down the hall to an office. I returned to the command post. Quix was there, waiting for me and glancing at the monitor banks.

"You're wanted back upstairs," he told me.

CHAPTER 49

Run-Time and The Mick

As we came out of the elevators, my sidewalk johnny brigade was still in the hallway, but they all looked even more nervous than the last time. I did what Phishy would have done: shook hands as I went along to reassure them all was fine.

I hadn't seen all of them in a while but Run-Time had three VPs for his company—two female and one male. The two female vice presidents—one Lebanese and one West Indian—were the "nice" ones who did all the "nice" things for Let It Ride Enterprises. Run-Time waited for me near my hotel suite door with his male VP, a stout blue-eyed Irishman, known as The Mick. He didn't shake hands but nodded when I arrived with now four armed guards courtesy of Quix. He did the "not so nice" things for the company.

We entered my suite again.

"Why are you gentlemen still here?" I asked.

The two men glanced at each other.

"You surely didn't mean that as it sounded," Run-Time said to me with a smirk.

"Mr. Cruz," The Mick said, "this scheme of yours was ill-advised from the start. Whatever plan you had has clearly gone awry."

"I would've agreed with you maybe fifteen minutes ago, but not now. I do believe my plan is moving along nicely despite the extreme stress they're trying to inflict on us. But what did you come to tell me?"

"We came to tell you to prepare to leave right away," Run-Time said. "In the brief time since we last met the crowd outside has increased again and so has the police presence. Whatever the protesters are going to do, it will be any moment now."

"The police will likely ground all hovertravel in the immediate area."

"But why are you here?" I repeated. "You're here because all the WHO conference attendees are still here. Government officials are not known for their courage, and megacorps avoid bad press like the plague. Why are they still here? Wouldn't they have left hours ago? The conference is big but not that important. They can talk about nothing at meaningless conferences any time they want."

"What are you saying, Cruz?" Run-Time asked.

"They're waiting for something," I replied, "and it's not to see the protesters break through the perimeter, police, and swarm in here."

"What then?"

"That's what we're waiting for. They have their own plan."

"A lot of schemes, Mr. Cruz," The Mick said. "Are you sure yours is better?"

"We've already succeeded with ours."

"You got what you needed?" Run-Time asked.

"We did."

"Then shouldn't we evacuate?" The Mick asked.

"We have to wait to see what their plan is."

"Is that wise?" Run-Time asked.

"Probably not, but we're going to do it anyway."

CHAPTER 50

BioTech Thugs

Bad news #1. I couldn't reach Phishy at all. He was supposed to get Fraggy's team on the first plane back to us, but wasn't answering his phone. Fraggy was a mess in his room, convinced that something had happened to them as he couldn't get in touch with any of his team himself. There was nothing I could say, but I did leave a couple sidewalk johnnies with him. Then I changed my mind. I had Quix send two security guards to stay with him. I didn't want anything to happen to him either.

Bad news #2. Prima was under tremendous pressure to connect with Mr. Incom. She was doing everything she could to stall, but the megacorps were relentless. I had to come up with something to help her.

Then there was the other piece of bad news. More heavily armed corporate soldiers showed up. They had turned the ground floor lobby into their staging area, but was it to prevent an attack or launch one? That was the question.

I kept everyone together in our hallway on our penthouse level. Quix gave me access to one of the video feeds of the lobby so we could watch the growing forces in the open lobby on my suite's TV screen. Johnnies sat and stood around it, passing minute-by-minute updates to those in the hallway.

"Mr. Cruz, what's going to happen?" one of them asked.

"We have to sit tight until it all blows over."

"What if the protesters make it to our floor? We're not armed."

"We don't need to be. We have our own armed security."

"I've never been to any kind of conference like this, Mr. Cruz."

"Neither have I."

Run-Time and his people had returned to his own floor because, according to The Mick, various corporate soldiers had "mistakenly" exited the elevators there before being turned back.

In my suite, I sat at one of the tables passing the time by trying to think of something to help Prima get out of her predicament. The problem would be once I did, getting down to the main lobby. It had quickly become a place no one wanted to be near if they didn't want to get shot.

"Cruz!" I heard my name from one of the johnnies in the hallway.

I got up from my seat and ran to the hallway. All the sidewalk johnnies in the suite followed me into the hallway. It was the same female security person who had challenged me before. She was armed and so were the dozen corporate soldiers following her.

"Hold on," I said as I walked to them and stopped to block her advance. "You're on the wrong floor."

"We're here to conduct a search of all the suites."

"No need. Already done and my people have been on 'round the clock watch since day one of the conference. Please leave this floor immediately."

"No!" she yelled, then smiled. She was saying: "What are you going to do to stop me" with her eyes.

I looked at her fellow corporate soldiers and knew they wanted nothing more than to bait me into a fight. Kicking one of them in the head wasn't an option here.

"You're not very bright are you. I have a lot of friends in this city. My city, not yours. I'd be very careful what you do next. I'd hate to have the Metro PD throw you and your buddies here in the same box then haul you down to a prison cell."

She kicked me! But I was ready for her and blocked it with both my forearms.

"Ah, you have some martial arts training," she said.

"Don't do that again."

"Or what? You're not armed. You only have two armed guards with you. They're no match for us. If I do that again, what will you do?"

"Do you think you're the first bully I've come across?"

"I don't—"

I blasted her in the center of her chest with my pop gun. I dove to the ground as did every sidewalk johnny. Quix's men opened fire on the corporate soldiers who were doing the same. Then there was a loud explosion.

My ears were ringing something fierce. Quix's men were on their backs, but so were all the corporate soldiers. Quix came around the corner with dozens and dozens of security guards with much bigger guns. I'd never seen Quix mad before. He reached down, grabbed the woman, and threw her down the hall—like ten feet with the one throw. He marched to her as she got to her feet. She yelled and kicked his head with incredible force. I heard the crack and winced. Quix was a cyborg and that side of his head was all steel. She screamed in pain even before he snatched and broke her leg with one bionic pummel, then she screamed even louder. He dragged her down the hallway and around the corner. All we heard was screaming then her voice got softer and softer.

When he returned, the other corporate soldiers were on their feet but Quix's men had the barrels of their weapons pointed at their faces and heads.

"Eject all of them immediately," Quix directed his men.

"We are authorized corporate security and you can't—"

Quick punched the man so hard in the chest that he coughed up blood. The man staggered back a few steps and fell over.

"Shut up," Quix said, then nodded to his men.

They escorted all the corporate soldiers from our floor at gunpoint.

"Get the woman too. She's lying on the ground floor. Lucky for her, most of her body is already cyborg, so she won't mind getting a new one."

CHAPTER 51

Afraid of WHO

To say we were relieved to have Quix on our side was an understatement. I thanked my posthumous mentor, Wilford G. aloud, for introducing me to my new friend Quix. I couldn't have done better than the ex-military merc. However, clearly things had gone out of control.

Quix and his men stationed themselves on our floor, uplifting the spirits of all the johnnies. They were their wise-cracking and chatty selves again. Some of the sidewalk johnnies passed around beverages to everyone.

I'd returned to my suite to continue watching the video feeds on the TV screen. It was now three different feeds of the outside perimeter. The growing crowds looked meaner. In the sky were more than a dozen circling Metro PD gunships.

"Mr. Cruz, can they open fire if they break through the gates," one of the johnnies asked me.

"Non-lethal."

"All those big airships to only fire non-lethal bullets," another johnny said. "They should fire tear gas at them now and disperse them."

"If they do that, then they'll charge," I said.

"We don't want that," he said.

"Anything from Phishy yet?" Sidewalk Sid asked me.

"Not yet."

"I hope he's okay."

"Phishy is always okay. When he does call in, he'll have a perfectly logical excuse," I said.

"Maybe he overslept and has his phone off. He's done it before."

"Maybe. He is Phishy."

Quix stood, back against the wall, watching the screen. He and all his men remained at a high state of readiness. I saw him touch his ear. Someone was saying something in his mic. He looked at me.

"Something's happening downstairs," Quix announced. "The World Health Organization people are there. Looks like they're about to have a press conference."

"This is it Quix," I said as I jumped up from my chair. "They're launching their counter-plan."

"For those of you who do not know me, my name is Peter Foil, the current president of the World Health Organization. People of Metropolis, I speak to you not from overseas but here in your fine city at the Utopia Convention Center in Opus Fields. I speak to you to inform you of a plot to strike at the very heart of your people."

Foil spoke with a deadly serious delivery. Behind him, stood police brass and federal higher-ups. But of particular interest to me were, for the first time, I saw all the WHO past presidents, including Mr. Timely. He was taller than Foil, as thin, but with a shaved head.

Before them were all the conference attendees of government officials, scientists, researchers, the biotech megacorps. Quite impressive for a hastily put together press conference. A line of the media at the front of the facing crowd. I spotted Raven and Mrs. Alonzee at the front. Other women next to them I assumed were more WHO wives and girlfriends.

Quix gave me a look probably thinking the same question Run-Time had asked me: ""What have you gotten me into?"

Foil continued. "The past few days there have been large protests around the convention center. Such protests are common for those of us in our business of public service. Even today, there are those who hate those of us who have dedicated our lives to protect humanity through science and research. That hate is so powerful that these protesters have in fact devised a method to use Nature against us, Metropolis's eco-system, and its people. Earth's natural rain is the medicine it uses to fight diseases that plague our planet. We have learned that these protesters may have unleashed a bio-threat in the rain of such significance possibly only a few hours ago with the intent to kill the attendees of this conference, but also threaten every man, woman, and child in Metropolis."

Gasps rung out in the main lobby area, including from the media.

"As such World Health Org will lead this joint task force with local, city, federal, international, and off-world authorities to bring to justice all these perpetrators, colloquially known as biopunks. People of Metropolis, that is what the World Health Organization was created for. We have never let you down and we will not fail you this time either. No bio-threat, or threat in general, on this planet is greater than the good and resolve of all of our collective efforts."

Foil's revelation was met by the applause from the spectators. The media readied to pounce with questions. However, I couldn't help think that the true audience wasn't them, or Metropolis's residents, but me. I noticed the quick glance at me from Mr. Timely.

Members of the Metro PD's top brass joined Foil at the microphone. I already knew what would be coming. Every last protester was going to be arrested using whatever force necessary. The Metro PD would hunt down every last person associated with the protesters. The word wasn't used yet, but soon it would be. *Bio-terrorists* were on the loose in Metropolis and their plot was to use this Andromeda Rain to kill us all. He revealed a top-secret government bio-program to the public without them knowing it, even using its confidential name. Foil was clever. I had used similar ruses myself in the past—reveal a secret without them knowing you had. The WHO was in charge of this Red Ball—a state of police activity for the highest profile cases—and before long, he'd have everyone they wanted entangled in their net and labeled a bio-terrorist.

But I was ready for them. At that moment, all I could think about was what Dot was thinking, probably watching the TV at Eye Candy, cursing me for getting myself involved in another high-profile, crazy case. I could hear myself saying to her: "But it's not my fault!"

PART EIGHT

BioTerror: What Does a Global Pandemic Have to Do with a Local Street Detective?

CHAPTER 52

WHO's Men

I saw Chief Hub appear from the crowd of onlookers. I had to talk to him, but knew there was no chance. All I could do was stay close to him until I could. Police officers filed into the lobby area to begin to disperse the media and the crowds. All were ordered to return to their hotel suites. I slipped by people headed for the elevators to follow Hub. I saw him approach the WHO President and the men shook hands.

"Chief, how long until your forces move in?"

"They're already moving in. We can watch from the conference security command center."

"Excellent." Foil saw me and smiled. "Will you be joining us, Mr. Cruz?"

"Thanks, Mr. Foil, I will."

With that I turned and walked away. No need for me to wait for them.

The group reconvened in the command post with the video monitor bank. Foil had an expression of satisfaction on his face. Mr. Alonzee was stoned-faced, along with the Victorian-suit wearing Mr. Zeno. Boyish, fez-wearing Mr. Geronimo had a smile and Mr. Euclid was giggling. Mr. Timely came in last and if looks could kill, I'd be deader than dead.

In my last case with Wilford G. there was a criminal named Mr. Candy. He wasn't one person but many different people. They all used the same name but were different. They probably acted differently, thought differently, planned differently. In this case, the criminal was actually a criminal board of directors. One was the chairman, but they all could act and did. Their style and tactics were different, but all was done in the service of their cabal.

However, I put them out of my mind for now. My focus was the same as theirs—the security cameras. Metro PD had launched their attack. To the eye it looked like giant balls of solid smoke descending to the ground and exploding. Protesters had pushed through the gates to charge towards the police perimeter and the convention center beyond. Where the giant balls landed people stopped moving, falling to the ground, covered in white film, coughing and blinded by the tear-gas like chemicals. But many of the protesters had their own gas masks and police and gunships fired on them from above. None of them would get through but wave after wave of the protesters kept coming.

"Chief, I am sorry, but we will need to quarantine everyone outside, including your men," Foil said.

"Has the decision already been made to quarantine the area?" Hub asked.

"We believe it appropriate to quarantine the district."

"Quarantine Opus Fields? On what grounds? Do you know something we don't?"

"If the question you're asking, Chief, is do we have an actual case of bio-terrorism? Then we do. Six cases."

Hub looked at him. "Six cases? When?"

"Within the hour," Mr. Timely answered. "They were believed to have the cold, but it's much worse, and is contagious. All six of them were protesters."

"Chief, our containment teams are already standing by," Foil added. "It's fortunate that this conference was here and all of our WHO's resources were already on the ground."

Chief looked at me for a brief moment. I noticed that more than one of the WHO presidents noticed his reaction.

Foil gestured to Quix, standing quietly to the side. "Sir, you are the chief of convention security?"

"I am."

"Until the crisis is over you will report to WHO security." He pointed to Raven. "This is Ms. Raven. She is the head of WHO security and is firmly versed in all WHO field containment procedures. Hopefully, this will not be a problem."

"None at all."

"I understand there was an incident on the penthouse level," Mr. Alonzee said.

"Incident?" Quix asked. "No incident I'm aware of."

"I believe someone was thrown off a balcony."

Quix stepped forward with his pecs moving on their own. "She slipped. I take security of any facility I'm in charge of extremely seriously. I tell you to do something, you do it. You attack or attempt to assault any of my security personnel, you might get hurt."

"Mr. Quix, no one doubts your professionalism," Foil said. "In fact, I insist that you remain on duty until the crisis is over. Though we may question the convention center's director on some of its recent hires, there's no issue when it comes to the ability of you and your men."

"Thank you."

"This elusive Mr. Incom made the perfect hire when it came to you."

"Thank you, sir."

"Ms. Raven please defer to Mr. Quix on matters of building security. WHO will have oversight beyond the center's immediate perimeter."

"Yes, sir," Raven answered.

"We should talk more, Mr. Foil," Chief Hub said. "Quarantine of an entire city like Opus Fields."

"Yes, lots of wealthy people who contribute to the police holiday fund."

"That isn't what I meant and you know it."

"Of course. Forgive my attempt at humor, Chief. Should we leave or should we simply ask Mr. Cruz to go away."

Everyone looked at me.

"I'll go back to my suite," I said. "It's good to finally see you in person, Mr. Timely."

He watched me closely without answering.

They all wanted to say something to me but held their tongues. I went around them for the door.

"Cruz," Chief called out. "We'll be talking a bit later."

"Yes, Chief. It's not like I'm going anywhere."

"That Mr. Cruz is the truest statement yet from you," Foil said. "Step outside the seal of this building and off to quarantine you go."

I left the room.

CHAPTER 53

Bio-Suits

The World Health Organization was a behemoth of bureaucracies. I had always thought the CDC was the powerhouse on the world stage when it came to bio-threat. They took the backseat to the WHO when things became real. The CDC was in the public eye; the WHO stayed in the background despite being the power.

I also learned, even more daunting, there was a WHO Earth and Up-Top had its version—WHO Space Command. Not surprising since Earth and Up-top always wanted their separate everything. But this was WHO Earth's show, and Mr. Foil was the general. My guess was they were going to try to so overwhelm me that I'd curl up in a fetal position, balled up in the corner, and surrender. They didn't know me well. That wasn't going to happen.

Normally, protocol was for CDC to take the lead but they skipped over them and went straight to WHO command. That told me that they knew Fraggy and I were working together and they were not about to allow him to run anything, even temporarily.

The main press conference was over but now were a series of on-the-floor briefings by WHO bio-containment personnel. They told people what to expect in the hours and days ahead as bio-decontamination units arrived. No one in the building was in any danger but we'd see their people in their white bio-suits, but not to be alarmed they emphasized.

A special team would also arrive to clear all attendees from the conference. After that, people would be able to leave. However, it was going to be a slow process. The priority remained the situation outside the walls and perimeter of the center.

"You are far safer inside here than anyone in Metropolis," the bio-threat person said.

Bio-threat, bio-containment, bio-decontamination—Fraggy told me they each meant dramatically different things but all the same to me as a layperson. Scary people in bio-suits were coming for you.

I couldn't leave. I couldn't risk not being able to get back in the convention center if I did. Fraggy was here and I had to keep him close.

I'd seen people in bio-suits before. I had seen them first when I was a child. The sight of them gave me nightmares for days. They were faceless forms coming to take you away. The ones gathering at one end of the main lobby weren't all that scary looking, but they did make me uneasy.

My instincts told me the WHO cabal was closing in on me. Phishy was still M.I.A., Raven was going to be Quix's second shadow, so two of my resources weren't available. There were so many ways for them to jam me up.

I headed to the hotel suite elevators when I remembered and ran back to main check-in desk. The two guards at the counter looked up.

"Where's Prima?" I asked.

"Sorry, she's been trying to reach you. We completely forgot with all this chaos."

CHAPTER 54

Prima Donna

They buzzed me back in and the door to the security command center was closed. The WHO presidents, Chief, and Raven couldn't see me. I ran down the hall to one of the conference rooms. I opened the door and the room was filled with the same megacorp executives, only they were sitting around, smoking.

"Sorry," I said and closed the door.

I ran to Prima's office. The door was locked. I tapped on it. "Prima, it's me."

The door flung open and she grabbed me. She slammed the door and locked it.

"Cruz," she whispered, but she was really yelling. "What have you gotten me into?"

"Lots of people are asking that these days."

"Why do you think that is? I'm trapped in this place, not allowed to leave. If I do, they tell me I'll be put in quarantine for six months to a year. In the room down the hall, I have some very seriously dangerous people threatening to put me in jail unless I produce the convention center's director. How do you suppose we'll manage that?"

"Prima, listen to me. Take a deep breath. Listen."

"You won't be the one going to jail. This entire ruse of yours is collapsing. It's failed so totally—"

"It hasn't actually," I said. "They're doing this to scare us."

"Cruz, it's working. These people could ruin me. A life's worth of work could be gone in an instant."

"Prima, I'm the fall guy."

"What?"

"If it gets that far, I'm taking the fall for it all. Not you or Fraggy, me. You have nothing to worry about. Let's walk back into the room and I'll do the talking."

"Prima, I'm not going to let you down. You came through for me. I'll come through for you."

Prima calmed down a bit.

"Do you even know what this case is yet? What's this case about?"

"It's about two murders, a case of bio-piracy—stealing a man's arm to get access to a building over three thousand miles away, framing a gang for bio-terrorism, leaving evidence that a new bio-terrorist cell is looking to strike Metropolis, and more."

"My God. More? How do you get involved in these cases? Ever heard of the phrase 'out of my depth.'"

"Oh course, Prima. But this isn't out of my depth."

"It isn't. I don't ever remember G. hunting down bio-terrorists and he was a detective for over 70 years."

"I'm not hunting bio-terrorists. I'm hunting crooks. That's what we detectives do. Bio-terrorism, or their ruse of bio-terrorism, is the cover."

"Cover for what?"

"That's what Phishy is going to tell us."

"Phishy? Our life and reputation hang in the balance based on your friend, Phishy? The one with the fishes on his shirt?" Prima closed her eyes and held her temple with her fingers. "I'm ruined. I'm ruined and I'm going to jail."

I opened the door with the executives and Prima followed me in. The executives put out their cigarettes and stood to face us.

"Have you reached Mr. Incom?" the man asked.

"Not by phone but by message. He will not be available until tomorrow. WHO will be quarantining all of Opus Fields."

The executive looked at each other.

"Why?" the woman asked me.

"There has been an outbreak outside among the protesters. At least three members have a contagious, unidentified disease."

"Disease?" another asked.

"Yes. A designer one. Created in a lab. WHO believes it was part of a broader plot to kill attendees of the event, possibly everyone in the convention center."

Most of the executives gasped.

"With all due respect, speaking with Mr. Incom can't be the priority," I said. "This situation has to be stabilized. Police are still in a gun battle with attacking protesters outside the center's walls."

The senior woman stood from her chair. "I've read your profile, Mr. Cruz. You are given to gross exaggerations to shock people and throw them off balance."

"Ma'am, all the WHO presidents and the Chief of Police are right down the hall from us. Outside in the main lobby WHO personnel, fitted in bio-containment suits, are gathered. WHO has also taken over the security of the center. Exaggeration? I don't think so. Rather than sit here smoking and wasting our time, you should return to your suites. That is the directive of Mr. Foil, the WHO President, and Chief of Metropolis Police Hub. Are there any questions?"

"No," the woman answered.

I turned with Prima following.

"Mr. Cruz," The senior man called out and we stopped. "You've bought yourself another day, but one way or another we will be speaking with your boss by vid-phone. One way or another. You have your one day."

"Assuming we all don't die from some bio-engineered disease. You all have a nice sleep tonight. Do call the main desk immediately if you have any unusual secretions from the body or start coughing up chunks of flesh or bone."

We left the room. Prima was trying hard not to laugh.

"I think I was grossly exaggerating again," I said.

She patted me on the back as she walked to her office and I headed out to the elevators.

CHAPTER 55

Fraggy

Again, I was taking no chances. Prima Donna was going to remain with Run-Time's people until this was all over. I didn't want her by herself in her office. When that was done, I decided I'd have dinner with Fraggy and take his mind off all his worrying. Quix had to recall his two security men.

It was night and we sat at the suite's dining table eating takeout Chinese food.

"I don't know about this plan that you said I came up with," Fraggy managed to say with all his grief.

"Fraggy, this is what detective work is about."

"You can keep it. I'll stay in my office and in my lab. I'm never doing this again."

"Sometimes things get tough, but that doesn't mean quit."

"For me, it does."

"Your people are fine."

"You don't know that. Have you heard from Phishy?"

"No, but that doesn't mean anything bad yet."

"Doesn't mean anything good."

"Let's keep calm."

"We're running out of time. How are we going to get out of here?"

"Fraggy, if you don't calm your nerves you'll have a heart attack. Let's watch a movie. Something with action and comedy to take your mind off things."

"This whole thing is a disaster."

"No, it's not."

"You said they know."

"I said they know we're up to something. They know about me, not you."

"How long do you think that'll last? I don't want to lose another body part."

I stood from the table. "Fraggy. Movie."

"How can you be so calm about this? There could be a plague right outside our walls."

"There is no plague."

He followed me into the living room as I scrolled past a list of movies on the TV control pad. "How do you know?"

"It's a ruse too. They panicked and they wanted to keep us here until they could figure out what to do."

"You come to these conclusions so easily. If that's true, the scope of it all. Protesters. Get the police involved. Shooting tear gas and bullets. That's a big ruse."

"Why is that strange to you? Isn't that exactly what we've done. A ruse on a massive scale. We've done it. They've done it."

"But we're the ones trapped in theirs."

"Fraggy, they are trapped in ours. They just don't know it yet."

"What? Trapped in ours?"

"Fraggy, we have to buy a bit more time."

"We don't have time."

"We need your team to figure this out."

"You figure it out. You're the detective."

"Not this time, Fraggy. I'm not a scientist. Your team will solve this case. Only them."

"We're relying on a group of recent college grads."

"Fraggy, it's your team. You said they were the best. I'm trusting your judgment. Having doubts now?"

"Where are they? I want to know that they're okay. Are they rotting in a jail overseas? Were they shot escaping the headquarters there? Did their plane crash?"

"Planes don't crash anymore, Fraggy. We have hovertechnology."

"You know what I mean. Something happened!"

"Yes, Fraggy. But they'll make it. We just need them to make it soon. We may only have tomorrow."

"Then what?"

"The conference will close early and everyone flies away. If we can solve this before then, we have everyone here trapped in one spot."

"You know what I'd do if I were them?"

"What?"

"Say we're the bio-terrorists."

"I thought of that too."
"You have?"
"Yes."
"Next time I have a great idea, please ignore me."
"How about a zombie movie, Fraggy?" I asked.

CHAPTER 56

Quix

I had called home every night to speak to my wife and Cruz Jr. It was a good thing I did because all communication was out and I wasn't particularly pleased with WHO upsetting my routine. However, Fraggy was having a good time watching his movie with a bucket of popcorn. At least someone was happy this quarantined night.

Knock! Knock!

I didn't like that sound, especially after watching a zombie movie, albeit comedic. Fraggy looked like he wanted to hide under his bed. I pulled my weapon from my jacket. Quix's men had retrieved all my weapons from the secret place Phishy had stored them in. I aimed my omega-gun at the door.

"Cruz, it's me so please don't shoot me through the door." It was Quix's voice.

I unlocked it and ran back around the corner for cover.

"Open!"

Quix came in and closed the door, locking it with the flick of his finger.

"Look at the two of you. Popcorn and movies."

"He's eating popcorn," I said. "I was trying to call my family."

"No outbound or inbound calls," Quix said.

"Have a seat. I'm sure Fraggy won't mind sharing his popcorn." I sat down at the table and Quix joined me. "Do you want him to listen?" I asked.

"I don't mind."

"Fraggy, pay him with popcorn. Get another container from the kitchen."

Fraggy moved to the kitchen which would give us some time to chat.

"How's your new boss?" I asked.

"You mean my babysitter. She's okay when she's not around, which is most of the time."

"What's the latest?"

"Cruz, I came to tell you that they mopped up every last protester out there."

"When?"

"Hours ago."

"That's faster than I thought."

"They aren't happy at all. They were looking for your friends."

"Bia."

He nodded. "They were looking for her and her people. Lucky for them you told them to leave when you did."

"They want to pin it on them."

"Wherever they're hiding better be good because the police will rip their turf apart to find them, and the WHO bio-suits are with them."

"Bia is too smart to hide anywhere near where they normally hang out."

"If they do, if they are, they'll be found. No doubts about it."

"They'll have lookouts on the street regardless. They'll know if anyone's close to where they're hiding."

"The other thing you should know is that the word is that arrests are imminent."

"Arrests? Bia?"

Quix shook his head. "Here."

"Here?"

"Here?" Fraggy stood next to us with a bowl of popcorn. "You mean us?"

"I don't know."

"It can't be us, Quix. There's nothing to arrest us on."

"Cruz, I'm telling you what I know. Arrests tomorrow. Don't know who or when yet. But you should prepare yourself."

"I can't go to jail," Fraggy said, almost hyperventilating.

"Fraggy, you're not going to jail. I seem to be having this same conversation over and over."

"With me? You never said that?"

"Not you, Fraggy." I turned my attention back to Quix. "If I needed to hide Fraggy somewhere, where would you suggest."

"You know as well as I do. All you could do is hide him on one of the floors with one of the megacorps. They know you're friends with Run-Time. They'd search your floor first, then his. No one else would hide him for you."

"I thought you said I wouldn't go to jail," Fraggy said.

"You're not going to jail, Fraggy. I may want to stash you somewhere to frustrate them, if they come for you."

"I shouldn't be scared of anything," Fraggy said to himself. "I'm the head of the Metropolis CDC."

"Fraggy, that won't help us."

"This whole thing is a disaster."

"You know something, Quix."

"What's that Cruz?"

"It's a good thing we know this convention center better than they do."

"Don't count on that knowledge going too far. They have scanners that can hear a heartbeat from one hundred yards."

"Fraggy," I said. "I'm going to teach you to slow down your metabolism so that you seem dead," I said, patting him on the shoulder.

"What!"

CHAPTER 57

Don't Make WHO Angry

Early morning, I was already up when I heard commotion in the hallway. There was loud knocking, but I didn't move from my oh-so-comfy sleeping bag on the bed. I heard a click and I knew that the front door was being opened. A corporate soldier came into my room, holding a huge laser rifle. Then Raven appeared, followed by another corporate soldier.

"Why are you in my bedroom? Raven, no means no."

"Mr. Cruz, I'll give you ten minutes to get presentable and meet us outside in the hallway. If not, we can drag you out to the elevator now."

"Ten minutes."

"We'll see you in a few."

The trio walked back out and I heard the door click.

The last thing I did when I stepped out into the hall was put on my tan fedora. All the sidewalk johnnies were lined up along the wall. Corporate thugs with laser rifles were in front of them, every other man. Raven stood there with her arms folded.

"Search the room," she said and a dozen armed thugs marched into my suite.

"Why are you invading my privacy?" I asked angrily.

"We'll go downstairs for a chat," she said and led me to the elevators. I followed with two of her men behind me.

I said nothing to them and vice-versa for the entire ride down.

We exited and I saw that half the open lobby had been turned into some kind of bio-containment processing area. We were buzzed in at the main check-in counter and back to the security command center. People were packed in tight, but Mr. Foil was who I was looking for. He was there with a self-satisfied grin.

What I was not happy to see was Prima with an armed guard on either side of her. Standing next to her were those same biotech megacorp executives. The man did say we only had a day. Quix sat on a chair surrounded by five armed guards. None of the other past WHO presidents were in the room, but there were plenty of police and Fed brass standing with Foil.

We were waiting for something. Raven's phone rang. She answered it, listened and hung up. "Not there either."

"Where's Chief Hub?" I asked.

"He's in the field," one of the police lieutenants answered.

"Chief Hub can't help you, Cruz," one of the police captains added.

"Also, your friend Run-Time and his entire staff have been detained too for questioning. They won't be coming to your aide either," Foil said.

"I hope you understand the gravity of this situation, Cruz," the police captain said.

"I do. It's all a very serious matter, according to Mr. Foil."

"Mr. Cruz, where is Mr. Fraggioti?"

"The head of the Metropolis CDC?"

"Do you know of another?" Foil asked.

"Cut the crap, Cruz!" a police captain yelled.

"How would I know?"

"You were in his room last night."

"Fraggy and I are old friends. We were catching up on old zombie movies. In fact, that area out there looks exactly like the bio-containment areas in the movie."

"Do you think this is funny, Cruz?" another police captain asked.

"No, I think you're funny. I think Mr. Foil is funny."

"Mr. Cruz, we're going to find Fraggy, as you call him," Foil said.

"Why? He's the head of the CDC. What do you want with him?"

"Mr. Fraggioti is wanted in connection with this incident," a captain said.

"That's crap, captain, and you know it. You've known Fraggy far longer than me and you let Foil fly in here accusing him of things."

"No one is accusing Mr. Fraggioti of anything, Mr. Cruz. He is wanted for questioning."

"I was sleeping, so how would I know where he is. Maybe he's sleeping in the bio-containment area."

"We will find him and locate your biopunk terrorist friends too. The ones you were seen communicating with on multiple occasions."

"Yeah, I told them to hide from you too. Sounds like you're not having much luck finding them either."

"I'll ask again," Foil said. "Where's Mr. Fraggioti, Mr. Cruz. We know you were in his room last night. We also know Mr. Quix over there visited you both last night."

"Mr. Quix wanted to know which zombie movie we were watching. He's a fan."

"Where is Mr. Fraggioti, Mr. Cruz?"

"I don't know. If you've been watching me, why don't you know?" I said.

"Mr. Cruz, the World Health Organization can detain you indefinitely."

"Not an American, you can't. Unless I'm sick with one of your convenient diseases you have no jurisdiction over me at all. Was that why you sent Raven to my room that night? She was going to stick me with something. Plant some germ in my clothes."

"Mr. Cruz, you do have a wild imagination. Unfortunately, your game has run its course. It ends today."

The captain stepped forward. "Turn around." I complied. "Mr. Cruz, you're being placed under arrest for suspicion of harboring terrorists." He handcuffed me and patted me down. "You won't need this." He took my omega-gun and turned me around to face them. "The phone you can keep so you can call a lawyer, which you'll be needing."

"Mr. Quix, I thought no one was supposed to have weapons in this center," Foil said to him. "Bad form on your part."

"Captain, Foil and his friends don't live in Metropolis. I have friends too, and I'm not going to forget that you put handcuffs on me. Wilford G. Jr. and all five hundred thousand officers in Metro PD will know too. I hope you know what you're doing," I told him.

"Captain, ignore him," Foil said. "The rantings of a little man with no power at all. Ms. Prima Donna is it? I want you to pick up this phone and call your boss Mr. Incom this very moment. The game is over for you too. There are a lot of things that are not adding up here. Your head of security, Mr. Quix, is not a head of security at all but an international street mercenary. You run a salon but are managing this event. Then Mr. Cruz is hired here for unknown reasons. We want to talk to this Mr. Incom. If you do not put him on the phone, we're going to put you in jail for fraud. Governments and megacorporate CEOs don't take kindly to scams. Is Mr. Fraggioti this Mr. Incom? Please call Mr. Incom now for us."

Prima looked at me.

"Mr. Cruz cannot help you. Please dial."

Prima slowly dialed trying to compose herself. My phone began to ring. Everyone looked at me.

"Can you help me answer that?" I asked. "You'll want me to answer the phone."

The captain fished out my mobile from my pocket and held it to me to answer.

I smiled. "Mr. Incom, how may I help you?"

Foil stared at me with such shock and disgust.

"Figured it out yet?" I asked. "The goal wasn't to get you to a fake conference in Metropolis, Mr. Foil. The goal was to get you away from the real World Health Organization Headquarters so that we could do a complete forensic search and audit—floor by floor, computer by computer, lab by lab."

Foil's mouth dropped open.

"You thought you uncovered our scam before we could do what we were going to do, when the fact was, we succeeded the moment you arrived at Metro International. I think you owe me a jelly belly for such duplicity," I said.

Foil clenched his teeth and pushed me to the ground as he ran out of the command center. Raven, all the corporate executives, and the corporate soldiers ran after him. After they emptied the room, the only ones left were Prima, Quix, two of Quix's men, and the three police brass.

"Captain, get these damn handcuffs off of me!" I yelled from the ground. "They're getting away!"

"What the hell is happening here?" a captain yelled.

Quix spent fifteen minutes throwing his cyborg body against the metal door until it was bent out enough for him to punch through it. It had been firmly barricaded from the outside.

When we finally got out of the command center, everyone was gone!

"Stay behind us," Quix commanded and told us all to stay down behind the counter. He joined his two men on duty and one of them handed him a laser rifle. "We need better firepower." One of the men disappeared. He looked at the captains. "Do you all still know how to shoot?"

"Don't be offensive," a captain snapped.

"Making sure. I know some of you go soft once you start wearing fancy dress uniforms and spending all your time behind desks."

His men returned with a bag of heavy guns. Quix grabbed one of the machine guns. The captain grabbed Quix's laser rifle.

"Yes, that's what you need," Quix said to him.

"I was a sniper," the captain revealed.

The other two captains grabbed machine guns too and so did Prima Donna.

"I can shoot," she said. "Don't worry about me."

"How many do you see?" one of the captains said.

"A lot," Quix said, staring out into the dark expanse of the atrium main lobby. He had bionic eyes or in-eye augmented vision contacts. "Their mission must be to keep us pinned down as long as possible."

"Cruz, try your phone," Quix said.

I shook my head. "Comms down again."

"Then we shoot it out," a captain said.

"Shoot it out," Quix said. "No machine gun, Cruz?"

I smiled. "All I need is my omega-gun."

"If you say so."

"In fact, I'll shoot the first round. Let them know we're coming and we're not happy."

I shot an explosive round without looking over the counter, then Quix dove over the counter and began firing. My round exploded and all we heard were yells, as a storm of gun and laser fire came our way.

Desperate people did stupid things. Desperate criminals did stupid and violent things. They weren't just shooting at civilians, but members of the Metro PD. Metro police were deadly enough, but shoot their own and they'd track you to the ends of the galaxy to put you in a body bag. Why were they so desperate? What did they want to keep us from finding out? What did a jovial cat burglar and a street detective, me, stumble upon that would make senior members of the largest health organization on the planet explicitly instruct their army of corporate soldiers to kill us?

For the next hour, Quix and his two men did most of the damage, using their intimate knowledge of the building, to gun down most of the soldiers. The captain who said he was a sniper on the force proved his worth by taking out all the soldiers who tried to shoot down at us from above. Prima, the other two captains, and me did our part taking out whoever was left. It was slow and brutal, but we did it.

However, Quix told us to stay put and we heard sporadic fire until we heard commotion from the hovertransport area. Metro PD stormed the lobby with hundreds of officers, and we knew proper protocol. We lay on the ground, face first, unarmed, with hands out. Chief Hub came in with his men.

"Chief," I greeted.

"Cruz," he acknowledged. Hub looked at the captains. "What's going on here?"

The three captains looked at me. "Maybe it's better if he tells you because I'm not entirely sure," a captain said.

"Chief, you need to find the WHO presidents."

"Why? Do you have your evidence?"

"I need a bit more time, Chief. I'm waiting for my people."

"Your people? Is that all?" Chief gestured to officers with a waving signal.

Officers escorted Quix and his two men back in.

"Quix," I said. "You better let Fraggy out before he suffocates."

"Where was he?" a captain asked.

"Storage closets on the penthouse level that aren't on the building plans and the secret passageways to get to them. Phishy called them our 'secret stash.'"

"He's with me," Hub revealed.

"Where?" I asked.

"Outside," Hub said matter-of-factly.

"What?"

Hub waved and then I saw them. PJ strolled in with a smiling Phishy! And a bunch of college-aged looking kids came in with them. The Cavalry had arrived to save the day—and tell me, finally, what the case was really about.

PART NINE

The Part Where Those Scary Guys in Bio-Suits Break Through Your Front Door

CHAPTER 58

Phishy

I was never so happy to see Phishy. He looked fine—no bruises, cuts, laser welts, or bullet holes. He stretched out his hands like an arriving movie star.

"I told you I could do it, Cruz!"

"Yeah, you did Phishy," I said as I shook his hand.

"You deserve a proper greeting."

Of course, it was coming and there was no stopping it. Phishy spun around doing his chicken dance. That was how he greeted me, with some dance jig. I waited until he had sufficiently amused and tired himself out. But instead of yelling at him to get serious, I welcomed the display.

The Chief and the police looked at me, then back at Phishy. When he was done some of the officers applauded. Phishy took multiple bows.

"Boss, don't expect any dancing from me," PJ said.

"You have people dance for you?" Chief asked me.

"That's just Phishy," I answered.

"You're a bit crazy aren't you, Cruz, and you hang around crazy people," Hub said.

"Phishy, who are they?" I asked. "Please tell me they are who I want them to be."

"You know who they are, Cruz. They're Fraggy's team! I brought them back all safe and sound." He said beaming with pride.

There were almost two dozen of them, probably not one of them over thirty-five. Most of them looked a bit rattled, as if there were some ordeal they had all survived.

"PJ?"

"Yes?"

"Chief, is the entire center closed? Can we use one of the upper suites to have a place for our guests to relax, freshen up, and get something to eat?"

"Use the penthouse level. We've already cleared that level, but I do have officers stationed at all the elevators."

"Thanks. PJ, you're in charge of our young guests. No strangers anywhere near them."

"Got it. I'll punch any suspicious people through the wall so they splat on the ground below when they fall multiple stories." She caught herself and looked at the chief and the police. She smiled. "Just joking."

"It better be just joking," the Chief said. "You're an ex-felon cyborg. Your arms are considered lethal weapons. Haven't you been cited for punching people before?"

"Oh, that's a long time ago," she replied. "I don't punch people anymore."

"Chief, she's not going to doing anything illegal in a convention center full of police. PJ, take charge."

"Follow me," she said to the kids and they followed closely behind her.

"I'll have Fraggy sent up too," I said to them. "He's here too."

That bit of news lightened their spirits. I could hear them talking to each other as PJ led them to the elevators.

"Are those the kids who are going to save us?" Prima asked.

"That's them."

"Then let's get on with it," the Chief said.

"We have to wait for Fraggy," I said. They both gave me the evil eye. "We have the records so we have everything, including the evidence."

"Cruz! What's this about?" the Chief shouted.

"Are you telling me that you still don't know? You must have an idea," Prima said.

"Chief, at the very least you have attempted murder of law enforcement and civilians."

The three captains nodded.

"How so, Cruz?" he said. "All the gunmen are dead and on their way to the morgue. Do you have some recording linking their actions with the WHO execs because we have no witnesses? I know them. They'll have their lawyers concoct some credible story why they ran off and will completely deny they directed any of the gunmen to kill anyone. They'll deny they even know who they are. Probably claim the gunmen work for the convention. We have no evidence to the contrary. Nothing to arrest them on, let alone convict them on. Is this your great plan you had me sign onto?"

"No, chief. The key is those kids. The WHO execs ran out of here because they realized we had full access to their headquarters. They're afraid of what we might find. It's big."

"Cruz, it better be. A big crime that we can get big convictions."

Prima signed. "Cruz, we've all gone out on a big limb for you. I agree with you that something's rotten here. They ran out of here like frightened criminals, no doubt in my mind; I've seen it before. No need to convince me there, but without proof, they'll walk and can still legally come after me, you, and the entire Metro PD."

I pointed at the elevator. "The key is those kids."

"Then get them relaxed and fed fast so they can tell us what this is all about," the Chief said. "But I know you, Cruz. I saw you ask those questions at the conference. You have an idea."

"Of course, I do. I may even know, but like Prima said: proof. We need the proof." I looked at Phishy who was uncharacteristically quiet and calm, listening to us. "Okay Phishy, you're on. I want to know what the heck happened over there."

Just as I had to let Phishy do his chicken dance, I had to let him spend however long he did, greeting all the sidewalk johnnies with his high and low fives, handshakes and fist bumps. I didn't watch this time because I would have gotten mad. I was as impatient as Prima and the police to know all there was to know.

PJ had Fraggy's team in one suite, the one across the hall from where mine was. I met Phishy in my suite. Sidewalk johnnies were buzzing around, but I had Phishy finally seated at the dinner table, stuffing his face with food, as I debriefed him. Of course, there were johnnies sitting at the table, standing around, everywhere listening and eating too.

Phishy's mission was to fly overseas to Europe and once Fraggy's team were able to sneak into the WHO international headquarters to review and record files, get them out of there on a plane for Metropolis as fast as possible.

"Everything was going good, Cruz," Phishy said. "They copied all the files first, which we thought was going to be the hard part, but it was easy. Then they acted like they were working like normal to review the records from the terminals. The guards never bothered them. They were working.

"Then one day, I always hung out in a hovervan in the street outside with my new buddies. Did you know they got johnnies over there too?"

"Phishy, focus. You were on stakeout outside the WHO headquarters. What happened that one day?" I asked.

"Oh, yeah. An army of hovercars show up and all these guys stormed in. Like way over a dozen, maybe a dozen or less, I think, maybe a few guys."

"Phishy!" I said. "Forget how many of them for now. What happened?"

"I didn't like it so I called the team and said don't take any chances. Get out. I told them to take the stairs, but these guys took the stairs too. Then I lost contact with them. Cruz, I panicked. I didn't know what to do, but I remained calm."

"What did you do, Phishy?" one of the johnnies asked.

"I waited. The team was hiding together in a lab. It took a few hours but those guys left the building and got back in their hovercars and flew away. That's when the team came out. They got in the hovervan and we flew away too."

"Why didn't you call in?" I asked.

"That was their idea. They took my phone and theirs and we tossed them into a river. They said we couldn't take any chances that we weren't being monitored."

"Then what? Why were you late?" I asked.

"Well..."

"Phishy?"

"We overslept and missed the plane."

The johnnies laughed. "Phishy, we thought something bad had happened to you and you tell me you overslept?"

"That's all it was. We made it. But then we couldn't get into the convention center. The team said we couldn't use any phones, so we had to wait until our opportunity came for us to get in. But it seemed to be getting worse and worse. But the cops cleared them all away, and here we are."

The johnnies clapped.

"Yes, Phishy. Here you are."

"I did it."

"You did it. You completed your mission. Now we can find out what bad things the bad guys were doing," I said.

CHAPTER 59

Fraggy's Team

I peered out of the convention center's observation level again with my binoculars. It was like the massive half-dome was sitting in an ocean of milk. Hover-robots had saturated every inch of the grounds with the chemical, spraying lane by lane. Now sweeper hover-robots were scrubbing the hell out of every surface from outermost perimeter to the center. The robots had started their bio-decontamination on the dome of the convention center first. In the distance, I could see an army of them waiting—people in bio-suits.

"As long as you stay away from me," I said to myself. There was something ominous about them even from a distance of miles away.

I'd heard that everyone detained by the police was taken to a new processing center set up in Wharf City, which made me laugh. That was a seedy district frequented by low-level crooks. But I guess it made sense since there were lots of large warehouses for Bio-Con to use. It would be a process-first, then imprison human assembly line. Even though WHO had disappeared, Metro PD would still have to follow-through with detaining, identifying, and questioning every last protester to make sure there were no bio-threats. That would take months, likely many to process nearly one million people. So Wharf City was going to have a crime rate less than the well-to-do Silicon Dunes or Silver City where only robots lived for quite some time.

In the air Metro PD police cruisers maintained an open airspace, which was a welcome sight. The main threat were crazy reporters trying to swoop in for close-ups or even to "combat drop" one of their street reporters past the perimeter to try to run into the convention center. It was to be expected with a near-total media blackout. One moment they were reporting that there was a possible outbreak of some unknown disease among the protesters around the center, right in the heart of Metropolis. Now WHO itself had disappeared and no one was talking. I didn't blame them for being so aggressive in trying to get answers. But the airspace had to remain clear. The Metro PD gun-ships were long gone and that meant the situation was calming down, not escalating.

I did wonder about Bia and her people. My guess was that WHO was going to pin the "outbreak" on them, and through that get me thrown into decon too. Off the grid for six months? I didn't even want to think about it, and there would be nothing I could do to speed things up. Bia knew how to take care of herself and so did her people. I was confident no one would find them until they wanted to be found.

My survey of the outer area was done. I put my binoculars back in my jacket and headed to the elevators to get back down to the penthouse level suites. Fraggy's team had enough time to relax and eat. It was time to work.

Fraggy had seen them earlier but was called back into action by Metro PD. He was, after all, still the head of Metro CDC. There were sixteen of the kids. Phishy might have been outside WHO headquarters in the comfort of his hovervan with his new European sidewalk johnny friends. The kids had to do all the work, then play hide-and-seek with security before escaping. I'm glad they simply stayed put and let the security come and go rather than attracting any attention by running or breaking out of the building. No one knew they were there until they were long gone. Their calm under pressure ensured our scam hadn't unraveled before we'd even begun.

The team didn't bring suitcases of clothes back from Europe; they had suitcases of data. My suite was being transformed into a busy computer room with one of the kids seated with three or more screens in front of them, some wearing headphones playing music, as they sifted through file after file.

"Listen up everyone," I said as I walked to the center of the suite.

They all stopped what they were doing to listen to me.

"As much as I'd like to let all of you alone to do your thing, we're on the clock. I wish we had unlimited time but we don't. Fraggy—" they started to laugh. "Am I the only one who calls Fraggy, Fraggy?"

They shook their heads "no."

"Okay then. He told you his suspicions. We know there's a cover-up. In my experience, sometimes I'ts best to start with a theory as to what happened. It may be completely wrong but it's a place to start. You can still go through everything at the same time, but being able to prove or disprove a theory can move things along much quicker."

"We're building a case," one of them said.

"Exactly. We have to be able to say what they did, how they did it, when they did, and if possible, why, which is most often common greed or any of the other deadly vices. Do any of you have any theories?"

Blank stares. Youth today didn't seem to have much in the way of imagination.

"Do you have a theory?" one asked.

"Yeah, the Rain," I replied.

"Andromeda Rain?"

They all looked at each other.

"None of you have any theories. What's wrong with mine?"

"Well, sir, I don't see how or why. The Rain is used to inoculate the environment and the public from infectious disease—epidemics, pandemics—to supplement local, state, and country-wide disease control measures."

"Also, not only people, sir, but animals and food supplies."

"There's nothing for anyone to commit a crime over, sir."

"Well, I'm glad none of you can think like a criminal, which means you're all good kids. But I have to be able to think like criminals, as a detective to catch them. Money."

"Money, power, and sex, sir." The kids laughed.

"The heart of most crime," I said. "Since I doubt WHO was involved in a prostitution ring, let's look at the money and power angle then. WHO has a lot of power all over the world, so let's scratch that one, too. Why are you all avoiding the obvious? It's the number one overwhelming driver for most crime."

"WHO is a not-for-profit, non-governmental agency, sir."

"So? There were plenty of megacorps here at their conference."

"You mean your conference, sir. How did you and Mr. Fraggioti get them to sponsor and participate in the conference?"

They saw me grin. "We're just cool. No, we put together all the right people to make it so they wouldn't say anything but 'yes.' But back to the megacorps—"

"Are you suggesting that the biotech and pharma megacorps are the ones pulling the strings?"

"Now we're getting somewhere. Do you believe it's plausible?"

"I do, sir. Every one of the past WHO presidents does work for the biggest one of them in the world."

"Biome."

"Yes, sir."

"But what could be the crime? I see no crime possible," another team member said with skepticism.

"Sir, what if the diseases that the Rain was tasked to eradicate were in fact created and released into the environment."

"Now we're really getting somewhere," I said.

"That's not a crime," one of the other kids jumped in. "That's unspeakable evil. No scientist would do that. We're talking about the World Health Organization. How would they get money from that?"

"Disease created. Cure created. Released. Disease cured. No one dies. Epidemic averted," another kid said.

"But where does money come in?" another asked.

"Ladies and gentlemen, not-for-profit doesn't mean no money. Don't the governments around the world pay for the Rain?"

"Oh, my goodness. He's right." One of the kids stood up. "We're talking tens, maybe hundreds of billions of dollars paid out from governments all over the world."

"And much of the research and development is contracted out to megacorps globally."

"They could be using entire populations of people as one big clinical trial."

"Ladies and gentlemen, you have the theory. Now go find us the proof so we can start sending people to jail. Because if it's not them, it will likely be Fraggy and me. Watching zombie movies in prison with Fraggy is not my idea of fun."

CHAPTER 60

Fraggy

Fraggy returned to the suite late that day, but not alone. While the first part of his team were kids under thirty, the dozen or so scientists he showed up with probably had grandkids over thirty—bald and silver hair all around.

"They have the top secret clearances to fully review all Rain protocols." That's what Fraggy told me and I actually knew what he meant.

The new joke on the floor was how many scientists can you fit in Cruz's hotel suite. They were all in there working. More monitors and extra vid-phones were brought in. The bedroom was now a vid-conference (no jokes please) and was already in use as they consulted with other lab scientists and field researchers from around the world.

"How's it looking?" I asked Fraggy.

He stood in the hallway for a quick break. In fact, the hallway was the designated break area. He was nibbling on a candy bar.

"I had always felt there was something not quite right with the payments, or even that the costs of things were being grossly overinflated. But if even one of your theories is correct...it boggles the mind at the scope. What it also means, even more disturbing, is this has been going on for a very long time. The Rain isn't new. The Rain was here before Metropolis was here."

"Corruption through the ages then."

"Criminality on a grand scale through the ages. I know some of the WHO presidents. None of them struck me as reckless and contemptuous of the mission. Our mission is to protect people, the cities, the planet, all its wildlife. This is such a betrayal of that mission. For money? They're all well-paid. Most of them are from wealthy families. They already came from money."

"Maybe the megacorps offered far more."

"It's depressing. You lose hope in humanity."

"Don't lose hope, Fraggy. We need you."

"I think we found out why they wanted my arm too."

"Why?"

"Apparently, I've been quite busy deleting financial records at the WHO headquarters. Somewhat difficult since I've never been to WHO headquarters."

"They were sending you a message."

"Yes. How nice of them."

"Seems to be a pattern. Revenge. Get back at anyone who threatens."

"Not a very uplifting thought. They're still out there. Have you heard from the police?"

"No," I replied. "All the police can say is that they are still in Metropolis but as to where, no one has a clue."

Fraggy had a pained look on his face. "I want all this to be over."

"Fraggy, we need that proof."

"Sounds to me that even if we find the proof, it won't be over."

"Don't you worry about that. Get me the proof for the Chief and I'll take it from there," I said.

The situation had taken a turn for the worst, but I wasn't about to tell Fraggy about it. WHO Earth was no longer running the bio-decon operation. It was now WHO Space Command in charge. Spacemen were running around Metropolis in bio-suits. I hated it! But there was nothing me, Metro PD, nor Metro government could do about it because a bio-threat alert had to be called. Chief Hub told me that it was no longer six people infected with the unknown disease with flu-like symptoms. More than a hundred were infected.

I didn't say it to Hub but all these new cases were curiously in the very districts of the bio-punk communities. I didn't care about the biopunk gangs because at least the good people they terrorized could live in peace for a while, but not all biopunkers were gang members. I felt it was another ruse to flush out Bia and her people. But then I started asking myself why? Why would it matter at this point? They could set-up anyone at this point.

I returned to the convention center's observation level to again look out with my binoculars. No longer was the massive half-dome sitting in an ocean of milk. It looked like someone painted the ground all around us yellow. So instead of being yellow-tagged we were being yellow-zoned. I didn't like it. I had thought the crisis was winding down, but that didn't seem to be the case anymore.

In the distance, the army of waiting bio-suits was growing. None of this was any good. I had managed to send Phishy and PJ away before WHO Space Command took control from WHO Earth. All the sidewalk johnnies who had been there with me from the beginning, I also sent away. I had put them through enough stress to last for an entire year. They needed to get back to their lives, but that meant we had no sentries anymore. Quix and his men had security duties on the ground floor to occupy their time. I was really the only armed security for Fraggy and his entire team, so I wasn't leaving the convention center anytime soon.

Prima also got out of there before the lock-down orders from WHO Space Command. At least my wife would be able to get the real news from her boss, Prima. The new lock-down also meant no comms.

I'd set an elaborate trap to snare the bad guys and it had worked, but now it seemed that the bad guys were gone and I was stuck in my own trap and couldn't get out. Fraggy had half-joked before that it was like we'd never get out of this convention center. It started to really feel that way. I stepped back from the window as hover-robots in the sky were now painting the ivory outer wall layer of the center's dome the same yellow color. I felt as if we were being buried alive.

When I came out of the elevator I heard shouting from around the corner. It sounded like it came from my hotel suite. I reached for my weapon. We didn't have armed security in the hallway anymore, but Quix did send one of his security guys to the room to connect the hallway hidden camera feeds to the main TV screen in the living room. We could see anyone who came off the elevator and who was in the hallway outside the door. It was better than nothing.

The door opened without me having to knock. There was an all-out argument with the scientists. Fraggy, however, was smiling.

"What's going on?" I asked.

"It's not conclusive," one of the bald scientists said.

Other scientists argued with him. Again, they were using terms, phrases, and words I never heard before.

"There's no other explanation," one scientist said.

"What do we have Fraggy?" I asked.

"I can answer," one of the senior scientists began. "We have proof that in more than one occasion the bio-contaminant in the field came well after the components were added to Andromeda Rain to eradicate it."

"That is not conclusive," the same bald scientist said.

"It is, sir," a younger scientist said standing up from her screen. "All we have to do is follow expenditures. You don't mass-produce a cure for a disease before it's even identified."

"Are you certain you have that data trial?" he asked her.

"Yes," she answered.

"We all looked at it, sir. All of us came to the same findings," another kid added. "Cures mass-produced and stored months, even years, before the disease that it was supposedly created to destroy. Unless they can time-travel we have our smoking gun."

Fraggy looked at me smiling. "We got it!"

"We have the what and how but not the who," the bald scientist said as others made sounds of annoyance.

"No, this is good," I said. "We need it all. Can you tie this scheme directly to the current or past WHO presidents, or any of the bio-megacorps they're in bed with."

"We can, but it'll take time," one of the junior researchers said. "If only we had more resources."

"Time is what we don't have a lot of," Fraggy said. "But do the best you can."

"Fraggy, gather up all the evidence. We needed the 'what' and that's what your team found. That mission is complete. Time to bring in an agency that has far greater resources than any we'll ever have—Metro PD. If there is a data trail to be found, they'll find any evidence far faster than us. Fraggy, send your team on a vacation."

Now, everyone was smiling. For Fraggy's team, the crime fighting ordeal was over.

None of us could leave the center, but the team could have their own penthouse suites to enjoy. Quix sent up one of his men with plenty of alcohol, so it was now party time for the researchers and scientists. Multiple room TVs were tuned to the same song playlist so the entire floor was shaking with their beats. I even spotted dancing scientists!

Fraggy wanted to talk to me in the hallway privately.

"Thanks for sticking by me with this."

"Of course, Fraggy. We have bad guys to catch."

"I was thinking about what you said about seeking revenge. We had to contact a lot of colleagues to confirm our findings. I'm sure they'll know by now what we have."

"They can't stop it. The police are after them too."

"Yes, but until they're all arrested, maybe even after that, we might still be in danger."

"We knew they were guilty. But what? Your team found that out. The police will do their part. All they need is one to talk and the police are very good at making people talk. They'll wrap them all up in a nice bow for court, then jail."

"I wish I was as confident as you."

"Fraggy, no gloominess. You put together the team. You uncovered their scheme."

"You already knew the plan before the team found it."

"I can think 'criminal.' That's how I catch them."

"You did say they would react violently."

"Is that what you're worried about? This building is surrounded by police. Quix and his men are on security detail. The evidence is in the hands of the police. Chief Hub is fast-tracking it personally."

"But we still can't go home yet."

"I checked in with the police scene commander. WHO Space Command will be clearing us soon. Maybe tomorrow. Then we're home free."

"Okay."

"Celebrate, Fraggy. You deserve it."

I should have been more of Fraggy's frame of mind. Wilford G. repeated it many times before: "Don't act like the case is wrapped up before the case is wrapped up. That's exactly when the bad guy pops out of the shadows to shoot you."

CHAPTER 61

Corporate Soldiers

I sat up in my bed in the dark. As always, due to my recovering germophobic tendencies, I was inside my sleeping bag on top of the bed. I only slept like a normal person in my own bed.

My wife was the only human exempt from my no other life-forms in my bed policy. Cruz Jr. was only allowed on top of the covers. The main benefit of the sleeping bag, however, was that it had all my weapons packed nice and snug with me.

Something had woken me up. It was almost two a.m. The hotel suites were enclosed without any outside windows so when the lights were off it was really dark, except for the green indicator lights of the TV, appliances, and all doorknobs throughout the suite.

The gunfire I heard made me rip the zipper down and jump right out of my sleeping bag. My pop-gun went on my left forearm, I grabbed my omega-gun, and I slipped on my karate slippers. I also grabbed my goggles and put them on. I did all this in the dark and moved to the door.

I wasn't in my original suite anymore but in the penthouse level furthest from the elevator, but closest to the atrium balcony. I crouched down and opened the door. A figure was already cowering there. Fraggy turned on the flashlight in my face.

"Turn that off, Fraggy!"

He did. "I'm sorry I didn't recognize you without your hat."

"You hear gunfire and you turn on a flashlight."

"Sorry, I wasn't thinking. Now I can't see."

"That's what you get." I looked down the hall and could see a lot of his team members in the hallway too, but they at least had the sense not to turn on their flashlights.

"Fraggy, get every one of them into the work suite now."

"But the gunfire?"

"Do you have a gun?"

"No."

"Get everyone in the work suite and barricade yourselves in there."

"What about you?"

"Forget about me, Fraggy. Take charge of your team. Anyone who comes through that door, kill them."

"Kill them?" Fraggy was beside himself.

"You heard me. Go."

"How? Kill them? We don't have guns."

"Fraggy, I don't have time for this. I won't be in the suite with you all. Get in the suite, look around for things to use as weapons. You're scientists. Use the scientific method and improvise. Go!"

Fraggy ran down the hall and I heard him whispering to the others. They all moved to the work suite.

I ran to the balcony but kept close to the wall. I stood slowly and peered over. I can't say what I saw made me feel good. I had seen assault teams with flashlights on assault rifles before. Police had them and so did others. What I saw on the ground were not police.

I bolted down the hallway like a madman. I heard someone cry out as the door of the work suite slammed shut. Hopefully, Fraggy got everyone in there like I told him to. I had to get to the elevator before it was engaged.

Around the corner I came, but it was already too late. The elevator was on its way down.

I heard a noise and looked. Fraggy was watching from a door ajar.

"Fraggy, what did I tell you. Is that how you barricade yourself in?"

"We didn't get everyone."

"Then get them. Have them help you. Someone is on the way up and it's not the police and it's probably not Quix either."

Fraggy and a few others ran out to other suites. At one point it seemed like everyone was in the hallway again.

"Get in that suite now. The elevator is almost here!"

They all ran in and the door slammed shut. I heard what must have been them moving furniture in front of the door. I hoped they realized that neither the door nor the furniture was bullet or laser-proof.

As I stood there waiting, I assumed that the gunfire we heard must have been Quix or one of his men firing in the air to wake us up and warn us. I had to make a decision: was whoever coming up Quix or his men, or was it a hostile force that somehow got through security?

Regardless of the answer, the logical place to be would be where I was standing, which was fine against an amateur but if it were hostiles—corporate soldiers—where I was standing would be the first place they'd fire at. I needed to be elsewhere—fast!

The elevator arrived.

If it were Quix's men, too bad. I couldn't let whoever was on the elevator get out. The elevator could accommodate an assault team of at least twenty. I might be able to hold out against that many, but not likely running around in pajamas, karate slippers, and hat-less. My main concern was Fraggy and his people. They were helpless and if something happened to me, there was no one to defend them.

The second the elevator door began to open I fired multiple rounds inside. Already, I knew it was bad news because there were no lights inside. They had disabled the lights. Quix's men wouldn't do that and the police don't sneak around. But they had had the same idea. Something round was thrown out as soon as the door began to open too.

Luckily, I could run and dive for cover as the stun grenade blew. Unlucky for them, when my explosive stun rounds exploded there was no place to run and hide inside an elevator. I heard grunts and yelling, then nothing.

I stepped in before the door could close and put the elevator on "STOP." It made a loud audible sound. No one else could come up this way to get at us.

I ran to the corner, already aiming my omega-gun, and stepped out into the hallway. Another team of corporate soldiers thought they could sneak up behind me from over the balcony. I cut down the ones closest to me, then machine-gun fired the rest of them. They fired back but I had cover and they didn't.

This was not a game by any means. I had to move quickly. I ran back to the elevator and shot them all even though they were down. Then I felt safe to use their own handcuffs to bind all of them together as a big mass. I popped back around the corner and handcuffed all of them too. I knew I'd have very little time so I started collecting all their weapons. Of special interest were the grenades. I took off one of the men's armored vest—he wouldn't be needing it anymore and took a bag off another for my newly acquired grenades.

I had all my weapons around me and I'd be the sentry for the work suite until help could arrive. The more time they gave me, the more mischief I'd be able to create. I propped up a few of the dead soldiers in the hallway so I'd have more cover. Over the balcony was where they'd have to come from. The stairwell was also near the atrium balcony. I jammed the door, but that was easy enough to break through. However, they'd have to come down the hallway. It was the only way.

All there was for me to do now was wait. How did I find myself in these situations? I was a street detective not an urban commando. This was ridiculous!

Something was happening on the ground floor. An explosion of gunfire erupted like the opening gambit of a world war. Bullets and laser pulse blasts. I hope our side was the one winning.

As I suspected, the bad guys were waiting for a moment. There was an explosion on the penthouse floor, which was the stairwell fire exit door, and a torrent of gun and laser fire down the hallway. Another team had probably scaled up to the floor. I knew this because the corporate soldiers in the elevator all had self-contained rappelling equipment, ropes and all.

I sat with my back against the wall and waited as they, however many there were, were at least halfway down the hallway, around the corner. I had all my grenades lined up in front of me and began pulling pins, then flicked grenades around the corner, one after another. When the explosions began, I reached out with my newly acquired machine guns and fired. I didn't use the laser machine guns so they couldn't see exactly where I was. I heard metal on metal so that meant they had metal shields, so I threw more grenades.

This was what I did for more than fifteen minutes. A battle royal between me and however many corporate soldiers. It was like it was never going to end. I heard a few more explosions, but it wasn't my grenades so that meant I had shot whoever was about to throw grenades at me.

They really shouldn't have given me all the time they had for me to prepare my mayhem. I hadn't used the laser machine guns because I taped all the ones I had together, jerry-rigged their controls, and was ready. I threw my creation around the corner on the floor as I pushed the button. Laser blasts, machine gun fire, and grenades was what they got. This went on for another ten minutes or so.

Then there was a click. I turned my head to see the elevator engage, doors close, and descend.

"Cruz! Stop firing!"

The voice over the speakers startled the heck out of me. It was like the Creator yelling at me from above. I turned off my laser machine-gun creation. There was utter silence.

All the hallway lights turned on, which also startled me. I took off my night goggles and gripped my omega-gun. I threw a cloth around the corner first in case a sniper were there waiting to shoot at the first thing that moved. I peeked around the corner and my mouth dropped.

The hallway was filled with corporate soldier bodies.

CHAPTER 62

PJ

I was pissed!

The magnitude of the attack was so overwhelming that it defied all bounds of normal criminal decency. There was a mountain of bodies in the hallway. I wasn't walking through all that. I was only wearing my PJs and karate slippers. This was so outrageous.

The voice over the speakers was one of Quix's men. Later, I'd learn Quix was shot in the jaw and couldn't talk, though he'd be fine later and would walk out of the hospital the same day. The reason there were no police was because the WHO Space Command disbanded them to complete bio-decon of the area, or as I would yell to their faces, "spray yellow crap over everything." I was mad and I wanted them to know it. They swarmed into the convention center in their bio-suits conveniently *after* we had a full-out gun battle with corporate soldiers where we could have been killed. Conveniently, none of the bio-suits could explain how the corporate soldiers got in, unauthorized, through their yellow zone.

Now, as a result of the mountain of bodies in the hotel suite hallway and bodies all over the main open lobby, courtesy of Quix and his men, we all had to be re-bio-deconned. I felt the blood surging through my veins I was so angry. These corporate soldiers breached the decon line and we had to suffer.

"I want to go to the hospital then," I said to the bio-suits.

"Were you injured?" one asked me.

"Yes, I am very injured being held hostage in a yellow-painted giant half dome. I want to go home."

"Sir, we can appreciate how you feel."

"If you didn't send the police home, this wouldn't have happened."

"The police were not sent home. Units are still on the scene."

"On scene. Do you see all this? Do you need to take off your bio-suit helmet? Because obviously you're having trouble seeing. How many bodies are here? How many on the penthouse level? You don't know because they're too many to count. We had a full-scale war inside here. This is a convention center! We're supposed to have quiet, boring conferences with simple breakfast, lunch with keynote speakers, dinner mixers. Not being hunted by corporate soldiers!"

"These were not corporate soldiers, Cruz." Police were now on-scene inside. I knew the coroners were going to burn me in effigy for all the work they were going to have to do tonight, and well into the next day.

"Who was there?" I asked the officer.

"None of these guys work for any of the megacorps. These were contract killers."

"But they're dressed like corporate soldiers."

"Not corporate soldiers."

"Guns for hire? From the street? Look how many of them there are."

"Somebody spent a lot of money on them and they're not going to be very happy."

"Cruz, you're one dangerous cat," another officer said. "You did all that upstairs."

"They shouldn't have left all that firepower in my hands."

"Lesson learned, but not really, since you killed them all."

"Are the counselors here?" I asked them.

"For your friends held up in the suite?"

"Yeah."

"Cruz, they don't need counseling. They seem to think it was cool being on the site of a gun battle outside their door."

"What?"

I went upstairs thinking Fraggy and his team were traumatized beyond belief. When they came out, only Fraggy was acting like a normal person, panicky and wanting to lie down. All the rest of the team, especially the under-thirties set wanted photos of the carnage and wanted me to autograph their sleeping clothes so they could tell their parents, friends, and significant others they were there when Cruz wiped out some army of corporate soldiers.

If it were up to me, they'd be home, but we all were going to be in the convention center for longer than we expected. Fraggy was right, it was like we were never getting out of that convention center.

"Don't be painting any of us with that yellow crap," I yelled at another bio-suit who I felt was looking at us funny.

"You're in so much trouble," PJ said to me.

Her face filled up my TV screen. Finally, comms were back on and she was the first person I called. She hadn't left for the office yet; she was home. PJ lived in my same apartment complex.

"Why do you say that?"

"If the case is that big and it involves bio-tech, that means big, big government contracts."

"PJ, it was like one of those commercials where the hovercar lands and a clown gets out and then another and soon all these clowns are exiting the same hovercar with no end in sight. These guys just kept coming, and that was just my level. Quix and his men had to deal with more on the ground level."

"How did they get in without him seeing?"

"That is a very good question. We're going to find out."

"Corporate soldiers."

"Gunmen for hire. Someone spent a hell of lot of money. The sheer number of them, sophisticated, well-armed, grenades even. Even with my omega gun, I might not have stopped them. But I stole their own weapons from them."

"See. I only work for smart bosses. You showed them."

"PJ, I'm mad."

"I see that. If you had bionic arms, you'd want to punch out the wall."

"The police have not found the WHO presidents yet."

"No, they haven't."

"I want them found."

"How?"

"I don't care how. Get Phishy and the Sidewalk Johnny Brigade on it. I want them found. I don't care if they have to fan out in Metropolis and physically walk into every hotel there is."

"Cruz, do you know how many hotels there are in Metropolis."

"Our friends like high-class. A lot of them are Up-Toppers."

"Okay that narrows it down a bit."

"What if they find them?"

"Tell me straight away. I'll decide."

"Okay."

"Also have them put the word on the street for Bia. The WHO boys are hunting them, maybe they can help us hunt the WHO boys back."

"Yes, good idea. Smart. What else?"

"I'm stuck in the place still. I'll call Dot."

"Oh, Prima is not happy with you."

"If I were her, I wouldn't be happy with me either. She got more than she bargained for with this case. We all have."

"You have. You had to take down an army by yourself. Where were the cops?"

"The WHO people sent them away so they could paint the ground and building with their stupid yellow decon paint. Could have gotten us all killed!"

"Government at work."

"Okay. There's your mission."

"Got it."

"I just can't figure out why they'd do such a thing. They've given a new meaning to the word over-kill."

"They wanted to get you for spoiling their scheme."

"Lots of people have been mad at me before. They didn't go through all this. It's out of character."

"So is surgically removing someone's arm, putting on a new one, flying it overseas, so you can break into a section of a building. All you have to do is kick down the door, or have me punch it."

"You have a point there."

"They're crazy."

"Insane crazy."

"Don't worry about Prima. I'll tell her what you faced today and you saved Mr. Fraggy and his people."

"PJ, don't tell Prima that I had a shootout with an army. Dot will hear."

"Prima speaks French. I'll speak French so Dot doesn't know."

"How do you know Dot doesn't speak French? Doesn't Cruz Jr. speak French now because of you? How do you know he hasn't taught her too?"

CHAPTER 63

The Grapevine

The next call was to the family—Dot and Cruz, Jr. Unfortunately, there was the sight of the Hellspawn in the background. If I had known, I would have audio-called only, but I wanted to see my family, even if it was on a screen.

"When you coming home?" Mommy-in-law Dearest asked me.

"Don't bring your germs back here," Daddy-in-law Dearest told me.

Dot yelled a bunch of rapid-fire Chinese at them. They yelled back.

"Cruzie, how are you doing?"

"I'm fine," he answered as he started giggling. His head turned and, clearly, he understood what they were saying.

"Cruzie, tell grandma that she has stinky feet. How do you say that in Chinese?"

He laughed and babbled something.

"We were not in jail with you!" Mr. Wan's big head popped on the screen, blocking my son.

"Get out of there. My son's talking to me. Dot get control of your ancestors."

She laughed and rattled off in Chinese at them. I was getting a headache.

The police, private investigators, and the media all knew the power of the streets. That vast network of sidewalk johnnies, street hustlers, low-level criminal info peddlers, cyberpunk hackers, corporate spies. It all created this invisible web that covered the entire supercity. It wasn't technology; it was people who saw and heard all. You simply had to know who and where to ask, and how much to pay.

PJ had Phishy put the word out that we wanted to know where the WHO presidents were hiding or any of their bio-tech megacorp allies. Then Phishy put the word out asking for Bia to help find them. Well, Phishy asked the right question. Someone from Bia reached out to Sidewalk Sid, one of Phishy's main guys, and he got the intel back to me.

They knew exactly where the WHO presidents were hiding. The Crystal Camelot Hotel. I should have known. It was very ritzy and popular with the European uber-wealthy set. Unfortunately, that part of town didn't have sidewalk johnnies around, because people didn't walk in that district. They drove, were chauffeured, or had whatever they wanted driven to them.

PJ said she'd handle it. What that meant I had no idea, but she told me to leave it to her. She'd have them watched. I wondered if she was dating someone at the hotel. I didn't ask.

When were we going to be allowed to leave this convention center?! It did seem like I was going to die here.

CHAPTER 64

Patient Zero

Sometimes in life there are those moments when time slows down to a crawl. It's your mind fighting the reality of the moment. You're desperately trying to rewind time so you could start again.

I opened my front door of my suite. There stood someone in a full body black changeling suit—the highly illegal, Up-Top clothing made of digitally coated fabric. Wearing it, one could blend into any surrounding or become virtually invisible. The person's build suggested it was a woman. She blew the dust in my face and was gone. I slammed the door shut, but the damage was done.

I dropped to my knees and remained as calm as I could. I stopped breathing, though I had already breathed it. My phone was vibrating. I fished it from my pocket and dropped it on the ground at my knees, answering it with a touch.

"Cruz!" It was PJ. "They're leaving. We think they're going to the airport now."

"Follow them."

"We're doing that already. Why are you answering the phone like this? What are you doing?"

"PJ, this is very important. I'll put my ear-piece in, but keep the phone going."

"Why?"

"I want to be at the airport when they arrive. It's very important."

"Cruz, what's wrong?"

"I can't talk more. I'm leaving the convention center."

"Leaving? They cleared you?"

"I'm ignoring you now and putting in my ear-piece. Direct me to where at in the terminal they are."

I put my ear-piece in and the phone in my jacket. I slowly stood up and exited the suite. I didn't care that the door was open.

I knew the woman was Raven. Was the entire early morning shootout a grand distraction to allow her to get into the building and wait for me? I'm sure they infected me with something particularly nasty and contagious.

What they didn't know was that Quix, his team, and me made more modifications to the convention center than just secret storage rooms on the upper levels to hide weapons and stash Fraggy when needed. We also had a secret parking bay with its own hovercar.

"Cruz, can you hear me?" PJ asked me. I was on audio only.

"Where are they in traffic, PJ?"

"Even better. I know their flight."

"I need to know the terminal and flight number."

"What's happening, Cruz?"

"I'll tell you when I'm at the terminal."

I'd never driven infected with a deadly disease before. So far I was fine but I touched my forehead and temple. It had started. A slight warmth.

PJ gave me the terminal at Metro International and Interspace Airport and I had the airline with flight number. I knew Metro International backwards and forwards. It had state-of-the art security but I wasn't trying to avoid detection. I wanted to attract as much of it as possible. My odds of success were slim, and that was assuming my body allowed me to do what I wanted before whatever disease I was carrying really started its happy dance inside me.

I had already hung up from PJ, but my mobile was ringing. I wasn't going to answer. The last thing I told her was to have them stall the take-off of that plane. I didn't care how she did it. I had to keep a singular focus on my mission. As a former illegal hovercar racer, I knew all the secret ways onto Metro International. There used to be a death race competition that passed through it years ago, until police shut it down. I knew all the sky lanes into Metro International, and I knew where all the Metro PD check-points were. I also knew the designated hovertaxi lanes. That was my in. Maybe the police would spot me, maybe they wouldn't.

I drove like my amateur hovercar racing days. Using other vehicles to block the view of mine from police, diving and rising when needed. I'd slow down and fast forward. Knowing all the shortcuts into the airport, I avoided most of the hovertraffic.

I had reached the sky around the airport. A space shuttle was landing. Normal earthbound planes were departing and arriving. The WHO plane was a private one so it would already be on the ground. I saw the shape of the aircraft at its terminal. It hadn't begun its taxi to the runaway yet but would.

Here goes!

I accelerated my hovercar and dove. Immediately, sirens sounded. Drones would be around me in moments. There was an explosion of thick gray smoke as if it were on fire but without the fire. I set the auto-pilot, touched down, jumped out, and let it go. The hovercar rose at a steady incline. Airport drones reached it, clamped on, and took the hovercar down, seizing control of all its controls. The hovercar hit the ground with a thud.

Airport police cruisers also reached the hovercar and surrounded it in the sky. Officers jumped out with weapons drawn as they neared it. I heard them yelling at the vehicle.

I stopped looking at that point. I had picked the spot for a reason. They couldn't see me because I was on the other side of a concrete decorative wall. I squeezed through the space, climbed up the hill, and landing on the ground to the baggage handling. I took off my hat and tucked it inside my jacket under the black slicker I was wearing. The look matched with any other Metro airport worker. I wasn't running. Not approaching baggage. A baggage handler on a hovertrolley paid me no mind, because I paid him no mind. I carried my electronic clipboard proudly in my left hand to look like an inspector.

As I neared the private plane, one big, buff security guard watched me. Then two more came out of the plane and slowly walked down the stairs.

"Inspector," I called out.

"Inspector? We're about to depart."

I shot him and the two other guards. Up the steps I went. To be considerate, I closed the airplane door and locked it. Outside the window I could see the three security guards, I couldn't read lips, but I'm sure it was all kinds of profanity. They were hit with mild stun rounds only.

I peeked around the side to the right and I saw faces staring at me. I looked to the left and walked to the cockpit. The cockpit door was closed but that left a steward balled up in a corner, shivering.

"You, stand up there. I need you to make an urgent call. Stand up. I don't have much time."

The steward stood up and faced me, shaking. Her eyes were on my omega-gun.

"I need you to call Chief of Police Hub and tell him that a Mr. Cruz, that's me, is on your plane and that you need to send a full bio-contamination team and quarantine this plane immediately."

"What? You have that disease on the news."

"I do. They were the ones who gave it to me."

"What?"

"Call Chief Hub now. I'm sure I'll collapse soon, so you better call before you do too."

She stood there looking at me with shock.

I walked towards the passenger area. I threw my electronic clipboard through and it was shot to pieces by someone out of sight. I fired around the corner and heard something fall.

"Hi Raven," I said as I walked down the aisle. She was lying there dead or unconscious. I wasn't sure but I took her gun anyway. I turned and walked to him.

"Mr. Foil."

The look on his face was priceless. He looked up at me, then looked down. He literally was at a loss for words. I looked around. Mr. Euclid sat in his seat, not too eager to eat any more of his jelly bellies. It was the first time I had seen Mr. Geronimo without a smile. Mr. Zeno was looking out the window with a sour face; he wouldn't even make eye contact. Mr. Alonzee and his wife looked like they were on the verge of tears. At the back, Mr. Timely glared at me.

"Mr. Cruz." Foil had regained his composure. "You have nothing at all. You may believe you've won, but you've won nothing. You have simply caused a lot of inconvenience. You haven't won anything. With all your friends of this fine city, you have nothing at all. WHO is a long-lived organization of prestige that existed long before you and will exist long after you. What does fighting global pandemics on the behalf of the people of Earth have to do with a little street detective?

"Mr. Foil, it's like this. I die. You die. Nothing else to say."

I found an empty seat and sat myself down. From the corner of my eye, I saw flashing red and blue. An army of airport police cruisers in the air surrounding us from all sides.

The steward stood in the aisle with two other men, obviously the pilots.

"Chief Hub said to hang in there," the steward said.

"I'm trying," I said. "Your passengers poisoned me with some virus. I'm suddenly having a hard time keeping my eyes open."

"They're here!" the pilot yelled, pointing.

Good grief! I didn't want to see them. The bio-suits had arrived. I was drifting away but not before all the windows and the plane itself was covered by that milky chemical.

My eyes closed but I felt a blast of air. The bio-suits were in. My last act of the day was to open my eyes to a hazy view of those bio-suits reaching toward me. They had what they wanted—me in quarantine.

I had no doubts that I'd make it. Those WHO criminals couldn't care less about me, but they were definitely not going to let themselves die. They'd calculate that they could beat whatever charges we'd file against them. So they'd save me to save themselves. That was the only thing I regretted: not seeing them all arrested and carried away in handcuffs.

CHAPTER 65

Decon Doctors

I knew I was lifted out of my airport seat. I knew I was being moved, likely on a hovergurney. I could feel the drizzle on my face. But that was pretty much it as I had zero energy and a fever came over me like I had never experienced before. Maybe I could have cooked some breakfast on my forehead.

That's all I remembered. When my eyes finally opened, I felt I had been sleeping for decades. I could barely move. For a few moments, I wondered if I could even move. Finally, I wiggled my fingers, then my toes. I looked around. I was in some kind of hospital. When I saw it, I was not happy in the least—I was hooked up to a very scary looking I.V. It was feeding me but also pumping other stuff into me.

I had closed my eyes but felt a presence.

"Mr. Cruz."

I opened my eyes again. A man stood over me. A woman also appeared at his side. Suddenly, it seemed all kinds of people were around me. Medical staff in white, tight-fitting clothes.

"How are you feeling?" he asked.

"Dead."

He smiled. That meant I was okay. I could breathe a sigh of relief.

"No need to worry, Mr. Cruz. You've come through the worst of it. We'll keep you here for observation for about a week, as you get your strength back and get you unplugged from the IV."

"How long have I been here?" I asked.

"Five days," he answered.

"That's too long."

"Your body doesn't think so. It had a battle to fight with the help of some medicine but came out the winner."

"Thanks. Was anyone else sick?"

"Mr. Cruz, everyone infected has been cured. On the plane and in the city."

"The plane," I repeated, starting to chuckle. "I had no doubt about that since it was the people on the plane that infected me."

The doctors glanced at each other.

"We heard something about that. You probably know much more than us. Our focus was you, here. Not anything else. Your case was more severe than anyone in the city."

"I'm sure it was."

"But no more of that. You'll be out of here next week."

"Can I have visitors?"

"Certainly, in a few days. Immediate family, of course. Don't overdo it though. We'll set you up with a phone. You can start receiving calls until you're ready for visitors in person."

"Okay."

"Get lots of sleep and get your strength back."

"One more question," I asked. "Where are we?"

"A place you're not too unfamiliar with. The entire Utopia Convention Center has been turned into Metropolis's premiere bio-treatment center with the best state-of-the-art treatments we've learned from decades of research and practice around the world and even off-world. The best of Earth's doctors are here, not to be too self-congratulatory, and you, Mr. Cruz, are the center's star patient. You have your own section."

"I'm at the convention center now?"

"You are."

Damn! I was back at the convention center again! How does one get away from this place?

CHAPTER 66

Eye Candy Crew

They did it. I had my own vid-phone screen on a movable arm attachment to my bio-bed. I could receive my calls! They'd also reconfigured the room so I'd have more privacy.

The first call was from Dot! She called from the Eye Candy break room.

"Cruz!" she greeted smiling, holding Cruz Jr. in her arm with his legs around her waist. He waved at me smiling.

"Hey Mom and Cruzie," I said.

"We have company," she said and the screen filled up with her co-workers and boss.

Prima Donna, Cyan, Pinkie, Goat Girl, and Lipps. Like my wife, always in fashionable attire.

"Cruz is back!" they all said.

"Cruz, you're alive!" Prima Donna said.

"Yeah, I made it. I can cross this one off my bucket list. Being exposed to an epidemic bug. The things criminals think of."

"I said it before, Cruz. Wilford G. didn't have half the exciting cases you've had," Prima Donna said.

"I bet he did, and then some. He just didn't tell you."

"Talk about a case," Goat Girl said.

"You guys know how to pick 'em," Cyan said.

"How long do you have to stay there?" Dot asked.

"About a week. Hopefully, it'll be sooner, if I have anything to do with it."

"Can't rush it, Cruz," Prima said. "Get fully rested. Consider it your vacation."

"What was it like out there, with the quarantine?" I asked.

"They quarantined Opus Fields and Crystal Cliffs. You want to make rich people furious, imprison them in their homes and tell them no hoverlimo rides," Pinkie answered.

"They also quarantined two other districts near Neon Blues," Prima added. "All over the news. But we all went about our business. Not like there was anything else to do."

"Those guys in bio-suits were busting down doors all over the place," Cyan added.

"They want to make a reality show with them," Lipps said.

"Reality show?" I asked, trying not to laugh.

"You're the real reality show, Cruz," Prima added.

"Cruz, I say you and the family deserve a long vacation—a real one," Goat Girl said.

"That's for sure." Dot nodded.

Cruz Jr. clapped his hands. "Vacation."

"What about the bad guys?"

"Cruz!" they said in unison, scolding me.

"Forget the bad guys," Prima yelled.

"How can I forget the bad guys? I'm lying in a quarantine zone. I'd like to know that they're sitting in jail."

"Ask the Chief about that," Prima said.

"What? What does that mean?"

"Cruz, I know I was mad at you," Prima said, "but you handled it well. Looks like when the times got tough, I was the one who was falling apart, not you." She hugged Dot. "Your man knows his stuff."

"He does."

"Are you all going to tell me about the bad guys, or do I have to call PJ at the office?"

"You might want to hold off on that one too," Prima said.

"What does that mean?"

"Get your rest, Cruz," Cyan said. "That's all that should be on your mind."

"What are you all not telling me?"

"Bye, Cruz!" the Eye Candy crew said in unison.

"Bye-bye, daddy," Cruz Jr. said.

"Wait!"

CHAPTER 67

Dot

Dot gave Cruz Jr. over to Prima. She was the only one left in the Eye Candy break room. Then she broke down crying.

"It was all my fault," she sobbed.

My wife was crying and all I could do was touch the screen.

"What was your fault?"

"I was trying to help by finding you a case and look what happened."

"Dot, stop crying. Nothing was your fault. Bad guys do bad things, but we caught 'em."

She managed a smile and wiped her eyes. "You should've heard what my parents said."

"Oh no. Do I want to know?"

"They said you're too much of a bum to die. Dad said bums are made of strong material. Too unbreakable to kill."

"Your parents. So bum is a term of endearment?"

We laughed.

"Okay, tell them that I appreciate they were worried about me, but I won't tell anyone."

"Yeah, they don't want anyone to know they actually like you."

"Dot, don't blame yourself. These were not the normal bad guys. But we're not the normal good guys. I was never alone. I had a good team with me. Prima, Run-Time helped, PJ and Phishy did their part, a lot of people helped on this one, new people I never met before. The Chief even helped us set this up to catch them.

"This thing they did with the germ attack. It was pure desperation. They knew we were closing in. If it was anyone's fault, it was mine. They caught me at my hotel suite. I opened my door without checking first. I violated my own training. Ma always said: 'don't open the door unless you know who it is.' She taught me that when I was Cruz Jr.'s age, but I let my guard down and got sucker-punched."

"But you made it."

"I did. Especially when our daughter is on the way."

She smiled. "The vacation will have to be postponed a bit I think."

"Yeah, but not by much."

"I guess I can't scold you for the 'save the world' cases anymore after this."

"I don't want any more 'save the world' cases after this. I'm tired. Maybe I will hire other detectives for the agency and have them do it."

"And what would you do?"

"Sit at my desk, do the books, and look pretty."

I'd succeeded in cheering my wife up. The tears were gone.

"No, you have to do it. Do what you do best. Catch the bad guys."

"Catch bad guys."

"So, when do I get to see my family in person?"

"You tell me."

"I'll have to see what strings I can pull to speed things along with the doctor."

"Yes, your son needs to see you. And his mother needs to tell her husband how much she loves him."

"He'd like to hear that in person, and tell her how much he's missed her and loves her too."

"Cruz, rest. No working. No checking messages or checking in with clients. You need rest."

"I do need to learn how to eat on my own again. They have me hooked up and plugged up to all kinds of machines." I smiled. "I'm lean and mean through my CDC IV diet. I'll write a book and become famous again!"

"Yes, all you have to do is first get infected by Plague. That's a very good sign. Your silliness is back."

"So what's this about PJ and why do I need to talk to the Chief?"

"And here comes the bad sign. You're working again, Cruz. Questioning your wife about cases is working!"

CHAPTER 68

Chief Hub

Chief Hub called me back later that day. I had my bio-bed in the inclined upright position. I'd been uplugged from all the IVs and had been drinking water straight from a big, clear pitcher. All I had to do was tap the screen of my vid-phone on the bed's arm attachment to receive his call.

"Cruz, you have a real problem. No other person would think to call the police to say hello after your ordeal. Did you even speak to your family?"

"First thing this morning."

"Why are you calling me and leaving messages then?"

"I heard a rumor that certain bad guys are not sitting in prison. You can understand if such a thing were true that I'd be highly upset after what I've been through."

"Your evidence from Fraggioti didn't get us there."

"What?"

"They came close but too much ambiguity. Would never stand up in court with the defense attorneys they'd be able to hire. We can prove the scam. The underlings who gave the orders, but there was no data trail of them directly giving the orders to the underlings. The bio-tech megacorps will never talk. Any witnesses we might have flipped ended up dead because of you and those mercenaries you hired. Their accountants are also far too clever for us to be able to prove kickbacks of any kind with their scheme."

"They shouldn't have come gunning at us."

"Yes, they shouldn't have."

"They get away? We stopped the scam but they get away."

"I didn't say that."

"They created a global scam to 'inoculate' populations with their Rain for 'fake diseases" they created from the start and they walk?"

"I didn't say that either. We're going to get them on communications fraud."

"Communications fraud? Like getting the murdering gangster on tax evasion?"

"Whatever works. There's going to be a lot of litigation around this case. They may not be in jail now, but they will be in a kind of jail for the rest of their lives defending themselves in criminal and civil cases. Governments don't like to be scammed, and especially for something as serious as bio-threats.

"Then there's off-world. Their laws are a bit different. Up there, circumstantial evidence is plenty to lock people away. Up there, the charges won't be conspiracy to defraud. It's outright bio-terrorism."

"They created diseases and unleashed it."

"It doesn't matter if they had the cure ready to go and no one died."

"I say we need that Up-Top law down here."

"Working on it."

"Then we did get the bad guys."

"We did."

"Chief, I suspected from the start that you knew more about this before me, or even Fraggy."

"Maybe."

"Were they already being investigated?"

"Why do you ask that?"

"I didn't have to do much coaxing to get you to help me put this whole fake conference together to trap them."

"I wanted to make sure there wasn't a real bio-terrorist threat against my city. You had a plan ready to go. Others couldn't get their act together. I was happy to let you barrel ahead, as long as we were there to keep an eye on things."

"Did the scam include WHO Space too?"

"They're the ones who investigate WHO Earth."

"So many things happening behind the scenes. Well, thanks Chief for helping pull this off."

"I should thank you. You're the one in quarantine, not me."

I smiled. "Yes, I took the plague bug for the team."

"Better than getting shot."

"Only slightly."

"Also, you should give that office manager of yours a raise."

"PJ?"

"That's the only one I know that you have."

"Why?"

"Don't you talk to your employees, Cruz?"

"I'm stuck in here, Chief, but I'll call the office."

"Your office? She's not at your office, Cruz. She's at the center there with you."

CHAPTER 69

PJ

I was long past unconscious. The bio-suits had me on a hover-gurney and covered my entire body with a plastic enclosure. Some of them kept passengers back as two of them push me out the plane's open door. The entire aircraft was under a giant white tent.

But, luckily, aside from multiple accounts as to what occurred next, I was able to watch the whole thing on digital video for myself courtesy of a CDC hovercam and the airplane's external cameras. People always forgot that PJ was called Punch Judy *before* she got her bionic arms. My ex-felon employee was a mixed-martial arts boxing terror who specialized in pummeling people taller and bigger than her to a pulp before becoming a cyborg. She was her gang's enforcer, albeit it is kind of laughable to call a punk posh gang a real gang but her street fighting skills were nothing to laugh at.

Bio-suits led the pilots and stewards off the plane—one bio-suit personnel to one exposed person. Then the WHO presidents and Mrs. Alonzee. Each bio-suit held each person on the arm as they slowly filed out of the plane down the steps. Other bio-suit personnel gestured them forward. All the WHO personnel knew bio-decontamination procedures fully. Strip naked, sprayed with chemicals, scanned, clothes burned—lot of fun to come.

Everyone heard a commotion outside. Something broke through the white tent. It was PJ!

"You!" she yelled at the WHO presidents.

Bio-suits rushed her. Big mistake. PJ grabbed one in each arm and threw them like ten feet away. She did her own rushing—at the WHO presidents. The men ran.

"Where are you going?" PJ punched Foil in the chest so hard, he collapsed to the ground, unable to breathe.

She ran and pushed a fleeing Zeno in the back, sending him several feet forward, crashing into a few bio-suits. She slapped Euclid, sending the man into the air, crashing into more bio-suits. Timely somehow had a gun, but bio-suits jumped him to stop him. PJ got to him and punched him unconscious in the head. There were too many bio-suits coming so she grabbed one and threw him into Geronimo, knocking both men into Alonzee and his wife. All of them were lying bruised, bleeding and unconscious on the tarmac.

"Strike!" PJ said triumphantly. "That's what you get for trying to kill my boss." She looked at the bio-suits circling her. "What are you going to do? Come on. Put me in quarantine. I know that's what you want to do. Put them in the hospital and me in quarantine. I like that."

Armed bio-suits rushed into the containment tent with laser rifles pointed at her.

"Oh, so you arrive after I do all the work! Useless! You better not shoot me and scuff up my bionic arms or what I did to them, I'll do to you!"

The armed bio-suits were smart enough to lower their weapons.

After I hung up with the Chief, I had one of the doctors find her in the center and put her on a phone. Later in the day, I'd have the great pleasure of watching video of PJ giving the WHO baddies what they deserved. For now, I'd have PJ tell me the story herself.

"PJ!"

"You're alive. I told them."

"PJ, why are you here in the convention?"

"I had work to do. You were acting all strange. I knew they did something to you. I thought you were shot. You looked pale, so I closed up and got in my hovercar to go to the airport too. I had to make sure you didn't need help."

"PJ, that would be the opposite of help.'"

"But if you were shot. Then I thought, no! They infected him with germs. That's what they'd do. All this epidemic talk and quarantines. I knew they were the kind of criminals who would do something so low. I had to get to the airport too."

"PJ, what did you do?"

When PJ told me how she punched her way through airport security to get to the huge bio-containment tent they'd erected over the WHO plane, that was entertainment enough. But when she told me what she did to the WHO presidents, I burst out laughing. That woman was getting a big, big bonus. I had to see the video for myself.

She was laughing too.

"They're still in the hospital and if I see them again, I'll punch them again."

"I feel much much better now, PJ."

"You're welcome."

"But wait."

"Wait what?"

"If I'm here, and you're here. Who's running the office?"

"Stupid Man."

Phishy was running the Liquid Cool office?!

CHAPTER 70

Parents

My reprieve from purgatory had finally arrived. I was cleared to leave the convention center. I'd never been to prison (the Wans and I were only "held" in jail for an afternoon for a "misunderstanding") but imagined I felt as they did on my "big day."

I woke up like a kid on Christmas. I had no belongings—clothes were burned and my weapons were in police storage. Still I was fairly weak when it came to walking, so I'd gotten my own hoverchair to zip around.

My trio of primary doctors arrived first thing in the morning.

"Ready to go, Mr. Cruz?" one of them asked.

"Ready."

They officially released me. In fact, I was the last patient of the center. CDC contract workers were standing by to tear down the entire operation. The location was back under their control, not WHO Earth or WHO Space. A CDC orderly walked with me as

I coasted along in my chair. I was looking around for Dot. Where was she?

Dot drove a new dark silver Bee, but I so saw no sign of her hover-speedster bug.

"Cruz!"

That was my Pops' voice. The orderly and I looked around. There were my parents waving from a hovercar a few feet above the ground.

My pops liked big hovercars. He liked his room. I was in the back with my folded hoverchair taking up most of the backseat. I got a kiss on the cheek from Ma and a hug from Pops before they helped me into the hovercar.

"Dot's been working on your homecoming party," Pops told me.

"Party? I want to sleep."

As we rose into hovertraffic, I looked back at the giant home dome of the convention center.

"I never want to see you again," I said aloud. "If there's ever an awards show on TV and it's at that center, I'm not watching," I said to them.

"You never watch award shows," my Pops said.

"That's true. Maybe it's a Karma thing. Movie-Town blames me for so many people going to jail and jumping off rooftops because of the scandal, they said, let's get Cruz. We'll keep him in our convention center and never let him leave."

"Oh, Cruz," my Ma said.

"It's true, Ma. Do you know how long I was in that place? I leave the building, then they want to quarantine me and where do they want to house me? The same building I escaped from. It's cursed. No party. Sleep only for me."

"Cruz Jr. will not let you sleep after not seeing his father for so long," my Pops said.

"I'll give him my hoverchair. He'll prefer that. I'll sleep. He'll play. I like that arrangement."

"You need proper food," my Ma said. "Look how skinny you are."

"Ma, I'll be famous. I'm writing a book about the Cruz bio-decon IV diet!"

My parents laughed.

"Cruz, what's this I heard about you naming your daughter Cruzalina?" Ma asked me.

"Cruz, our granddaughter is going to be named Cruzalina?"

"PJ! No, her name will not, and will never be Cruzalina. Don't listen to PJ. Dot and I have the name but not that."

"And don't name her after any super hero either," Pops said. "You young people are into all these fads. Simple names. Not street names like gangsters."

"Ma, we're going to name her after you."

My mother turned around smiling, as I nodded with my own smile.

"We're naming her 'Ma.' I like it myself. Might confuse kids and her teachers when she gets to school."

I don't know what came over my Ma, but she tried to hit me in the shoulder in my post-decontaminated state.

CHAPTER 71

Hellspawn and Cruz Jr.

My day of freedom wasn't so free. The first half of the day, I was in the custody of my parents for breakfast and lunch. Hanging out was fine, but I wanted my bed.

We returned to the Concrete Mama—home! The apartment mega-tower was like a chunk of granite set down on Earth from space. It was the no-frills monolith tower of legacy housing. If there was ever a planetary shockwave from a nuclear blast or an asteroid crash, the Concrete Mama would still be standing. It had been home for over fifteen years and was now my family's home when Dot and I got married. It had been passed on to me from my maternal grandparents; my parents had their own.

Residents of the Concrete Mama weren't rich or working-class as with most living in the district of Rabbit City. Because of my so-called fame and Dot's arrival, I liked to think we had classed up the place. We used to have lobby johnnies, but they were a thing of the past with our doorman, Mr. Post, an ex-cop, the building hired a few years ago after me leading the interviewing process. He too classed up the place, along with Mr. Jax, the night doorman.

I used to live on the 100th floor but needed a bigger place, so I switched places and now lived on the 150th floor, but kept my same apartment number: 9732. Home Sweet Home.

But now, the parents turned over custody of me to the Hellspawn! Why were they even in my place? I beheld a very peculiar thing when the two sets of parents greeted each other. They were all speaking English to each other.

"Ah, I see how it is," I said. "When I'm around it's Spanish and Chinese. I'm going to bed, but where's Cruz Jr.?"

"Your wife has him," Mr. Wan said.

"Where are they?"

"Party planning."

"Not this party again."

We'd left the hoverchair in the car so I had to hobble around at sub-light speed.

"You walk like an old man!" Mr. Wan yelled at me.

First would be my super sauna shower. Lukewarm water shooting out of the main floor and ceiling vents, from the side nozzles waves of hot steam would blast out. I'd be in my super sauna shower for an hour.

Then to bed under three fluffy blankets. Cruz Jr. wasn't here so this was my chance. I'd leave the parents to converse in English to each other while I slept my first night in a long time under my own roof and not in that damn convention center.

My case. I'd have to think of a name for it when I did return to the office, after days of rest. Assuming there was an office left with Phishy running it. I couldn't worry about such things. I was home at last.

The feel and smell of my fluffy blankets on top of me. I curled myself up to form a pocket of pre-sleep bliss. All of a sudden, something was walking on the top of my fluffy blankets. That something sat down hard. That something started jumping up and down.

"Cruzie, I'm going to stick you in the dishwasher."

I just heard laughing and clapping.

"Oh Cruz! We found your son!" My mother-in-law was yelling in my bedroom so loud it was like daggers in my eardrums."

"Really?"

Cruzie started jumping up and down on top of me again.

CHAPTER 72

Quix

My Open House-Welcome Home party day had arrived. I was racing Cruz. Jr. from the elevator down the hallway to the office, each flying our own hoverchair.

"See, Cruzie. Your pops can race a hoverchair too."

I opened the main door and we both coasted in. With my medical recovery chair, Dot and I couldn't get away with not allowing him to use his recreation one. He loved his hoverchair a bit too much. I told him I wanted to see him running around like a normal hyperactive kid. We didn't want no fat kids in the house.

I looked at the PJ reception desk expecting to see Phishy but instead it was Quix.

"You're not Phishy!"

Quix laughed and stood from the chair. "Phishy's here. He went to get party stuff from his vehicle."

Inside the Liquid Cool office were scary looking cyborgs (Quix's men), sidewalk johnnies, college kids (Fraggy's team), senior citizen types (more of Fraggy's team), and biopunkers everywhere. All of them chatting nicely with food and drinks in hand. Music was playing from PJ's boom box.

"Isn't that..?" I began.

"Blues," Quix answered.

"Don't know if PJ will like you playing anything other than her French ska music on that."

"She gave us permission already."

I got out of my hoverchair; Cruz Jr. was jetting around like a crazy person grabbing food. I walked to Quix to shake his hand.

"We made it, Quix."

"We did."

"You look all healed up."

"I've been shot before. My jaw is metal anyway, so I didn't mind it too much."

"Shot before. I'd say most of us in this room have been shot before, including me," I said smiling.

"But you're the only one here who's survived a real personal bio-attack."

"Don't remind me. Not something I'd like to repeat ever. How did your men do?"

"I was the only one who was wounded. They made it through fine."

"Good. Case closed."

"We didn't get a chance to talk, Cruz, but I have to say you did a solid job that night against the assault team."

"That was a bit of luck."

"Much more than that. You neutralized far superior forces all by yourself, no back-up. Most military guys I know couldn't do the same."

"Lucky."

"Where did you learn to shoot so good?"

"Video games."

He laughed and patted me on the shoulder.

"When I was a kid, I had to occupy my time."

"Then you occupied yourself with the right pastimes."

"You did give me the time I needed. If you didn't warn me with the gunfire."

"They were coming in so fast and there was so many of them. I had to warn you somehow. We couldn't even get to the elevator fast enough to shut them down, but you turned the tables on them."

"They ended up sending me all the weapons I needed, and grenades. I did thank them but they couldn't hear me."

Quix smiled. "G. would have given you a thumbs up on this case."

"Yes, he would."

"Though you should make up your mind as to your profession. Cop, soldier, or detective."

"Detective, please. I don't know how I get caught up in these things."

"It was a good op. They were fooled completely."

"Those government agencies and megacorps aren't as smart as they think, if we could fool them with our fake conference and lure them from all over the world. And the punch line: we made them pay for it and think they were running it."

"Is there really a Mr. Incom?"

"No, it's an identity I invented from another case."

"Well good work. Look forward to working with you in the future. Any client who can stand shoulder-to-shoulder with me and my men with a machine gun is okay in my book."

"Machine gun? We get machine guns at this party? Where?" PJ had stepped through the door, holding bags of party food in her arms.

CHAPTER 73

A Freak Show in My Office

My parents arrived; they had driven me to the office. Then Dot and her parents.

"We did it!" Bia yelled when she came through the door with Bolt, Zip, Handy, Breech—walking with his new bionic legs, and other bio-borgs.

She gave me a big hug.

The Eye Candy Crew showed up. Never had all of them been out of the salon together before. Goat Girl was in her professional appearance, but Twinkle also showed up wearing dark glasses.

"Don't take it personal, Mr. Cruz, but if any of your cop friends show up, I'll likely disappear out the door," he said shaking my hand.

"I won't take it personal at all," I said to him laughing.

Fraggy also showed up. He told me and I had to make the announcement.

"Ladies and gentlemen, Fraggy has been promoted. He's the new president of WHO Earth!"

Everyone applauded.

Finally, Phishy returned. Through the door he came with more sidewalk johnnies, including Sidewalk Sid, and several sidewalk sallies.

"I'm back!" he said. "Cruz!"

"Hi Phishy. Good to see my office is still here in one piece."

"You know what that means." He ran to PJ's desk and turned up the music. "Cruz Control, please." He was looking at my son.

"Why are you looking at my son, Phishy?"

Cruz Jr. descended in his hoverchair and jumped out.

What I saw next was deeply disturbing. It wasn't just Phishy spinning around doing his chicken dance. He had my son at his side doing the same thing. Everyone was laughing and applauding.

"Phishy, what did you do to my son?"

They danced to blues music. But there was nothing sad here. We were having a party. Another case solved! Until the next one.

Cruz's next case is what? A three-armed man? You'll have to see for yourself in ***The Moon Is a Good Place to Die! (Liquid Cool, Book #8)!***

THANK YOU FOR READING!

Dear Reader,

I hope you enjoyed my **Liquid Cool** cyberpunk detective novel, *BioPunk Blues*.

<u>**Can You Write Me a Review?**</u>

I'd greatly appreciate an honest review on one or more of the following sites:

Reviews are the best way for readers to discover good books. My writer's motto is simple: "Readers Rule!" Thanks so much.

Always writing,

Austin Dragon

CONTINUE THE ADVENTURE

Get Your Next *Liquid Cool* Books!

These Mean Streets, Darkly *(Liquid Cool Prequel Short)*
Liquid Cool *(Liquid Cool: The Cyberpunk Detective Series, Book 1)*
Blade Gunner *(Liquid Cool, Book 2)*
NeuroDancer *(Liquid Cool, Book 3)*
The Electric Sheep Massacre *(Liquid Cool, Book 4)*
I, Alien Hunter *(Liquid Cool, Book 5)*
A.I. Confidential *(Liquid Cool, Book 6)*
Biopunk Blues *(Liquid Cool, Book 7)*
The Moon Is A Good Place to Die *(Liquid Cool, Book 8)*
Write Me a Murder on Jules Verne's Island: A Liquid Cool Cozy Murder Mystery *(Book 9)*

Liquid Cool Box Set *(Liquid Cool Prequel and Books 1-3)*
Liquid Cool Box Set 2 *(Liquid Cool: Books 4-6)*
Liquid Cool Box Set 3 *(Liquid Cool: Books 7-9)*

Liquid Cool: From the Crazy Maniac Files mini-series

Classic Cyborg (Book One)
Digital Samurai (Book Two)

Also by Austin Dragon

See all my books in science fiction, horror, and fantasy at: http://www.austindragon.com/books

ABOUT THE AUTHOR

Austin Dragon is the author of the *After Eden* Series, including the *After Eden: Tek-Fall* mini-series, the classic *Sleepy Hollow Horrors*, the new epic fantasy adventure *Fabled Quest Chronicles*, and cyberpunk detective series, *Liquid Cool*. He is a native New Yorker, but has called Los Angeles, California home for the last twenty years. Words to describe him, in no particular order: U.S. Army, English teacher, one-time resident of Paris, political junkie, movie buff, Fortune 500 corporate recruiter, renaissance man, dreamer.

He is currently working on new books and series in science fiction, fantasy, and classic horror!

<u>Connect with Austin on social media at:</u>

Website and blog: http://www.austindragon.com

Pinterest: http://www.pinterest.com/austindragon

Goodreads: https://www.goodreads.com/ADragon

<u>Other books by Austin:</u>

See all my books at: http://www.austindragon.com/books